The Story of
ERVIN
JAMES

BERNETTE SHERMAN

The Story of
ERVIN
JAMES

MOUNT HOPE MEDIA, LLC
Georgia

Published by Mount Hope Media, LLC
Georgia
www.MountHopeMedia.com

ISBN-13 Paperback (6x9): 978-1-954636-02-6
ISBN-13 eBook: 978-1-954-636-01-9

Cover design: Image of man playing fiddle, unsourced, circa 1900. Image modification for cover by Carolann McColley. Picture of house taken by Rebecca Washington. Cover design by Bernette Sherman. Additional photos in book provided by Rebecca Washington and Dorothy Elo.

Library of Congress Control Number: 2021931655
Printed in the United States of America

Special thanks and appreciation to the following for graciously reading this story in advance and providing your helpful input. Where provided, I've added their words below as well.

Glenda Pierce Harrison, an alumnae of Virginia Union University and Howard University, a member of Alpha Kappa Alpha Sorority, Inc, a strong advocate for girls and young women (https://olivetreeforgirls.org). She is also a proud descendant of Junius Pierce, Tenner James, Archie James, Robert James, and of her great, great, great grandparents, Ervin and Nora James.

Beth Hermes, fellow author, teacher, friend and founder of PenDragon Literary.

Bernard James, fourth generation Sidney James (son of Ervin James) descendant.

Rebecca Washington, great-great-granddaughter of Ervin James and my ever-supportive mother.

Dedicated to the family and descendants of Ervin and Nora James.

Contents

Prologue

Off a well-traveled highway in Florence, South Carolina stands a marker. A traveler can turn off U.S. Highway 76/301 and onto a dirt road that winds around an open field and forks to the left. A cemetery sits between trees and bushes, the final resting place for bodies who over generations sought to find peace, to find safety, to find a place they could call home.

Back around the main road, if you drive too fast, you'll kick up dust and may miss one of the few remaining homes, mostly unoccupied; a reminder of days gone by, when Jamestown (now Jamestown Historic District) was a thriving community of more than 200 Black people who farmed, planted and tended to fruit trees, hunted, and kept livestock. A haven founded by Ervin James.

Resilience and strength are in our DNA, put there with every drop of pain, every sound of laughter, every heartbreak for simply existing, every hug that heals. We carry on, growing stronger generation to generation. We've overcome in some way or another every obstacle, but our stories remain hidden in the back of history, footnotes to narratives we haven't been the center of. This story is about the strength, pain, and heart of a man born a slave but who left a legacy for generations to come.

This story is based on the life of Ervin James. It is for all of us who struggle, break, and find the pieces to put ourselves back together recognizing the story, lessons, and beauty in scars seen and unseen. Each of our stories is different, but if we are here today, it is because our ancestors have carried in them and passed on to us their DNA. I urge you to remember and honor the resilience and strength you carry in every fiber of your being.

In writing Ervin James' story, I honor his voice, the language and dialect of a man born and raised in slavery, and who lived much of his childhood in the south. I honor the language born from struggle and the use of verbs in a more natural way for those forced to take on a foreign tongue, while making sense of that tongue through a language stored deep within their souls.

This is how I am related to Ervin James. My name is Bernette Sherman (1976), the daughter of Rebecca Washington (1952, Mark Hudson), who was the daughter of Rosabell Moses (1921, Ezekiel Washington), who was the daughter of Rebecca (1886, Peter Moses), who was the daughter of Eli (~1865, Hannah Davis), who was the son of Ervin James and Nora James.

Notes about the Language and Voice

Now put to rest your ideas of traditional literature, forego the lessons learned in your English classes, and allow yourself to forget the formality of English. Yes, let it go as you slip back to an era when most people didn't go to school, being illiterate was more common than being able to read amongst all people in this land, regardless of race, and survival was the goal of a harsh reality. The rules you may be accustomed to are bent and broken. You'll also notice his use of the English language changes some partway through his story. This is intentional, based on the effect of being in a different place.

You'll notice that the language and voice of other characters are unique to them and are often shared in a "diary" stream of consciousness type voice, usually present tense. There are also instances where Lilly and Ervin are in the same chapter and the best voice for those moments is present tense. I chose to leave one chapter in particular (thirty) in the present tense. You may understand why when you read it.

The purpose of this story is not to create a typical literary work, but to create an inspiring piece that speaks to people where they are through conditions that, on some level, are relatable to the experience of being Black in America. This is #ownvoices.

The Story of
ERVIN
JAMES

Virginia to Charleston

I was born in Virginia near the river. The fields stretched out for what seem like forever, looking like a sea a corn. It growed high in the summer sun begging for somebody to end its misery. Only ones that did was us. Like we took they heat and took it for ourselves. We done harvest it once but they want us to help some more while we still here. I looks up at the cornstalk taller than me and mama and on up to the clouds where God must sit. I wonder if he sitting on a fat cloud now looking down at us. Mama nudge my arm and tell me to get the corn off the lower part of the stalk and stop staring off. I look up again and the cloud moving. Must be God floating away too.

Mama was a good cook. That's what everybody say and I ain't like nobody food much as hers. She turn that cornmeal to gold. I had a brother and a sister too, but they was older than me. Greta was my sister. She ain't long turn ten when she got send off some moons past in the winter. My brother Ethan been seventeen. He gone too. I ain't never seed him again after mama make me go back inside when they start hitting him with that whip. She sayed wasn't nothing nobody could do cuz the misses ain't like the way he looked at her. I telled mama Ethan ain't look at her no kinda way but she ain't believe me. Sayed since the misses sayed it, it was so and I was a liar. I sayed I wasn't and she hit me cross my face and telled me I better learn fore I wind up like Ethan. Then she walk off huffing and her shoulders all tight.

After that it been only mama and me, but we was together. I ain't knowed my daddy. They sold him after she start getting full in the belly with me. Mama sayed daddy was strong in the head, the heart and the body. She talk bout him and she get this piece a candlelight in her eye then it go away like somebody put a snuffer over it. She act sad to talk bout him. She sayed master ain't been happy bout it. He had a sweet eye for my mama. I seed how he look at her when he come and check on the cooking. The master wife ain't like that or how mama was so good in the kitchen and how she been in the house all the time or that the master liked her. Greta was good in the kitchen too or starting to be. She ain't like that my sister was too much resembling the master and couldn't stand to see her. But Greta always been smart, a good learner and quiet so I figure Greta got someplace fast.

I figures that's why she had that scratchy looking man to take us off too. I ain't been but eight when we leaved Virginia and started to South Carolina. Only me and mama.

That man skin looked like leather faded in the sun and his beard been gray and rough. He bought us to take back south, further south. Some spose to go on to Louisiana. That's far as his line was going. I walked behind bigger men, like my brother was. Or what I imagine how my daddy been. I wasn't big though. I ain't never really been that big. Guess they ain't figure I'd be all that strong and so I wasn't worth keeping. Specially without a mama and with my mama.

We walked forever it seemed. We started walking on the full moon after they celebrate America being free. We walked in the woods and in fields. We pass farms and fields full a animals. I seed the south part a Virginia long the river and taste salt in my mouth and it tickle my nose. Men and women on the wooded roads look at us like they ain't never seed a sight like it. Dozens of black men and women and children walking with ropes and chains. They ain't never sayed nothing and ain't wanna catch a look in the eye neither.

It been hot but that ain't matter. We stopped along the way to work fields to earn our food while we was marching so they could sell us. Some younger men and some older men tried to run chain together but they ain't make it. Not far. The men riding with the horse beat 'em enough to scare us but not enough to leave marks. They ain't wanna leave nothing that might scare off the buyers. That's what mama say. Cept once.

We been going til a full moon come back and this man we nickname Rice ain't come back from the woods when it been time to go. They yell for us to keep walking and they catch back up with us. They taked three big men. Two was hairy and look like the old gray beard man. Like they was his boys. The other look like he try to grow hair on his face too but it ain't work so good.

Dogs and horses took after him in the woods where we peed and they sayed to us, Walk! Slow.

We walked like they sayed and the dogs start barking loud and the two they leaved with us taked off too. Next thing I knowed I hear some noises like fighting then a gun go off. The gray beard old man unhook his horse and done gone off after the sound and his other men get closer round us. Gray beard stop where we can see still him cuz them three men come riding back. He waving his arm in the air then we stop. He looked at something can't nobody see. He get off his horse and then back on and one after another they come riding back like a parade. Mama scream when the last horse start coming.

What's wrong mama! I asked her.

Women crying and screaming but they wasn't saying why.

Then that one who can't grow no beard come riding round all us slow so everybody can see but ain't nobody wanna look.

Look! Any one of you niggers think you wanna be free? Who wants to be free? Tell me now and I'll show you the only freedom you're ever gonna see. It'll be at the hand of this shotgun. I'm sick of you niggers thinking you can run! You belong to us. Bought and paid for. I say where you go and when. Let this be a warning. We're done going easy. I'd rather kill every last one of you then see you running off free and screwing up the makings of a great nation.

He drag Rice by his feet tied to the horse saddle. Blood cover his whole shirt and they ain't even close his eyes.

Take a good long look. I don't want to do this to anyone else. But I will. Remember this is what freedom looks like. Let's go.

Mama say don't be scared for us or nobody. It was just the way it was and we ain't had no choice. She sayed that one day things was gon change but it wasn't the time yet. I wondered when it was gon be the time. I wondered when God was gon come and save us and take us to the promised land like they talk about in church. I wondered if I had to be like Rice and die to see it.

That old slave buyer and seller rode up ahead of us in a carriage, his head covered from the heat and his feet not having to bear the hard earth. Meanwhile our feet was bleeding and we had to stop to wash and rinse them and rewrap them if we needed. I still can't figure how we made it. I guess we ain't have a choice if we wanna live and not die in the middle of nowhere. Even then I knowed it wasn't alright. It was never alright.

When we got to Charleston we couldn't hardly see ahead cuz it was raining so hard. Mama sayed God was crying for us and angry bout the whole business. Rain on my head ain't never been so sweet. The rain make the heat drip away and I feel clean. I was tired but it give me some strength. If I was bigger I might could escape down that river in Charleston and they might never find me. But I wasn't old enough or big enough to do that without mama or those dogs find me. And mama wasn't escaping nowhere. She was scared to even think bout it or talk bout it. She just as soon walk away and do anything else stead a listen to other people talk bout leaving or even wanting to leave.

She never sayed to me why but I seed her back. I wondered how they was gon account for that at the market. The man who brought us to Charleston ain't seem bothered. Maybe he figure she ain't gon run when she got me. I reckon she won't.

I got washed top to toe with a hose that stung like pine needles dipped in ice. They ain't give no warning. We shivered in that long skinny red brick and concrete hall in two lines on either side. Women and children on one side and the men on the other and that been it in that room side them men trying to sell us. We all naked like I came out my mama. The men got cleaned, women got cleaned and they ain't care nothing bout our nakedness. They rubbed oil onto most of us. The children they ain't bother with. They took a rag and wiped our teeth one

4

after another. I close my lips and that ugly man sayed, Open up boy! Ain't got all day!

Mama look at me to open my mouth. Same nasty rag going in and out of our mouths. They made the women put they hair back neat as they could and rubbed a black oily goop on it, making it look even darker and shine like it do in the sun. The little bit a silver hair round mama forehead disappeared.

Then they start taking us out. Mama keeped my hand in hers tight. She sayed I need to stay close so they keep us together cuz I's young. Mama look scared though. She heard things bout South Carolina and how it been a mean state. She wished we woulda been sent bout anywhere else than where we was. My hand hurt in hers but I ain't let out more than a slow breath cuz I's scared she'd loose up and then somebody might snatch me away from her.

Ellie Porter been her name and she been bout 34 years old. She was pretty with deep brown skin and soft brown eyes. Pretty enough the men in there look at her wrong like. She had full cheeks and a round face and a pretty smile that made people get settled and calm when they seed her. Made them feel she was safe. I think that helped her be in the house to cook and be round much as she was. Let me be in there with her and my sister til they sent her away. That bout broke mama. I think she was glad when master sent us away together, but not when she found out where we was going. I heard her cussing him under her breath and then saying, God forgive me. Then cuss them both, master and the misses, right again.

The old white man with the rough beard was probably only fifty but that seemed old to me. He called mama and me into that room with all them white men and women dressed in suits and hats and fine dresses standing round staring at us and pointing and whispering. We ain't never seed nothing like it and I ain't knowed what to do.

One a them big strong young men that tried to run was already in there standing on some wood so folks can see him. He still look mad and look at me in my eyes when I walk by. I wonder where he got taken from and where his mama been cuz he been around Ethan age.

That man with the beard telled mama to get up there on top a wooden box and for me to stand with her. I walk up next to mama and they start coming round to look. I tried to hide behind mama but he pulled me from back a her so they could see us. He offered us both together as some special. I heard people asking questions and then men come up demanding mama open her mouth and cough and spread her legs and lift her arms. She had this dingy piece a cloth round her top and another one round her waist and legs like the one I had round my waist and legs.

They ask me how old I was and pulled my lips apart to look at my teeth and gums. One telled me to make a muscle with my arms and I looked at mama.

He yelled, I'm talking to you boy, don't look at your mama. Answer me.

Eight, I sayed and he nodded.

He had eyes that ain't look evil. He walked away and studied another boy Cotter who was ten and came on the trip with us but ain't had nobody. No mama or brother or sister or auntie. Nobody. I ain't knowed where he got picked up from neither.

Another man come up asking bout us. Other men and women. They'd be talking bout money and how much for Ellie, how much for me. Together. Just Ellie. They'd ask mama what kinds of things she can cook and how long she was a cook and the old white man swore she was the best cook south of Tennessee and that I was smart and well behaved.

They keeped asking bout us separate and he keeped saying we was a package. He sayed, I don't separate at that age. Not good for my business. But nobody bought us. Somebody got Cotter and that older one remind me of my brother Ethan. I knowed he went to a plantation like we leaved. Mama say he gon be put right out in the fields cuz he young and strong. I ask her if they gon do that to me and she ain't answer at first then she sayed, That's what they do Ervin. Take our strong men and work them til they ain't got nothing to give.

We stayed in that damp room behind the hall they was making deals and sales in for a week, waiting for somebody to pick us. Mama was getting nervous. Others keeped going. She sayed if somebody ain't buy us soon they might not keep us together. I cried all night long. My eyes was puffy and red the next day when I step back on that block. That man who make me talk to him and not my mama was there again. He had two woman with him this time. The one was his wife and the other his sister. His sister was studying my mama and his wife was studying me. They keeped going back and whispering.

I couldn't talk to mama. I only could hold her hand. I squeezed it cuz my nerves been so bad my stomach hurt and I was like to lose that nasty mush they give us. They oiled me down that day and it was hot in that building. I remember the sweat sitting in little balls on the oil on my shoulders and chest and flies coming in and out.

They seemed to talk and look and talk and look forever fore they started talking to the old white man who bringed us there. He looked back and forth at me and mama talking to the man and the women between looking at us. We been standing there all this time, other men and women poking us and making mama spread her legs and raise her arms and asking bout how old she was. The old gray beard man sayed she was twenty-seven knowing it was a lie but it raised her price if she had more years to bear children.

A man was in front of me asking how big my daddy was and I telled him I ain't knowed. He was asking me something else when the old white man came and sayed, These two aren't for sale anymore.

I looked at the man with the two women. Mama grabbed my hand til it folded in hers and I ain't let no breath out. I ain't know what was gon happen. The man walked over and sayed I'd be coming with him and his wife and that mama was going to his sisters.

Mama screamed, No don't take my baby. Don't take my baby. He's only eight. God no. Please.

I just cried but ain't no sound come out my lips.

The man telled mama to gather herself and for me to stop the crying. He said his sister live less than a mile from him and we'd see each other. Mama stopped breathing and I been scared she might pass out.

We're leaving all together. I don't need two servants. But my sister needs help around the house and she's agreed to take you on. It's not easy work and we don't suffer laziness. He turned to me and sayed, I expect you to work hard and to help in whatever way is needed.

I ain't answer. I ain't nod. I just standed there, my hand in my mama's, looking at his feet. It was the only place to look. Black shoes that looked worn but that he done polished to come buy us. They wasn't rich looking like the master we had in Virginia. I slowly looked at mama and she couldn't look at me. Her eyes was swoll almost shut.

Is she gonna be a problem? The sister ask bout mama. Are you gonna be a problem? I'm doing you a favor you know, so you're not separated from that boy of yours. Or should I let somebody else come and get ya, and who knows when that'll be or who it'll be.

No ma'am. I won't be a problem. I promise. Mama voice been like a whisper but that woman heard it.

Good, she sayed and mama squeezed my hand.

The man sayed something to the old man that selled us. Then the old scraggly man give mama a handful of clothes and send us to the back room to get dressed and be collected while they finished business.

Mama ain't had no voice. She got dressed like she did the day after they selled my brother and how she got dressed when they selled my sister. That's how she got dressed. I ain't say nothing either. Wasn't nothing to say. We wasn't all the way separated. That been good enough. Her new misses sposed to be walking distance. That mean I gets to see mama on Sundays and maybe some other times. I's still scared though.

I ain't never been without mama or somebody I knowed. Back home in Virginia I knowed everybody on that plantation. I knowed everybody who worked the fields and in the house. I knowed the people in the workshop. Everybody been like family but that's over and now I's gon be the only slave at this white man's house with his wife and nobody else. Mama gon be alone too. We wasn't the last ones there. But we ain't say nothing to noone when we leaved. No goodbyes or see you later cuz we ain't know and it wasn't good.

Mama came out first looking at the ground like she'd done every day since coming there. I glanced up and looked at the woman who was my other owner and then quick back to the ground. She whispered something to my new master. He turn and look at me and sayed, Did you look my wife in the eye just now, boy?

I stayed hushed. He asked me again and sayed I better answer him when he asked a question. I sayed something bout I might have but it was a mistake and I was sorry. He telled me that I best learn to respect her and where to look. I just sayed, Yessuh, and followed behind mama. Her owner walked in front of us to the carriage and my owners walked behind us like they been proud.

Arriving at Master John's

They dropped mama off and her owner rolled her eyes when mama hugged me tight. She sayed to be a good boy, to speak only when spoken to, and to work hard. She got this serious look like she might hit me on my rear and sayed, Don't give them no reasons. Don't give them no reasons.

When mama was gone I looked back at her, watching while she walked to the side door. She stopped there with the lady talking to her. We started off again but I could see her new owner pointing things out from the step like she was showing her around but not really going nowhere. Mama nodded but she was looking back at me too. I could tell, but she was scared to look too much. I think her owner wasn't so nice. But we was close.

We turned left down a street with light colored dirt, only bout ten feet wide, maybe less. Then he turned the cart left again into a long driveway. Trees was on both sides, some of them scraggly and then there was a big magnolia on the right side, half covering the house with shade. It looked sad, but it was still pretty. Like mama.

He stopped the carriage and turned back to face me. Now look here boy, you can call me Master and my wife you can call Misses Charlotte. She'll see to your needs being that you're still a boy, but don't expect to get spoiled or more than you need. We don't have room for greed or laziness. Everyone pulls their weight around here. And if you work hard you'll be fine. I'm fair. Hard but fair. We don't have a big ole plantation like the one you probably came from. Fact is, we just have a garden we tend to with our daughter and I got my workshop.

That's where you'll be mostly. My wife teaches piano lessons too. You'll help out wherever else you're needed.

I nodded, not really understanding everything he sayed. I just heard work, work, work. It ain't matter though. That's all we was to them. I hated that we'd turned the corner and I couldn't see the house mama was at no more. I could walk it easy but I wanted to see it cuz then maybe some days I'd catch a glimpse of her outside or something.

Now I know you're worried about your mama, Master sayed.

I wondered how he knowed. He looked out the side of the carriage like she was coming up the street and I looked too.

You'll get to see her regular on Sundays and my sister brings her family over quite frequently for dinners and such. She'll be busy with her work and you'll be busy with yours. You'll hardly have time to notice she's not around.

I ain't believe that part but I ain't let him know.

There wasn't no small slave houses anywhere I could see. Where the carriage stop I seed a barn set back from the house and I figured that's where I'd sleep. I sat where I was. I wasn't moving til they telled me to. I ain't wanna give them no reasons, like mama sayed. Misses Charlotte ain't look at me or speak to me. She got out the carriage and walked through the front door.

A big girl or youngish woman looked out at the carriage. She was trying to see in the back, probably at me. She was curious like. Her hair was light brown almost yellow and pulled back into a bun. I was scared to look any more than this.

Alright you go head and get out now, Master said. I edged my way to the end of the wooden bench and jumped off the back of the carriage. I guess it was more a cart since nothing was covered up or closed. I waited behind the cart for him to tell me where to go. I was scared. There wasn't nobody I knowed and nothing I had.

He sayed, I'm gonna show you round the workshop while Misses Charlotte fixes dinner. Then we'll eat and you'll get settled in.

He turn his head to face me and looked me square in my eyes. I bout peed myself. I ain't know if he was gon be like that

11

man on the old plantation that beat my brother til he droop from that pole with blood running down his back and ole Nellie had to put this nasty ointment on him. Or if he was gon be better than that. I ain't wanna get beaten or killed or selled far away from mama.

Look here boy. I know you scared. I see it in your eyes. I know you're just a boy. I'm gonna tell you two things that you'd do good to remember. We ain't rich so we work hard and everybody has to do their part - I said that before. And the second is that I'm hard but I'm fair. I said that too. But you need to remember that. I know this ain't easy but it's the way it is. I need help and you're it. I'll treat you good as I can but you gotta do your part. And you should be happy.

He look at me like I was spose to say something but wasn't nothing to say.

You'll learn a trade. Not every slave gets to do that.

I wasn't sure what a trade was. I ain't know if I was gon learn to trade things or that he might trade me for someone else.

Misses Charlotte came out the back of the house and called out, John. Master answered. She sayed, Make sure you bring him round this door for dinner. We can't have nigras coming through the front.

Master paused a second. I think he shook his head a little bit and sayed okay or of course or something like that. He wasn't thinking bout that. He was already thinking bout showing me the place I'd be sleeping - the barn in the back of the house. The house was simple but we walked right by it.

He pushed the door apart and the smell a wood come out. Sawdust. I sneeze a few times and wipe my nose. Wood was everywhere. Big pieces, cut pieces. Small and medium. Some was shaped like things and others was already in furniture.

Come on in boy. This is my workshop. I make furniture for the rich folk in town, some businesses, and other stuff. I do good work but if I want to make enough money I need help. You ever been in a woodshop before?

I shook my head.

You do talk don't cha? I got these two women round here who never stop but they just go on and on gossiping. Well you're gonna learn how to make furniture too. Help me keep up with the work. Seems everybody wants something new.

I wondered if I'd be in the fields but there wasn't none. Then I thinked bout mama in the kitchen at his sisters house.

He showed me round the shop. The wood cutter, a saw, horses set up in pairs, three sets. He had a big board standing attached to two wooden poles on T stands and they was anchored to the ground. On it was leather stretched from the top to the bottom and clipped. He had another one that was smaller but nothing was on that one. A big wooden table had all manner of furniture in different shapes. Some almost done, some he was sanding, others he was putting together. Some he was staining.

What do you like to do boy?

I looked at Master. Nobody never asked me that before and I ain't had no answer since I ain't never had time to like doing nothing. Since I could remember we was always doing something somebody else like for us to do. When I could sit long enough I separated bushels of corn - the good ones and the bad ones. Whether they was bad or not I couldn't tell at first but then I got to know that too. I used to sit beside Greta and separate them and she'd take out the bad ones and put them to the side to feed the hogs and stuff. This was different. By the time we leaved Virginia I was in the field picking corn beside mama. Hot sun and long days.

I ask what you like to do.

I like picking out the good corn from the feed corn suh.

I mean for relaxing, he sayed, like I ain't had no sense.

I shrug cuz I ain't knowed what that word mean.

You don't look like you eat much boy or did they just not feed ya much?

I wasn't sure how to answer that. I pulled on my shirt a little and then took a step back away from everything he showed me waiting for him to tell me what to do or where to go next. He ain't seem angry far as I could tell, just stressed. That's the best way I can describe it. I was scared to ask him nothing or say nothing.

Okay. Well, let me show you the garden.

It was pitch black out and he wanna show me the garden. Cept for the moon, wasn't no light to see it by. Like he ain't knowed morning was gon come. He just keeped on talking.

We usually just grow for ourselves and then we trade or sell the extra. It's not much more than that we can do with it. But we got more land we can use if we get to that point. Right now, we just don't have the hands or time to work it. Just me and my wife and my daughter. That's all we got.

I wondered why he ain't have no more kids. Everybody had lots of kids and he just had one girl and she was already big and he was already getting old like his wife. Maybe they wasn't that old but he was older than mama by more than a few years.

He put his hands in his pocket and look like he was gonna say something else but then ain't let nothing come out. He looked at the field that needed to be tended to and then at the grass beside it that he coulda been farming and making money off of. Then he sayed, Alright let me show you where you gon be sleeping and let you get cleaned up for dinner.

I was confused. We ate after rinsing our hands best we could and putting some water on our face. I figured that's what he meant.

He took me in the backdoor and on the side was an inside outhouse. He sayed he built up this kind of toilet that was a tube. Sayed he used some kind of skin and barrel and the main outhouse was outside. That the inside one wasn't for heavy work. I guess that meant it was just for peeing. He looked at me and sayed I could use the outhouse for my business. That the inside one wasn't for my use.

He took me just past that to a room in the back. It was big enough for a mat on the floor and there was a box and a bible on one side when the door open. I remember seeing a book like that when we had church, but I ain't knowed what he expect me to do with it. I opened the box then shut it real quick cuz I ain't asked him.

It's okay. You can open that. It's yours. Misses Charlotte wanted to make sure you had that before you came. You got another set of clothes in there for when it's time to get cleaned up. Misses Charlotte doesn't like it dirty in the house and doesn't like work clothes being worn when you're not working.

He stop and look at me with the candle hanging in front of him. He nodded like I ask him something then sayed, You know, she's glad we got you. You'll be a help in that garden. There's a lot of work to do out there. We'll do that tomorrow matter of fact and then we'll get started in the workshop when the harvest is done or it's down to where the ladies can handle it. If I don't get these orders done it'll be worse than a few ears of corn and collards going to waste.

He looked at me like he was waiting on something else.

Thank you suh, was all I could say.

Alright now. You put on those clothes over there in that trunk. And then put your clothes by the door. I set you up a table outside this room for you to take your dinner. Now we got some rules in the house. You can't go into the living quarters. You can come in and out that door we just used and you can come far as this little area outside your room. There's a chair in your room for sitting and a table right here for eating.

He made a small table and chair for whoever was in that room to eat by themselves in that dark corner. He looked at the table and where it sat and then back at me. We have candles. Now you met Misses Charlotte. My daughter is Priscilla and she's approaching sixteen. She does take gentlemen callers now and one very seriously. He may come around here. You let me know if they do anything they shouldn't alright? He waited again like I should laugh or something.

Yes suh, I whispered but I wasn't telling nobody nothing. Don't give them no reasons. Nobody. I knowed the woman run the house and that's why I was here now. Cuz that mean woman in Virginia ain't like my mama. Women send you away when they ain't like you. I ain't plan to cross neither of them.

Alright I'll leave you be for now. I'll knock on the door when dinner is ready. It'll be out here on the table. Make sure you put those clothes by the door so Misses Charlotte can see to them.

I wondered what she was gon see about them. The holes? Just look at them? Or actually clean them? They ain't been washed altogether clean since we leaved Virginia. I wondered if the clothes in that trunk had holes in them too. Master walked out the room and pulled the door shut. I standed there looking at it. I was still there when he knocked on the door saying dinner was sitting there. I ain't move. Even though my stomach been flat and making noises the whole ways from Charleston wasn't no food gon settle it. I wanted mama. I wondered if she was gon try and see me but then I remember she ain't seed where they bring me to.

Wasn't no windows or nothing to see out. I ain't knowed if it was light or dark out now. A lantern was in the corner but that been it. I was scared to sit down in the chair or touch the chest or even the bed. I ain't never had nothing of mine before or a room or a bed or even a chair. I sat in the middle of the floor and I only woke up when Master John opened the door.

He seed me there and sayed, You can't sleep there all night and you need to eat for your strength. Misses Charlotte wouldn't be pleased if that food wasn't eaten. Now take off those dirty clothes so they can be cleaned. Put on the night clothes in the trunk since it's so late.

I knowed only one kinda clothes. They must be same as day clothes. He keeped the door open this time just a crack and then stepped away again. You need to eat something boy. You need to be strong.

My stomach growled. I was scared to close the door and standed behind it for a while fore getting up my nerve to go back into that trunk on the floor. There was a white dress inside for sleeping and then a pair of trousers, socks, shoes, and a white shirt and suspenders. I looked at the shoes and put them beside my foot. My feet had never been in shoes. At the bottom was heavy boots. I ain't never had my feet locked up. Mama had some for when she worked in the house and came into the main parts to serve meals or help with guests or sometimes when she was sent into town to the market. I never went into the main part of the old master's house or step foot off that plantation til we was gone for good.

I took the shoes and the white dress and hide myself behind the door so he couldn't see me getting undressed and back dressed. I heard stories bout some masters taking in boys for other reasons.

I hurried up and put on the dress after I taked off my shirt. Then I taked off my pants. I put the shoes on my feet and put my clothes by the door like he sayed to. He musta been listening out for me cuz he asked me if I washed up. I ain't say nothing cuz I ain't knowed what I was sposed to do.

Did you wash your body boy? he asked me with his hands cross his chest.

I wondered if that's what he wanted me like this for. He came into the room and looked around.

He pointed to the corner where a bowl sat on the floor. Right over there. That's your wash bowl. Before you get dressed for the evening or put on your other clothes you make sure you wash up. Either Charlotte or Priscilla will fetch the water daily. There's a rag right by the bowl.

I only washed all the way up for Sundays and only after other people done used the water. This water was all mine and I got new water every day. I wanted to tell mama.

Alright go head take off the night dress wash up and put it back on. He standed there like he was waiting for me and I standed there too. He looked down at my feet. And you don't need those shoes on in the house. Those are going out and company shoes. Sometimes you might need to look more presentable.

I took the shoes off and put them back in the trunk. I was hoping he'd go. He looked at me and then he pulled the door shut this time. I took off the dress and kneeled down by the bowl of water. I put my hands in it and then put the water on my face. I put my hands in it again and touched my shoulders and my chest. I could see the water marks when I touched my thighs.

I picked up the rag and put it inside the water and it soaked up enough to where it was dripping and I pulled it all the way out and ran it over my face and my neck like mama did. Then I ran it over my chest and my arms then down my legs and feet. I looked back at the door then I cleaned my other parts. I put the rag back in the water and pulled it back out watching the water run down the rag into the bowl and some onto the floor. I think I stayed there with that water for a long time til my stomach started growling even louder I finally put back on that dress and went to the door.

I opened it slow and peeked out to see if Master or Misses Charlotte or Priscilla was around. Then I went to the little table and looked at the plate sitting there. They musta thinked they was feeding Master. I ain't never seed so much food on a plate. She had put peas and mashed potatoes and there was some kinda meat. Ham I think. And it ain't been the worst part of the pig. It was regular. Not the best, but regular. I sat down and picked at it. Mama was the best cook anywhere. I looked at the peas and the mashed potatoes and picked up a pea at a time to put in my mouth.

Don't pick at your food. Foods not easy to come by and I won't have you wasting it and playing in it, ya hear? I looked toward the voice and it was Misses Charlotte.

Yes ma'am. It's good ma'am, I telled her. I wasn't hungry no more. But I ain't wanna make her mad.

Of course it is. Now eat up.

I picked up the spoon on the table and put some mashed potatoes on it and put it in my mouth with her watching me. She made sure I swallowed it fore she went back where she come from. I could hear her say something like he's finally eating. He must be starving, such a skinny thing.

I wasn't skinny. Least I ain't think so. But Master John was bigger than most men. Maybe that's why I look skinny to her.

Well, leave him be for now. I know he's hungry. He'll eat. Tomorrow we'll get him out there to help you pull the vegetables up and sort them. It's a long day so he needs to be full and rested.

Well, I need to be rested too, she telled Master John. As does Priscilla. You as well. It's getting late and you are past due on the orders from the Johnsons.

I wasn't trying to be in they business but I couldn't help it. Even with mama working in Master's house we never slept the night there. We shared a cabin with Masie who kept the house and with Masie's husband and kids. The master's wife was fine with Masie. Masie wasn't pretty at all and never smiled and when she did she still wasn't pretty at all. She just cleaned like the Misses liked and ain't say nothing. She watched the Misses kids when the Misses had her lady friends over and did whatever else she needed to do. And then when Masie's oldest daughter was old enough she helped in the house and with Master's younger kids.

Eight of us been in that cabin when Greta, mama, and me was all there. Masie and mama would cook together and sing together sometimes when they got back late in the evening. Mama would tend her little garden where she grew peas, carrots and yams. She had one chicken too. One the master thinked wasn't gon make it and sayed mama could have. Mama gave that chicken life and that chicken gave us eggs. There was chickens here from what I could tell by the coop in the back behind the garden. He called it a garden but it ain't been the kind a garden mama and Masie had. It been big enough to feed all us plus two more cabins, at least.

Mama. That been all I thinked about.

I ain't been sure what to do with my plate. My stomach couldn't eat everything even if I been hungry but I ain't want Misses Charlotte mad at me.

Suh, I whispered. I sayed it louder, Suh? I standed up and tiptoed to the edge of the end of the little hall and peaked round the corner. Suh? I sayed even louder.

What is it? she called back.

I...I...I need to go.

Well then go on then.

The whole place was covered up in darkness and I ain't know what they had round there.

I spose cuz she ain't heard nothing she sayed, Take the light in your room boy. Make it quick.

I wrapped the food up in my shirt sitting on the floor by the door and stuffed it under my night dress.

Don't go out there barefoot now. You'll have to wash your feet up again. You got boots in that trunk. Put 'em on and then take em off and shake them at the door before you come back in.

Yes ma'am, I called back. I put the wrapped up clothes and food on the floor and put the boots on my feet. They flopped like they was for someone five years older than me. I shoved the food back under the dress and tiptoed out the door holding my stomach with one hand and the light with the other.

You don't need to move like you sneaking. Are you sneaking? She was standing looking at me with her hands crossed over her waist.

No ma'am. I just gotta use it ma'am. I got to the door past the inside outhouse and then opened it. She came behind me and waited in the doorway watching me. I was glad cuz maybe nobody or nothing would take me with her looking. Then I might not ever see mama. I went to the outhouse and closed the door then slid the clothes out of my dress. I shook it into the hole before sitting down.

I couldn't hold my breath long enough. I think Master John had just been in there not too long before. I knowed the door had open and shut and that musta been it. I finished up and shoved my dirty clothes under the dress and ran back to the house fast as I could.

What you runnin from? she ask me. Ain't nothin chasin you boy. She almost look like she wanted to laugh but she put her chin down and rubbed it with her hand.

Then she look me up and down and sayed, Take the boots off here and shake them off.

I ain't wanna take the boots off and was scared to sit down.

Take the boots off so you don't bring nothing back inside. I woulda had to sit inside the door she held open to take them off and she mighta seed my balled up shirt. *Don't give them no reasons.* I ain't want her to sell me away. I sat down carefully, holding my stomach. I slipped off one boot and then the other. I shook them from where I sat.

Give them here boy. That's not gonna do nothing to shake off no dirt. She grabbed the boots and slammed the bottoms together outside the door. Now you get to bed. It's an early morning.

I held my stomach and ran back to the room and I dropped the clothes by the door. I went inside and standed behind the door looking at it and the bed. I grabbed the blanket from the bed and laid down on the floor.

Ellie

They just rode off with my baby. Took him somewhere close by they sayed, but I ain't knowed where. I ain't knowed how many days til Sunday. He had these people who I ain't know and I had these people I ain't know. And that Misses Shelly.

She was a mess I soon figured out after they dropped me off. The outside looked alright but inside it look like a woman ain't lived there in years. She act like it been alright when we walked inside. Holding her head up and bossing me like I done it. She was walking through the rooms looking for something when kids started coming out to see and look at me.

Is this our new slave mama? A girl who looked a couple years older than my boy asked. She looked curious and proud like they'd done something special. Her skin's so dark. Can I touch it? she asked Misses Shelly.

Of course, Misses Shelly sayed. She's ours.

The three younger kids reached for my face and I let them touch all over my skin. No choice. They asked if they could feel my hair under my scarf and bonnet cuz they heard it was like wool or cotton. Misses Shelly said yes again so I took off my hair covering and let them put they nasty fingers in it. They snagging it and yanking it. Misses Shelly could tell it musta hurt cuz she wave them off me and say it been enough. The older boy stayed where he been when he first come in the room like he ain't care and went back to whatever he been doing.

What's she gonna do mama? the same girl called out to Misses Shelly.

She's gonna help me around the house and with you all. She came back to the room we was in and we was still in front of the door. Where's your daddy?

Out. He had some business. The bigger girl shrug her shoulders like it wasn't nothing.

Misses Shelly got real quiet for a moment. Then she asked if he'd been gone long.

Yeah, the littlest girl sayed. We're hungry mama. What are we gonna eat?

Well, Misses Shelly sayed with this big smile cross her lips, We have Ellie here to help. From what they said, she's an excellent cook. Let's see what we have in the kitchen for her to fix you up some dinner. Why don't you two show her the kitchen? Ellie, follow them.

I just thought how she ain't have something cooked up for those babies already, knowing the trip was gon be long. That oldest girl coulda fixed something for them.

Yes ma'am, I sayed. I knowed a kitchen and there wasn't nothing I couldn't make. That littlest girl acted like she got a new doll. She ain't wanna leave my side. Misses Shelly disappeared somewhere and the bigger girl looked at me from the table where she sat. Then she started asking questions. She ask bout where I come from and how old I is and what my favorite food is. A thousand questions. I barely answer one fore she asked another. I don't know where the younger boy gon off to. He sneaked away somewhere but I figure he be back for supper. I ain't see Misses Shelly again til I put the food on the table. When I seed her she look like somebody done cut onions up in her face. I ain't pay it no mind. Wasn't none of my business.

Still a Slave

(Now listen, I know they think I was born here in South Carolina. They ain't got no record of me fore then. To the world I ain't much exist fore Master John and Misses Charlotte picked me out in Charleston. But this should set that record straight. I was already eight years old when I came to that house. That's how I could be helpful.)

Master John came knocking on the door and wake me up out my sleep. I startled something awful. It was pitch black in that room and I ain't remembered where I was. Mama usually wake me up or my sister til they taked her away. But it wasn't never a knock on a door.

Time to get dressed and eat your breakfast. It'll be out here in a minute. Here, he sayed fore opening the door. Take this fresh lamp and give me the other one.

I picked up the light that was burned out and traded it with him. My finger hit his and I sayed, Sorry suh.

He act like it wasn't nothing and closed the door. Then he called back through it, When you're done eating, come on back to the field. Your boots are out here by the door. Those are your work boots.

I ain't know bout no work boots. The men in the fields on the horses wore boots but nobody who worked outside in a field wore them. They just had some ole simple leather shoes. I taked off the dress and put it on the bed to look at it. It was clean. I look at myself. At my arms and my legs and wondered if I been skinny like Misses Charlotte sayed. My stomach start talking again. Wasn't nothing gon change but maybe I get to see mama soon. And if I wasn't eating and got skinny she'd be upset and worried and I ain't want her upset, not at me.

I put on the pants and cracked open the door. These sposed to be good pants and I ain't certain whether I should put them on. They clean but they scratchy on the inside. I rubbing my legs when I open the door wider to look and see if somebody out there. My clothes sitting on the floor in a neat pile and sure enough Misses Charlotte standing at the end of the hall to where I couldn't go pass. Her hands folded cross her stomach like she knowed something. I grab the clothes real quick and get back into the room and close the door. I ain't know if maybe she knowed and just ain't say nothing or maybe she understand and ain't say nothing. I ain't even see the food she set out too.

I put on my old clothes. They was clean, smelling like soap. I sucked in the smell of the shirt then I buttoned it up. I unfolded the pants and there was socks in with them. I ain't never wore a pair of socks. They was scratchy and brown and too big. Musta been some of Master's socks cuz they went bout up to my knees, scratchy the whole way. I put on my boots and then tried to put the pants on and they wouldn't go over so I took off the boots and put on the pants then the boots. My stuff was still had holes but it was clean.

I opened the door and peeked outside to see if Misses Charlotte was still there but she'd gone. A plate with a cup of water was on the table. I looked at all the food and wondered who could eat this much. But I was hungry. She musta heard me sit down cuz she came back to the corner and sayed, Now you better eat this morning cuz there's not gonna be another meal like this til dinner and I'm sure you don't want to be hungry. We don't waste food round here, you understand?

Yes ma'am. I picked up the fork and waited for her to leave, picking at the eggs on the plate. She walked away satisfied. I shoved a forkful a eggs into my mouth. They was good. And there was toast with butter and two pieces of real thick bacon. I ate everything. I ain't knowed how hungry I was til I started eating. I ate too fast and gave myself a stomach-ache almost.

Miss Charlotte walked past me carrying a hat while I was drinking up the water. She looked at the plate and then sayed, See you outside. Your boots and hat are at the back door.

I leaved the plate where it was on that table. I was putting on the boots when I heard her come back. She musta been getting my plate and cup. I put the hat on but it keeped sliding down my forehead and covering my eyes. Misses Charlotte come behind me and pulled it from the back so it sat more behind my head. She walked past me and towards the garden. She had on her work clothes too. I standed up and walked behind her. Priscilla came out behind me. She wasn't too happy to be out there neither.

Master John already been out there. Baskets was set out for us. They crossed our body so our hands was free. He sayed he made them himself and then Misses Charlotte gave him a look like he was lying. Then he sayed, We made them ourselves.

Misses Charlotte asked me what I pulled before. I telled her I sometimes helped with corn but ain't been in the fields much without my mama and ain't never worked by myself.

She look at me almost nice and sayed, Well your mama isn't here now so you'll need to follow my lead, okay? There's corn to pull, and peas. She pointed to another basket laying there and sayed I could use that one for peas after the corn. And that we'd start with corn. There musta been four rows of corn stretching 40 feet each. Master John wipe his brow and walked to shade of the workshop.

I worked behind Misses Charlotte all morning, pulling ears of corn and listening to her complain bout how small some was and how she wasn't gon fetch a good price for some and how some was only good enough for the hogs. Priscilla keeped asking if we was done yet and her mama would say, Look around Priscilla. Does it appear we've finished? Priscilla would sigh and look at the sun in the sky. She finally sayed that somebody was supposed to be coming to call on her and she took her leave. Misses Charlotte muttered something under her breath bout we all got something else we might rather do. I don't remember his name now.

The sun got past midpoint in the sky when Misses Charlotte finally sayed to put down the baskets. She come back out with a warm piece a bread and a piece of bacon. We drank water Master John pump from the well and then I sat by the house in the shade. Misses Charlotte take up on a bench under

25

a tree and Priscilla still ain't come back out the house. I reckoned she wasn't planning on coming back out. I heard her whispering to her mama, Why do I need to stay out here all day if we got him? Otherwise what's the point of having a slave if I have to slave too?

Her mama just sayed, We need every hand Priscilla, and you have two.

After a while Misses Charlotte standed up and called to me that it was time to get back started. I followed her back to the field, wasn't no garden, and we picked up the other baskets. The holes was smaller in it so nothing fell out. I looked at the troughs we already filled up with corn to sell, corn for us, and corn for the hogs. We separated them while we was filling up our baskets along and along. I'd never picked peas. I quick figured out I hated picking peas. We worked side each other. She'd pick from one plant and I'd pick from another. I watched her to see which ones she picked and ones she let stay. I wanted to ask what to do with the ones she done leave behind. They looked like ones mama would bring back and make pea soup from.

She keeped checking my basket to see how I was coming. Finally she sayed, You gotta pull the leaves apart to see what's behind them. Sometimes they hide.

I had a better view being I been shorter than her.

We're gonna get through these rows and then we'll pull up the squash and the zucchini.

This was different than the big plantation. There was a whole bunch of corn. Corn everywhere and then only in mama and Masie's garden was there some other stuff, but that was just for us and special occasions.

This was a lot of different things and I wondered who all ate this. I wonder who they was gon sell it to. Back on that plantation in Virginia we sometimes separated out the corn what wasn't no good for market and threw in some good pieces cuz we knowed we'd get the pieces that wasn't going to market. If we ain't want it all to be the worst, that was the only way. Mama would sing out there or hum when she was working and I'd sing too. She got that sweet voice when she sang.

I musta lingered on one plant too long cuz Misses Charlotte sayed, I think you got everything off that one. Move on to the next.

I moved to the next one and started again.

We've never had help before, she sayed. Not like this. It's a little strange. We're not bad people. We're not. We're normal people who need help and...and that's why we got you.

I ain't say nothing. I couldn't imagine nothing good bout owning somebody just to have help. People could be help and be free. People could be help and be paid. That wasn't no excuse and in my book that made her and all the people like her bad people and if not bad they wasn't good. She put that bible in my room I guessed. Maybe to help her feel better bout what she done. I wasn't gon say nothing cuz it wasn't my place to say it and mama sayed not to give them no reasons. So I wasn't.

You understand me don't you, Ervin?

That was the first time any of them called me by my name. I ain't heard my name since mama sayed bye. I wondered did they know my name. Not that it mattered. I was just help. A slave.

You understand me right? She stopped picking the peas off her plant to look at me.

I looked down at the plant in front of me and whispered, Yes ma'am. It was the only answer to give even if it been a lie. She seemed satisfied so that was fine. Long as she felt fine I'd be fine.

Master John walked out the workshop carrying what looked like the back of a chair. He held it up in the sunlight studying it, one eye squinted. I wanted to be working in there with him and not out here with her. There wasn't even any senseless gossip or complaining now that Priscilla was inside. And I was right. She ain't come back out. I wondered if her caller had come or if she was just getting ready for him. I wondered how long it would take for the sun to start leaving the sky so we could stop. I wondered if mama was looking at the same sky right now and thinking bout me too.

We got round to the yellow squash finally and I kneeled in the dirt. My feet was tired in those big boots and I wanted them to feel the earth beneath them but instead they was locked away. I wanted to see my mama. To look beside me and see her face and not this white woman who took me from her like she was doing me a favor. I pulled a squash off the vine and put it in the basket we used for the corn and then keep going down the row on my knees picking up yellow squash. They had so much. I wondered the last time they came out here to do this.

I think she was reading my mind cuz Misses Charlotte sayed, We're several days behind and the rain has been good. We got a good yield this year. We'll be able to plant more next year now that we have an extra set of hands.

I picked up another squash and put it in the basket. I couldn't even think bout next year.

Charlotte

Dear Lord, there's another child in my house. Young one. Give me the strength only you can give Lord. I know that you make no mistakes. I know you give no more than we can bear. But God, it pains me to look upon this child's face and to know he misses his mother. Lord, help me to see the good in all things, even this. Help me to be a tool for your will and your purpose. To be a blessing and not a curse. His age isn't but a couple more than my Benjamin's. I need strength to look at him or talk to him and I pray in time you will grant me the strength to be a proper Mistress and to help him grow strong. I pray you will allow me to have a son of my own, God. To carry John's name. I pray you'll give Charlotte a brother and let me keep another child. I know you owe us nothing and we have all we have because of you. I only ask you find it within your grace to do this for me, for us God. That I might not look upon this child with sadness and longing for my own. Help me to complete our family and honor my husband with a son to carry on his name. Thank you, God. Amen.

Sunday

I woke up extra early cuz it was Sunday and that was the day to see mama. I put on the clothes Misses Charlotte sayed to wear today. The good clothes with the dress shoes. We was going to church and mama was gon be there. We all got up and had breakfast. I was in my corner by myself but I knowed me and mama was gon eat together later. Master John sayed, Sunday's time for family. It's important.

It ain't make sense how they thinked that was important. And still mama ain't with me. I guess in they heads it musta make some kinda sense or else they wanted me to think it did. Either way, there wasn't no sense to it but I'm fixing to see mama anyway.

I took the rag and washed up my face again after eating and wiped my teeth down all around til they squeak like Misses Charlotte show me to do. I was sposed to do that first but I ain't remember. She telled me to meet them round front when I was ready and to grab my bible. I picked up the black book and clopped outside and round the house. They was all waiting by the cart. They looked fancy and Priscilla looked like she was eager to hurry up and go. I figured that man she like was gon be there.

Jump on up in the back E.

They done taked to calling me E like Ervin too much or too formal. Least they ain't call me boy most of the time, unless they was upset bout something or irritated. It'd be worth annoying them though sometimes. Not too much to give them no reasons. Just a little bit. But none of that mattered. We rode on past where mama living and I ain't see nobody there. I was hoping they was already at the church. My stomach hurt I was so excited. But my stomach been hurting all week off and on. I heard Misses Charlotte whispering to Master John that she think I's just homesick and I'ma get over it after a while. I miss mama. I don't understand Misses Charlotte or Master John. They confusing white people. One minute they act like I'm a person and the next I'm a slave. Only way I figure it is they confused.

A church come up on the left side of the cart and a bunch of people been standing round outside. I was looking for mama. Looking where all the slaves was gathered it was hard to tell. They was bunched up together talking. I figured out later they only look this happy on Sundays. A white man leaned up against the church making sure they wasn't talking about nothing they shouldn't be. I seed her. She was watching the road that come up to the church. She seed me too and I waved. Big with both hands and she come running towards the street. A white man called after her and she slowed down a bit yelling back something. The man went back to smoking on some cigar. Guess they was a little kinder on Sundays.

The cart stopped next to some of the others and I jumped out and ran to mama and she run up to me. I hugged her hard and tight cuz I never wanted to let go and she hugged me hard too. She was crying when she pulled back. She looked at my face, my eyes, touched my skin, and looked at my hands, feeling my wrists and arms. Then she seed my owners and dropped her head down, saying nothing and taking my hand. She led me back to where the other slaves gathered. She started smiling as we walked towards them. This here Ervin, my baby boy. He at they house. She nodded her head towards Master John and Misses Charlotte. Misses Charlotte watched us. She looked at mama's and my hands, locked together and then turned her eyes to Priscilla who was making funny eyes with some boy.

Be a lady Priscilla.

She held her bible tighter to her belly with one hand and Master John took her elbow as they walked into the church.

A few minutes later after they was all seated we sat in the back. I was wondering if the slaves had they own church but one of the other slaves sayed they only did it once a month when the traveling minister come through. Otherwise we was in the same church as them. They pretty much ignored us back there

31

and we ignored them up there. Cept we couldn't talk and had to sit there and listen to something bout treasures in heaven and working and toiling paying off. I don't know what else they was saying. I was too busy thinking bout how mama was doing and what I wanted to tell her when this was over. We had all day together and I wanted to show her what I'd learned in the shop. It wasn't much but I learned it still. I wanted to show her my room and my bed and my table and chair. I wanted to sit outside at the table and chair set that Master John and I put out the night before so that mama and I could eat together. He put it on the inside of the shed in case it rained, as it liked to do.

I wanted to tell her bout the water in my room everyday and the too big shoes and boots and the scratchy socks and how I picked everything from corn to collards that week and how much I hated it.

When church let out and we was waiting to leave I started to tell her all that. Then her master let her ride back with us. They family followed in their carriage. We ain't say nothing in the cart but when we got back to the house I started talking again. I talked to mama in whispers. Misses Charlotte had mama come in and wash up so she could help serve everyone. When everybody was served mama fix our plates and bringed them outside to our table. It was the best afternoon I ever had in my life. I never wanted it to end ever. She talk bout the kids she was watching but she ain't wanna talk much. The kids she watched was running round but they couldn't get in no trouble she sayed. She laughed and sayed when she get back she gon have to clean them up and get them to bed.

The little girl keeped coming over, wanting to show mama stuff like yellow flowers growing from weeds, a junebug, and a handful of dried up peas. Mama was nice and would smile and look impressed. Sometimes her daddy would call her back and tell her to leave Ellie alone for now. That it was Sunday and meant for family but that little girl was confused too. She asked me how I knowed her Ellie and I sayed, She my mama.

She was even more confused. Why come you don't live with your mama? She asked like it was a normal question.

I looked at mama.

Now don't you worry bout that chile. You go on and play with your brothers and sisters.

She skip off and mama just pressed her lips together and held my hand. I showed her the spindle I had made smooth and even. I sanded it down myself after Master John had cut it to size. I had her run her fingers over it from the top to the bottom to see how smooth it was. She sayed it was nice and that it was good to learn to do something like that. She was happy I was gon learn a skill. She sayed, You know they got some slaves out here what can buy they freedom cuz they knows a skill. Keep that in mind Ervin. I did.

Mama started taking up the dishes and putting them inside and Misses Charlotte let me stand in the kitchen and help her clean up after dinner. I ain't never been in that part of the house. I seed the kitchen mama cooked in at the plantation but not that one. I guess I ain't need to since I had no business in it. Misses Charlotte took care of her own house.

I don't know where the hours went that day. They never went that fast during the week when we's working in that field or all day in the workshop. The hours never run away so fast but fore I knowed it, the sun was setting and mama's people's were saying they goodbyes. Next I knowed they was all set to leave and I hugged mama tight like before and she did the same. Be good and keep learning all you can, she sayed. And I mean *everything*. I see you Sunday.

Her owner chimed in and sayed, actually this week you'll see him Wednesday. I'm doing a ladies night at my house and he can help you out since Charlotte and Priscilla will be there and John will be out doing men stuff. Mama smiled big as I did. Wednesday.

Ellie

(I wasn't even thirty five years old and everything I'd ever loved in my whole life had been taken away from me by force. I hated them, every single one. The ones who act nice and the ones who let you know how they really felt. All of them was evil for what they'd done and what they allowed to be done. I ain't sorry bout how I felt. That was how I felt. They took away my husband, they took away my first born son, they took away my daughter, they took me and Ervin away from our other family and our friends and then they took him away from me. How else would I feel? If it wasn't for them, maybe I coulda been some kind of happy. Some kind of content.)

I got nothing but pain inside my heart. Pain at losing my loves, my babies. Pain at taking care of somebody else's babies while ain't nobody taking care of mine. What are they doing to him? Are they feeding him? Are they treating him okay? Is he sleeping? God, I want to die some days but he's out there. They sayed I'll see him soon and I know he's nearby so that's what keeps me going. God why you do this to me? Why you set me up with all this love in my heart and just take it all away? What's the point? Why you do this to us? I thinks that if your heaven is any reflection a this earth then it ain't someplace I wants to be.

That woman who bought me is a nasty woman. Nasty in every way. I been here almost a week and I can see it without no denying. She don't keep up her house, her children or hardly herself. Those babies running round here dirty and uncared for while she sulking after that husband of hers. He ain't care two cents bout her. I already knows he gots that wandering eye. I hates it. I don't look at him or talk to him. I just do what she asks me to, which is everything cuz she ain't fit for mothering. Here I is taking care a her four kids and her brother got mine. Taking care of four kids who gon do to me the same way they parents did when they growed up. But maybe if I love them they won't be so evil and mean. Maybe if somebody love them they might have a little more kindness. But I ain't got no more love to give. They done ripped it all outta me.

That oldest one already got his daddy's ways. He only fourteen and disrespecting his mama like his daddy do. He go and come like he please and don't do nothing to help out. They got a bit a money and I spose he think he smart and going off to college and won't need to do this lowly kind of work like even helping out his siblings every now and then. He definitely an ass in the making. Shelly sad and lonely I guess. Her husband don't get why so he figure she just can't handle it. He don't know really cuz he ain't hardly ever here. He off working and come back. Then he take off his clothes and leave them for the wash. They smell like other women, but I won't say nothing. I figure some part of her already knows. She ain't ugly. For being so pale, she pretty. Just don't do nothing with herself. She ain't got no excuse. I don't do nothing with myself either, but I ain't got no means or reasons.

She got those other three who spose to be studying with that tutor who come by twice a week. They take piano lessons once a week and other than that they ain't doing much. They play in the yard, gets filthy but happy it seems. They's ten, six and four. I's just glad they ain't no actual babies. I don't thinks I could stand it. Cleaning house, washing clothes, working they little garden with the oldest girl and cooking. I make sure they get bathed and dressed and taking they lessons. I wonder what they was doing last week fore I come cuz they looked like they ain't washed up in two weeks. White people ain't got no excuse. If you can have a slave you ain't got no excuse.

I's looking for tomorrow. Tomorrow is Sunday and they promised we'd be visiting tomorrow. I'll see my Ervin finally and hug my baby after hugging her babies, least that youngest. I don't think she understands I aint free. She ask me to play dolls with her and chase her in the yard when I'm putting up the clothes on the line. She thinks I's free like she free. I ain't. Least she got that sense a freedom bout her and she know I ain't like her but she love me still. Like she done got a best friend. She do make me laugh cuz she so funny and silly and just so hungry for

35

some attention. The six year old be singing all the time but if somebody come round she shut right up like she scared. I telled her she ain't gotta stop singing on my account or nobody else account. She smile but then she still stop. Maybe she figure out she can sing when other folks around. She gotta pretty little voice.

They all keeps me so busy the only time I gets to myself or my mind is night time. And those nights is long. I just keep going for Sundays. Cuz then I gets a piece a my heart back. I gets it back when I see my Ervin and see his smile. And touch his skin and hold his hand. And then I hold onto it all week long.

The Workshop and Fiddle

Priscilla, Master John's daughter, got married when I was bout sixteen. She married some man from about an hour ride this side of Charleston. He was an attorney but from what I gather not that good a one. Mostly chasing around people seeing if he could help them collect on things owed or wrongs done. People in his circle liked him enough. They had a bigger wedding than Master John wanted, given her husband got a big family. I figure she be happy as any of these women are married. None of them seem all that happy if you ask me. I don't know why people always getting married so they can be right miserable. I think I stick to myself. Less to worry bout.

Mama was there. That's when I first noticed she ain't look so good. We sitting outside at the wedding talking and waiting for them to finish up and she keep fanning herself, but in October. It wasn't even that hot. Not like it get in South Carolina. Mama sayed there wasn't nothing to worry bout. Just must be that thing what happen to women her age. She got hair gray all round her edges now and none of that goop they put in her hair when we come woulda covered it up. Still her face ain't changed a day. I go by and see her most days. Been that way for a few years since I got big enough to walk by myself.

We sit outside and talk in the evenings til Misses Shelly call out the window saying it's time to make my way back home and for Ellie to finish up her work to close down the house for the night. It ain't so bad being able to see mama like this. She don't have it like I do, but I think she likes that we get to see each other. The kids done got big so she ain't gotta run and chase them so much.

37

She done take up sewing. She got Misses Shelly to take it up too some years pass. Mama sayed she had to do something cuz Misses Shelly was gon drive both of them crazy. Misses Shelly got a knack for drawing up those dresses and mens pants. She takes newspapers and cuts out patterns and then they sew up clothes and sell them to the people in town.

Now you look at Misses Shelly and she seem like she like herself some, take care of herself. And she act like she can't live without mama. She asks mama bout fabric styles and colors and the way they feel. Mama likes it, keeps her mind off things. Off not being free. Off my daddy and Greta and Ethan. They go up to the market twice a month and set up and sell they clothes and then Misses Shelly packs them into trunks and she and mama haul them to ladies nights and they sell them there too. Shelly start giving mama a few cents for every dress they sell. It ain't much but mama been putting it away. She tell me I better do the same if the time come.

I will. I do. Master John give me a fiddle when I turned ten years old. He liked to play one and since he figured he wasn't never gon have a boy of his own and Priscilla barely liked learning piano he might as well teach someone how to play so he could have someone to play with. Misses Charlotte don't like the fiddle much. Say it don't go well with her piano. She tolerate it if we outside, so that's what we do. Master John and me goes out to the shed and we play the fiddle at night after work and dinner and visiting with mama is done.

He play good and I play good now too. Not as good as him, but give me a little while longer. Sometimes Misses Charlotte yell out the door and remind us to keep the time or that we ain't syncing up together. Master John look at me and roll his eyes. I can't tell if he likes her or not but they tolerate each other well enough. They don't fight. Probably cuz they don't talk much.

We played at Priscilla's wedding with a couple other slaves and white people. Mama was so proud of me. She telled everybody I was her boy up there playing the fiddle. She keeped pointing at me. I noticed how much she was sitting down then, fanning and flushing. I figured I'd ask her bout it the next day. That night I was on the fiddle and ain't nothing else matter.

After we done finish playing Master John had people coming up to him and looking at me and talking to him bout something. Later when we was riding back home Master John sayed I played real nice up there. Several other people thinked so and let him know as much. Wondered do I play other places.

Really? They sayed I play nice? I ask him.

Yeah, they did E. Let's talk about it later. It's late and my bride here looks tuckered.

Misses Charlotte sit straight up. Who're you calling tuckered? I think you speak of yourself. I could've danced another hour.

I heard them chuckle to themselves from my seat in the back. Play other places. It sound like a good idea.

Next day, mama wouldn't say much bout how she was feeling and I tried to get her to talk bout it but she sayed there wasn't nothing to talk bout so we made talk on other things. Her being a seamstress and my playing fiddle. She sayed how everybody loved my playing and I telled her Master John wants to talk to me bout playing, maybe other places.

She sayed, Sometimes masters will pay for that kinda thing, Ervin.

I smiled and sayed, He gon start giving me something for my work in the woodshop. I done got good enough to do some pieces all by myself. He can spend more time selling.

That's a good thing Ervin.

We got more work. Mama, if he know how to do it, I know how to do it. I might not be good as he is yet, but like I'm getting good on that fiddle, give me time.

You gots two ways to make money and save Ervin.

I smiled back at her. Mama was happy bout that. She sayed one day there won't be slavery and having a trade would be good. Knowing how to do more than farming would be good. She sayed she hoped she see it in her lifetime cuz there been so much talk bout it. I smiled back at her and sayed maybe it would be or maybe in my lifetime.

We talked bout what we'd do if we was free. She'd sew clothes, maybe still working with Misses Shelly but get a fair wage. She sayed she'd get a nicer place. Her little cabin outside the main house was so tiny she could barely turn round without hitting the stove and bed.

It done got smaller cuz her hips got bigger, I teased her.

She push me on my arm and sayed she wasn't gon make me no more pies I keep talking like that. It wasn't the first time she joked bout it but still made both us laugh.

I telled her I'd play the fiddle at night and build furniture and caskets during the day. She ask me if I was gon stay working for Master John.

I ain't wanna work for nobody cept myself if I can help it.

She laughed, Well I hope you know they ain't gon let no black man be his own boss.

I ain't sayed nothing bout that cuz I ain't want it to be true but I knowed she been right.

I can make most anything Master John can make and by the time I'm all the way a man I'm gon be just as good. I'm doing what you sayed mama. I'm learning all I can. I be in the room when he talking to those men sometimes bout what he want. We go pick up wood and materials and I'm in the corner. Sometimes I hear them making that business talk. Making deals and negotiating. It ain't that hard mama.

But will they listen to you? Negotiate with you? You ain't a white man. White men is the only ones white men will listen to. Trust me, Misses Shelly gotta go through the women to sell to the men cuz they might listen to their wives some but they ain't gon listen straight to her.

When I'm free mama, I'm a have my own stuff. I'm a make money my own way and I'm a make it so I ain't the only one.

She looked at me with eyes full a pity. Like I ain't know no better. She start picking with this dried blister on her thumb, feeling where the skin done got thick and hard from pushing needles. Then she start up one of them new coughing spells and I asked her to tell me what was wrong. She finally say to me she ain't have no answer. The doctor come by and he ain't know what it was so she ain't know either.

Next day I asked Master John bout mama, see if he knowed something mama wasn't telling me. He shook his head and sayed he didn't know no more than I did. I was bout tall as him now, but he was still a much bigger man. I was lean and strong but he was big and strong.

Don't worry too much E. These things tend to pass and people get better. Your mama's strong. She musta been real proud of you last night.

Yeah she was, couldn't stop talking.

He laughed and sayed, Nobody missed you on that fiddle.

Master John stopped cutting this piece of wood for a bit and look me square in the eye. E, your good. Good enough to play for other people. Now I know a lot of white folks don't like it, but I think it's alright for a man to earn something of his own. Just like it's important for a family to know each other. Those things are important. You listening to me E?

Yessuh, I sayed back.

Now after last night I'm thinking we have some opportunities. Farming and woodwork and Charlotte's lessons, those things bring in a decent living but we could actually make money to have and not just spend. You following me E?

No suh, I sayed being honest. I ain't know the difference.

We ain't rich E. You know that. Some folks have lots of land and slaves and don't have to work as hard as we do just to make a living. That's not us. We're simple folks. We work hard for what we have but we don't have extra. Pretty soon you won't be able to fit my hand me down shoes and my pants will be up past your ankles the way you keep growing. You eat like a man now. You coming along like a man and work like a man. Means you need man stuff.

He seemed fine with talking bout me becoming a man when men was free. I was a slave and that mean I can't be a man. I ain't sayed nothing but looked at the piece of brown leather on that board I was stretching. I brushed it. Some cow give up its life for that piece of leather to sit on that board so that we can make a chair and somebody could sit on it. That was the way things was. Some people gave up they lives for other people's enjoyment.

Master John? I finally sayed after he start back to work.

41

Yeah?

I can't be a man, suh. No matter how big and strong and grown I get or how much I eat or work. I can't be a man.

He looked at me then. I ain't look back. I studied that piece of leather though there wasn't nothing much more I coulda study. I tightened the pins to make it straight. I smoothed it under my hand. I taked up one of the seats we cut yesterday and started sanding it. He ain't sayed nothing yet. I wonder if this was the thing to finally make him mad. In all the years I ain't never seed him get angry enough to really scare me. But that silence. I ain't wanna look up his way. I finally peak out the corner of my eye while I turn the seat to work on another side. He was standing there his back to me like he was thinking real hard or just wasn't sure what I meant or what to say. I was bout done sanding that chair bottom when he finally sayed something.

Why do you say that E?

Master John, you know a slave can't be a man. Men are free.

He tensed up like he was bout to get mad and he hardly ever got mad. I thanks God he ain't like that. Some of our friends at church they got masters with tempers so bad they'll hurt them for looking at the wrong spot in the sky. Master John required a lot of me, of everybody and himself but he was fair. When we ain't have enough because the crops wasn't good in a year, they never gave me less than I needed. Everybody got a little less. He sayed it ain't make no sense to not be fair. I wish he also thinked it ain't make no sense to not be right. Cuz it wasn't right I couldn't be a man and free.

We worked in silence for hours. Usually we talks on all kinds a things. What to plant, who wasn't paying on time, what accounts was over, why the wood got more knots or was harder to smooth or cut. Where the best wood was gon come from and the price of it. We talk bout what girls I like at church and the weather. Talk bout most anything and everything we think of. Master John ain't had many friends. He ain't think most people was worth much. They talk one way and act another and he wasn't keen on that. He always sayed, Be a man of your word and let that be what lead in front of ya. You ain't got nothing but your reputation.

I wished there was more men who thinked like that but in South Carolina there wasn't. Even though it was the twenties nothing changed. Things seemed to be getting worse in fact. They wasn't bringing in slaves from across the ocean but it was busy at the ports. I seed more at church and not just babies and the ones born here. They was coming in from other places like I was.

The top of the seat was bout smooth and we was starting to lose light. Master John put his saw down and sayed, Sit down, E.

I sat down in the chair I maked for myself and he sit in the one he maked. The chairs we played fiddle in at night. Sometimes I knowed Misses Charlotte wasn't sure bout our relationship. A slave and master shouldn't be close cuz one gots to know who has the power. That wasn't never a question. A black man in the south as a slave can't have no power and even if I was free I wouldn't have none either. I'd take free though, any day.

E. I know this ain't gonna make much sense, he started. But I really don't like the institution of slavery.

I looked at him confused cuz here I was sitting up in his workshop a slave.

Now hear me out, he went on. When we needed help we had two options. Well three, but the first one didn't work out. One of the two that was left was to hire someone who came in every so often and we had to pay for the labor time by time. We tried that for a few years and it left us scraping up cash to pay somebody or not being able to get the work done consistently like we needed and we'd end up losing money. I knew people who had slaves and the thing they said was that when you need help they are there and can do a variety of things. They weren't going somewhere or not showing up for work cuz they got a better offer or just decide not to show.

You means they ain't got no choice Master?

Well, in a sense. Yeah. But it's not like that.

That seem exactly what it been like to me. But I ain't sayed nothing.

Now, E, I know you don't agree being you're in the position you're in. But I'm a fair man. Besides we don't want something bad to happen to you. These folks would eat you up alive if you were free and walking round here free. They couldn't handle it. You're actually safer having someone accountable for you. In the south black people are mostly slaves, that's the way it is. There are some who've earned their freedom or were given it. But most of them are mulattos. It's just not usual.

Some of the ones I knowed ain't have it no better than me. They was free but can't be out after a certain time or in certain places and was still working the same land they worked when they was slaves, barely getting by. But they was free. Most was scared to go anywhere cuz they might get caught and sent somewhere else as slaves, they papers destroyed. I heard stories.

He looked at my hands and sayed I was real good with them, better than he was at my age. He was bout thirty years older than me but he looked older.

Ervin, you are a man or will be soon. Whether you are a free man or a slave, you're still a man. We're all equal in God's eyes. I can't change the way the world is, or how other people think. I can't. You know all those years ago when we came and got you we had to convince my sister and her husband they needed help so that you could still have your mama. We weren't sure we could and I wasn't going to be the cause of you being separated. This slavery business can't go on forever. It's not natural for men to hold other people like this, I know it. I'm complicit in it but I know it. Can I give it up? You up? Not without going under. Honestly, I couldn't afford to pay you what you worth.

E, you're better than any of those ole white boys out there. Why? Cuz you learned from the best. So how could I pay you what you're worth? I couldn't. This workshop, that little farm, this house, those old horses and that cart. What you've seen since you've been here is all I've got in this world, and I don't have any sons to pass it on to. I've got a daughter but nobody who'll carry on my name by blood. You've got my name E cuz you're part of this household, even if you are a slave. One day you might be free, ten years or fifty years, I don't know. But one day you might be. And in the meantime, you work for me. I'm a make you an offer E. Cuz you will be a man and a man needs to be able to provide for himself and his family. A man takes care of his home come hell or high water. He provides. And I know my views aren't popular. Maybe that's why I'm not that popular cuz I know if I speak them business will dry right on up and I won't be able to provide.

I was listening. Waiting for what he had to say. Cuz in the end if it wasn't my papers for freedom, it wasn't nothing I can hold to.

You are mine on paper E. That's just the way it is. You work for me but, in my opinion, when you turn twenty-one you become a man. That means you gotta start earning for yourself too. We got asked to play at the Marshall's daughter's wedding in three weeks. Well they had a group but they want us to come in with the fiddles. They're going to give me a dollar and we'll split it so I get seventy cents and you get thirty. I have to arrange the business and opportunities so consider that my manager's fee. He smiled like he do when he being funny. I let my head wrap round it. Thirty cents for one little night of playing the fiddle. That was more than some made in a whole day.

What you think about that E?

I sat in my chair. I picked up something else to sand while I's sitting cuz my hands gotta stay busy.

I think that's okay. I get to keep it? I looked up at him. He was okay with me looking him in the eyes when I wasn't trying to challenge him.

It's yours. Keep it, save it, do what you want with it.

I ain't wanna smile and let him know how happy I was. I couldn't help it though. My lip turned up just a little on one side. It was dark so I hope he ain't seed it. I'd start saving so when I was free I'd have some of my own money.

Master John?

Yes?

Can I tell you something?

Of course.

I appreciate what you doing. I do. I don't like being a slave, wouldn't nobody like it. I don't like that I'm scared to fall in love or have children cuz of what might happen.

Master John looked down.

Sometimes I wonder why God even put us here if we all equal in his eyes. Why would he curse us if we equal? It don't make much sense to me. But I believe you when you say you fair. I believe you don't like that there's slavery but at the same time Master John, you a part of it so I am too. I ain't been round long as you and I don't know all the ways of things but I figures at some point God gon have some kind of reckoning and he gon ask people what they did for the least of those. He gon ask how they helped the strangers in they land. He gon ask these questions fore he let anybody in through them pearly gates and there's gon be a lot a folk disappointed bout not getting in. Master John, I plan on being on the other side of those pearly gates.

I sanded the top of a chair we'd be staining the next day. I put down the wood after a bit and went to the box I keeped my fiddle. At night I bringed it in my room but I always had it out here with us when we come to the workshop cuz that was our routine. We'd play a bit waiting on supper and then afterwards when I got back from seeing mama, depending on the night. I picked it up and Master John sayed, Not tonight. I think I'm a head on in.

Master John

They call it a peculiar institution. Slavery. The south is peculiar. Indeed. I'm not a high priced gentleman. I'm a carpenter with one slave and an average piece of land. I considered myself an honorable and fair man my whole life. In both my professional and personal affairs, but I don't know so much right now.

I pray God that I haven't done wrong by you. I pray that all I have done will be forgiven and that you will make me a better man. I pray that you will let me see my errors and correct them as best I can and harm no one else, lest it be an honest mistake. I pray you give me wisdom to not make those mistakes and not harm anyone. I pray you make me better than the men who hurt their slaves. Lord don't let me be like them. I pray you give me the strength to do what is right when it is time and to know what it is that I need to do.

Lord tonight you rebuked me through the tongue of my servant. As the master, I was made the student and he the teacher. Lord, why did you send this boy to me to turn into a man? Why did you make it so that I was the one who took him in? Why when I am as imperfect as I am did you lead me to him? God I want to serve you right and do right by your children, all your children. Have I sinned against you by owning him when your word says it's okay? If your word says it's okay why do I feel guilty? Why do I feel that it is not okay in my heart? Why do I feel as if I have not done right by the least of these? Why do I feel I have not done right by the strangers in my land?

God I pray for peace and understanding and wisdom. Help me to know what is mine and right to do each day, and especially when a moment comes when I am called to stand up and be your servant God. I am imperfect like this peculiar institution, but God you put me here in the south where this institution is the way of the land. How am I supposed to be here and in this land and not be a part of it? God show me the way. I pray. Amen.

Stones

Every year since I was bout twelve years old we started clearing back land for more room to plant. Master John and me would spend a full day cutting down a few trees and clearing away the brush. Usually it was a patch of maybe twenty by forty feet to push the farm back. We'd almost doubled it and I was faster in the field but Priscilla wasn't round no more and like Master John sayed, sometimes the day-laborers was unreliable.

This year when it was time, Master John sayed he had to think bout it. Was it worth it or should we try to play more gigs? We was making better money at that and the time we save with all the farm work we can easy use in the workshop. Master John had a good reputation all through South Carolina as a carpenter and people knowed I was his help and that meaned they knowed we'd get work done.

I never much like the farmwork but if we wanna eat, we gotta do it. But I love the fresh vegetables and sometimes it was peaceful just picking and not thinking bout nothing or thinking bout everything. Didn't have to get it right like with the woodwork. It seem it was something Master John did cuz he thinked he had to but if we just planted enough for us and to trade that would be enough.

He ask me what I think and I sayed, Less we gon be like those big farms it ain't worth bothering.

He keeped on looking back in them woods. Maybe it's better not to disturb it anymore. Let's leave it alone and do the things we're really good at. Misses Charlotte's piano lessons are going well and near everybody sends their kids to her.

Made me think bout Misses Shelly. Since she ain't have nobody else at home it keeped her busy with something to do.

Master John tell me everybody need something to do, keep they mind busy. Otherwise the devil take right on over and make ya crazy. He thank God my mama got Shelly sewing.

We only have one daughter, you know that E. I don't have any heirs other than her. One day when I'm gone she'll get this land and the house and the farm. She probably won't want it, she never liked this kind of life. Why she went to the city. When the time comes you may have a choice. Stay here or not. But I don't want those woods cut back anymore, you hear? I'm telling you now because I don't know when else I'll tell you or how long any of us have. My daddy only lived til fifty so I don't take anything for granted.

Why you don't want it cut back no more Master?

He paused then and taked a deep breath. I'm gonna show you something. Charlotte might not like it. She doesn't like to talk about it, but it's a reality.

The piano floated outside to us, some child pounding out notes in they first few lessons. I was used to it now, the sound of bad playing.

Walk with me, Master John sayed.

He walked past the farm area and into the woods. I followed him through the trees and the sun shined down between them. It wasn't dense but the shade was good. He stopped at a large tree bout thirty feet back from where we'd cleared. He stared at it, looking up through the leaves then back down it to the roots that stuck out the ground and rocks.

This is where we laid our babies.

I looked at the ground near Master John. There was seven stones. I bend down to see what was on them and seed where he carved dates on them and names. Two was older than Priscilla and the other five woulda been younger. Two of those woulda been after I come.

I looked at Master John. All these was yalls?

He nodded and his eyes got wet. I had a son who wasn't much younger than you when you came. But he wasn't ever well, and when he caught that fever, well there wasn't a thing the doctor could do. Said we could try and make him comfortable. That's what we did. That's all we could do and then we had to leave it to God.

There was boys names and girls names. Over my years there I seed Misses Charlotte get fat and lose weight a couple times but figure she just ain't knowed how to manage her weight.

Maybe that's why Misses Charlotte don't smile much and always look a little sad. God had taked her babies too leaving her with just one, like my mama. But she had a husband and a home of her own and God had done it, not man like with mama. Still, I feel like losing your babies is the worse thing no matter the reason. It made mama not like God so much. I think it made Misses Charlotte try to like God more.

My sons are in the ground, Master John sayed and touch the stones gentle-like. My daughters are in the ground. My one living is a three hour ride away. I don't have parents anymore and the only family I've got is Charlotte and Shelly's family. That's it. E, none of us got much so we got to hold to what we got in this world. I don't want her cutting back anymore. These babies deserve the shade of the tree and the sun poking in like it does. It's peaceful.

He was right. It was.

Back in Virginia mama had two rocks behind our cabin. There wasn't nothing on them. I wondered how Master John did it since he couldn't read neither. Guess he knowed his numbers and maybe his letters. Misses Charlotte can read some. Mama ain't knowed no letters. She had two rocks out there right behind the house where the shade of the house covered them. They lay side by side and the grass ain't never grow over it. Mama never liked us playing back there neither. She ain't never sayed what it was but now I knowed. No wonder she ain't trust God much, he ain't saved nothing for her.

I nod at Master John and sayed, If the time come and I need to, I'll tell Misses Priscilla not to cut back no more.

Misses Charlotte

I wasn't thrilled about taking in that boy. I knew we needed help, but we'd never owned anybody, and there was something about it that bothered me, though everybody was okay with it, it seemed. Just didn't seem natural, owning another person. Even if they aren't considered people, in the bible we're all people and equal. But we needed the help and John needed it. He's a quiet man, keeps to himself mostly. Cordial enough but he likes his peace and quiet. We talked about it for almost a year before deciding to do it. Now this talk from those abolitionists makes me second guess our choice. But all our friends and associates have one or two, at least. Some have many more. Most don't treat them all that good, not better than the animals they own.

I made John promise we treat him like a human because he's still a child of God. Now John seems to be thinking this thing over again. It's too late though. We committed and purchased him. We got papers saying we own him and we can't just turn him loose. We already know the wolves will be ready. I told John as much. It's like if I were to try to go out there without a husband. Who knows what would come of me and my safety. I can't go and come as I please without cause and reason and people knowing it's okay with John that I am. And I'm free. At least more free. What would come of him?

My parents never owned any slaves and neither did John's. They preferred to keep out of the whole business. They'd rent them from others though, but didn't want anything tied to them. I wonder how God looked on that. I wonder how God looks on us. We've done as right as we can by Ervin but there's rules to follow. My friends told me the rules and I set them up like that when he came. He never had friends around to play with and Shelly didn't let her children play with E either. Said it was inappropriate. Only time he seems content is when he sees his mama or he sees other slaves on Sunday. In honesty that part doesn't seem any no worse than the rest of us.

John works day and night and only rests on Sunday. That's just the way it is. I'm not for slavery but I suppose in my position I can't say I'm against it either. I'm already in the business. Now John wants to make some things right but I told him he can only do so much. He's one man with one slave, he doesn't have a plantation like Washington did in Mount Vernon, or even worse, that Jefferson. He's just one man. Freeing one slave or paying one slave won't amount to more than removing a cubic inch of sand from the beach. He says it's something. I reckon he's right but it's not my fight. Outside of these walls my words don't matter much.

I feed him good, make sure he's clean and looked after. We just ask that he work as hard as we do. But like John said he'll be grown soon and every man deserves some self respect in taking care of himself. That's what my daddy always said too. I don't know how that's supposed to work for someone who's not free. I don't know what that means for me and John. I figure we'll figure it out as we go and God will lead the way.

Affairs of White Men

Ellie

He off and gone again. He got a trunk full of trinkets and stuff he found for those rich folks who say they need it. They don't need half that stuff. They want it. Just like they want everything else and figures cuz they can pay for it, they got a right to it. I wonder where he found it. Where he got that stuff. Did he steal it like they steal people? Misses Shelly don't even bother trying to make no excuses for Master Daniel. She never has and I wondered if it's cuz she ain't got no excuses or just too tired to care.

She say she don't get involved in his affairs. I figures that mean two things but I ain't say that to her. I wash his clothes when he gets back from the road. I finds the hairs that sho don't belong to Misses Shelly and his clothes don't smell like musk. I figured he laid up with somebody when he gone traveling. Specially since he go to Charleston so much. That's where the money is and those high class ladies. I remembers. I ain't been back but a couple times but when we have our ladies nights there, I see how pretty they are with they hair all done up.

I thinks that's why even when we come back here Misses Shelly seem to make more effort. Think she trying to get his attention but it don't matter. He pay bout as much attention to her as he do his girls. They think a daddy just somebody who come home here and there and pay for they food and clothes. Now Misses Shelly do some of that too. Master Daniel got at least two others I figure based on the different scents. I knowed when he go to Charleston he come back smelling one way and when he go up past Marion he come back smelling a different kind a way. I wondered if Misses Shelly pay any attention. I figure he don't give her much chance since he come in and take off those clothes quick fore she or the kids can even give him a hug and a welcome home.

I wondered if he got some other kids too. He keep complaining bout how expensive running that house is and I thinks it ain't got no more expensive than it was so why it feel more expensive, lest you got more expenses somewhere else? He seem to be gone more and seem like his business is doing well but we don't see no difference here. In all the time I been here, I don't see no difference. Cept what me and Misses Shelly done. They say to stay out of the affairs of white men and I do, but those affairs seem to come right back here to us, whether we ask for it or not.

Those kids need they daddy. They need to see a good man round the house sometimes. That oldest boy done took off and act just like his daddy. I don't know how many girls he got round South Carolina. And now that he finished with his apprenticeship he don't seem to know how to stay settled nowhere. He come round here every couple weeks like I still owe him his laundry getting washed. I does it cuz well, I ain't got no choice but sometimes Misses Shelly tell him that I got more important things to do than clean his dirty drawers. I laugh in the other room cuz he get all frustrated asking whose gonna do it and she say he can do it, the tub is in the backyard. I don't come out then from what else I'm working on cuz I don't want him to see my face seeing his face. He'd know I been laughing.

He growed up handsome though, like his daddy. Trouble like his daddy. Got a good head for business like his daddy. But lawd he too much like his daddy so I feels bad for the women who love him cuz he don't know nothing bout loving nobody back. He just looking for what he can get and make from anything.

We making good though, me and Misses Shelly. All this time and we was making good. People know us now. They love the stuff we make and sell. I love to make designs and dresses and when the ladies put them on they feel so pretty. I stand back but me and Misses Shelly know. We knowed it's like when women around white men, we gots to stay outta they affairs. When a slave around any white people we gots to stay back from they affairs.

I's just as smart as she is, maybe smarter. I gives her ideas and we talk bout how we gon do this and that and sell what we make or who to talk to and where to go. Then she gotta do it cuz ain't nobody listening to no slave or doing business with me directly, not round these parts. Cept for Misses Lucy and sometimes Misses Mary Lee. Lucy talks to me. I think after talking with Misses Shelly she done figured out that it ain't all Misses Shelly so she ask me bout things or bring me a dress directly to fix up. Misses Mary Lee got her stuff wrapped up at church on some Sundays and fore I leave she give it to me and tell me what she need. Maybe they'll spread the word. Misses Shelly don't mind cuz she split whatever I make whether I make it myself or with her.

It's alright though. I ain't much up for all that talking and smiling and carrying on with them ladies like Misses Shelly do. She make all them feel special and beautiful when half of them looks like hogs in a dress. Anyway it ain't none of my business long as I get my earnings cuz I'm putting them away for my someday. Don't know if and when it'll come since I can't seem to get better. Sitting and sewing and talking with Misses Shelly is enough for me. And being in the kitchen cooking, my favorite other thing to do. That's bout all I can muster these days and even standing in that kitchen get tiring.

Misses Shelly asked me if I'm okay some of those days when I guess I looked like I was through. I wasn't okay but there wasn't nothing nobody could do. The doctor came back round to see me more than once but he can't tell what's wrong. Thinks I gots something going on with my blood and my lungs. I don't know if he right or wrong. I just knowed my body weak and I can't do much for long and this cough won't go. Nothing ever come up, just cough like I can't catch my breath sometime. And then there be a pain in my side, sharp. It last a long time. Doctor sayed maybe it was more than one thing and he hoped it would pass. Wasn't nothing he give me since it wasn't nothing he could name.

I felt like it wasn't that important to him. If it been one of them white people he'd of figured it out, but me, wasn't no thing to him. I think it's a thing to Misses Shelly even if only cuz she scared to run the business by herself. If I was her I'd be scared too. Sometimes she don't make half a sense but she gots good ideas and drawings and she good with them women. I can't do what I do without her. We need each other and I'm a little afraid.

My boy keep asking me what's wrong. I can't tell him cuz I ain't know nothing to tell him. I spend as much time as I can with Ervin. He the only thing I got and my body feel old even though it ain't. I'm barely in my forties and I feel like I'm winding down but I don't want to. I's the only thing he gots too and lawd knowed he don't deserve no more hurt in his life. That's one thing I'm thankful for. Misses Shelly and Master John let me have my boy. Even if he ain't lived with me he been in my life and I been in his.

I seed him at least every week and sometimes a few days a week when he was young and now that he got older we see each other almost every day unless it's planting or harvesting time then some of those days stretch so long there ain't time for visiting. Now sometime he going sneaking off other places and don't show up but for fifteen minutes fore he gotta go. He done growed up strong and tall. Almost tall as his daddy was and look just like him. He got that same smile and his cheeks raise up like his daddy's did when he smiled but ain't wanna smile. I'm so proud of him. The things he can do with his hands. He and Master John kind a like me and Misses Shelly.

I thanks God for that. I thanks God every day for not selling us to some people in this town or to one of them plantations. Some of our friends got it so bad that they just wanna die. They rather die than keep living like they do. Some did. They tried running off but they got caught and when they come back they ain't never the same. All the life gone from them. Like corn husks leaved to dry up in the sun. I hates being a slave. I hates not being free to do what I wants and be good at what I do on my own. But ain't nothing I can do.

Shelly

Daniel can't understand. None of them do. How I feel about her. The rest of them saw me wasting away and with all their politeness and rightness never said or did a thing. Never offered me anything but that I was blessed to have my husband and children. They were likely laughing behind my back. Knowing my husband was off doing whatever he does and that I was hardly a good mother to those kids.

All this time Ellie's taken care of my children, my house, and then started taking care of me. I can't tell her how I feel since it's not right, her being a negro and all. I have a business now and even if he doesn't think it's much, it is. I do well. We do. In spite of everything she can't have, she helped me have this. Something to wake up for in the morning. Something to look forward to the next day. She made me somebody better because she let me be her friend. I never had a friend that helped me like she does. Friends that will gossip? Yes. Friends like her? No.

I'm a little scared though. She's got this cough and she has these tired spells, but the doctor doesn't know what it is. I wish I could do something but there's not much anybody can do. She's strong though. And she hardly complains. Ellie has barely slowed. Not like I imagine I would've if I were in the same condition. I don't ask her to do as much as I once did and when it's time to cook I sometimes help. She tells me I can learn to make some of what she makes if I want to. I try but it never turns out the same. I think she has a special gift and that man in Charleston was probably right all those years ago because I don't taste cooking as good as El's anywhere.

Besides bringing dresses and pants we always bring food. The women like our parties because the food is good and when the food is good they buy because they're so happy. El and I figured that out together. She is so smart. I didn't know before her that negros could be smart like that. I guess I never met one before really. No, I met them. I never knew one before. Not before her and E.

I can't wait til our next trip. All the way to Charleston. I hear her humming now. That's what she does when she's sewing. She hums. I never know the tunes and when I'm around she doesn't say the words, least not in a way I can understand. But it seems to be alright. She doesn't cause any trouble with it. And it seems she works faster when she's doing it and Lord knows we have a lot to do. I'm trying not to stare at her on the other side of the room that used to belong to my oldest boy.

It's our own shop. The kids can't come in unless they're coming to help out. The oldest girls help out when they can and everybody knows when we have our shows we aren't to be bothered except when absolutely necessary. Ellie told me I could get them to respect that if I told them flat. She was right. She's right about a lot of things. I just hope she's not right about being as sick as she thinks she is.

Ellie

I loved and hated that place. Charleston what it was called. Evil place. You could feel the pain a hundred years in the making all bottled in that city. They was pulling on my arms begging for help and wasn't nothing I could do to help them. I just acted like I ain't feel nothing but it would stick. It would stick like the pain and cries when they taked my babies. When they taked my husband. When I seed them rip away other babies and mamas and daddies. Those kinds of pains stay with you. They settle into your spirit and into your bones and ain't nothing can get them out. I think they growed up in there somehow. A whole nother life. I smiled best I could but there wasn't much to be happy bout when you ain't got no life of your own.

I had it better than most, I knowed it. So I wondered how they even survived and went on. I wondered how I woulda been if they'd of taken my Ervin away too. I think I woulda just crawled up right then into a ball and died. He the only reason I'm alive now. I thinks bout my babies I laid in the ground in Virginia. My boy and my girl. They ain't never knowed the pain of slavery. Ain't never suffered over another. Ain't never feeled the life drug outta you for no more reason then you was born in the wrong body. They was born free in they minds and died fore they first breaths. Early like they knowed it wasn't worth waiting round and coming here. There wasn't nothing worth coming for.

My mama lost babies too and she lost my sister when she was four and I was two. She ain't speak for months, that's what Aunt Greta whisper to me when I been old enough to understand. I understands better now. I ain't wanna speak to nobody neither. I swore I'd never bring another child to this world. Why would I when they wouldn't be nothing but hated and treated like animals. I sayed I wouldn't but I did. I sinned against myself and I did. But that pain stay. It stay with you always. Ethan. Greta. Robert. All stoled away from me but stuck inside my heart, likened to break it. Coursing through my blood.

I tries not to think of it. But it's there. I sew and it's there. I cook and it's there. I clean up after them and it's there. No matter where I goes or what I does, it's there. Stuck inside. They don't know what it is that gots me this way. Sick in my body but I knows. God knows they did this to me. Poisoned me in the spirit. Poisoned my heart with they hate and pain and hurt. My body can't do nothing else with all the pain so it's crying. Breaking.

My boy's almost a man. He handsome and strong and smart and I'm so proud of him. He play that fiddle like nobody else, that's what I say. And give him some more time and he gon be a master carpenter too. They won't call him that though. Cuz they won't. But he's gon be so good. I thanks God that Master John did right by him, by us and ain't steel my son away or hurt him. That my Ervin had a chance and that I had my Ervin. He's my heartbeat. I feels him in my sleep. I feels him when I'ms awake. When I'm doing anything he's there too. Helping me through all the other stuff they put inside me. He help to ease the pain. The idea of him makes me want to keep breathing even if the hurt is more than I think I can bear. God gave me him. Let me keep just one.

Some don't know what it's like to be free. I don't know really either but I imagine it must be like when a baby bird gotta leave the nest and they mama start pushing them to the edge and that bird don't know nothing bout flying. Thinks it's gon die falling to its death. But then it look up and probably see God and then it start flapping its wings trying to get closer to God. That must be what freedom feel like. A bird think they falling and trying all they can to get to God. I want freedom. From this pain in my body. The pain in my mind. From always being in shadows and can't never see the light cuz somebody like Misses Shelly step in front. Don't even see she tying my wings even if she thinks she doing me right. Like the rain telling the ant I ain't gon flood you but a little bit cuz it's just how rain is. Ain't nothing you can do bout the rain cept get wet. Complain if you can but it don't matter. Rain don't care bout nothing but getting everything it see wet. That ant just got caught up. Rain gon rain. It's not thinking bout nothing but what it do. I'm tired of the rain. Tired. I wanna be like that bird, head towards the sky, stead a sitting in sticks, dirt, and poop.

It don't matter much now. I knows my time ain't long. I got to see him now. I got to see my Ervin grow strong and proud. He ain't always gon be where he is. God done showed me he got plans for the one he saw fit to leave with me. That was a promise that I spect God to keep. He let everything else be taken away and destroyed so he better keep this promise for my Ervin.

Misses Shelly and me did good on our trip to Charleston. Sold everything we had with orders for more. She ain't stop talking the whole way and alls I can do is listen a little cuz I don't wanna hear nothing bout next month or the month after or the holidays coming up. I don't wanna hear her talk bout fabric and thread and her sketches or tell her bout my ideas. I just wanna think of Ervin and Greta and Ethan and Robert. I wanna think bout them and how I knowed them in my heart and what I remember. I wanna try to see Ethan's face how I remembered him. He was Ervin's age last I seed him. I wonders what he look like. If he doing okay. If he alive out there somewhere. I wonder if Greta found a good home and if they treating her okay. I imagine she made it okay. She was always so smart and pretty. I thinks of my Robert. The only man I ever let my heart love. I see Ervin and I can't help but think bout him. I see his smile and he got his daddy's hands. I thanks God for giving me a little bit of my husband back in my son.

I thinks bout my mama and my daddy. I knowed her all my life and knowed my daddy til he got taken away. He wanted freedom too much for the master to put up with. Sayed, That one there is too much a risk to keep around. He'll rile up the other slaves.

Daddy always sayed every man deserve to be free. I put my head back and close my eyes while she still talking. I can see them. They in heaven right now and they at peace. Sitting round not having to work less they want to. Mama smiling at me in her garden. She used to love that garden. She growed tomatoes and cucumbers and peas. She sayed she ain't growing no corn but she'd grow other stuff and we eat it all. She had two chickens and they give us fresh eggs.

They liked mama. Our master let me come in the kitchen and cook with her, passed it right down to me. Like it's cooked into my blood. I stayed in that kitchen. When mama got too old to do the cooking, she sit right beside me and help me cut up vegetables, get the meats ready and anything else she could. She told me I was a good cook and never forget that. She sayed, Cooking and good food is a way to people's hearts. Remember that Ellie. Never go wrong with it.

So I cooked like it was my way to be free.

Guess it helped me get this close. Riding side Misses Shelly.

Daddy. I see him too. He don't look tired. He don't look angry. He look peaceful and unbothered. I wanna look like that one day too. Like they look. At peace. I don't know what it feel like but I imagine that what they look like must be what it feel like.

El? El? Ellie? What's wrong Ellie? Misses Shelly cuts into my waking dream cuz she been talking and I ain't been. She sound worried.

Nothing ma'am, I says back and start looking at my hands. The hands that served and slaved all my life. Taking care of other people's bellies and babies. Taking care of they homes. Making them feel comfortable. Helping them feel good.

I thought something was wrong. You got so quiet.

I thinks whether I wanna tell her something. She wasn't gon understand if I did. No matter how good a white person she think she is, she still own me so don't understand the pain that alone can give. Don't understand how I can't never feel free or at peace so long as I'm alive like this.

Ain't nothing wrong. Just resting my eyes and thinking. About what?

Nothing.

You can't be thinking about nothing, El. You can talk to me.

This woman think we friends. You can't be real friends with somebody who own you. We gets along cuz we gotta. I gotta. But we ain't friends. I needs her to do what I can't do and she own me and need me so she can do what she do. That don't make us friends. She alright but friends is a stretch.

Misses Shelly I's just thinkin bout Ervin and how he almost a man and thinking bout whether he gon get married one day.

Well I'm sure he will. He's got a trade. And everybody knows him so the girls will be calling. I hear they already are.

I smiled with my lips pressed together. I hoped she was right. I hoped he met a nice woman and had a nice life, as nice as possible. I hoped he'd see freedom one day and have something of his own. I ain't sayed that to her but she ain't press me no more. I was tired. Too tired to make conversation.

We got back near home and I asked Misses Shelly to please go by Master John's so I could see Ervin.

It's very late El. You can see him tomorrow. I'll give you time.

Misses Shelly, I know it's late but I need to see him and tell him something important.

The driver is tired too. You're tired and I'm tired. We'll go in the morning.

Misses Shelly. I need to see my son tonight. Please. I won't be long. I promise.

I thinks she seed my eyes and feeled like she should say yes, cuz she telled the driver to take us by her brother's house. I don't know why but I started crying then. Like it was just waiting to come out.

Now you're going to see him El. Why are you crying?

I don't know Misses Shelly. I don't know.

Your illness must have you all messed up and, maybe you're going through that thing women go through in their forties.

Maybe. My body had failed me and I was too young. I tried, I did. Sometimes we ain't got no control over things.

They was in the workshop. I could hear the fiddle pulling up to the house. He and Master John doing what they did. I knowed they was surprised to see me and Misses Shelly come up that late. Ervin come out holding his fiddle, looking curious. He ran over to help me out the carriage. I was weaker than I used to be and couldn't make that step alone. My body was thin and frail and my hair tied up under that bonnet was thinner than it had ever been. He ain't mention nothing bout it though. He believe people deserve dignity. He held my bony arm and walked with me back to our table. Master John ain't sayed nothing after coming over to talk to Misses Shelly. She likely telled him not to bother us. She can be smart that way sometimes, makes her good at selling to them women.

Ervin helped me sit down.

Sit right here next to me Ervin so I can look at you good.

Ervin put his chair right by me so I can see in his face.

The moon was full and it light up in his eyes. They still wide. I looked and held his hand. I wanted to be close to him. That's all I wanted since the day he came out my body. Screaming and hollering, us both. They ain't think he was gon make it. He was early and small and so weak. But he had a cry. And all I wanted to do was hold him and keep him safe. Keep anybody from hurting him or taking him away. I was scared he'd leave me after figuring out what he done come into. I sleeped with him on my chest so I could feel him breathe. I lived with him attached to me til he got too heavy and then I keeped him by my side.

Now here he was. I touched his face looking at the hair on his chin and over his lip. Master John had teach him to shave but it been all day now. He wasn't just turning to a man. He was a man. He growed up and I got to see it. That was all I ever wanted, to see my babies grow up and be some kinda happy and okay. To know they was loved. I missed that with Greta and Ethan. Ethan was seventeen when they took him away but they'd snatched him from my arms when he was young. Made him do all kinds of things when I was pregnant with Greta. That evil woman punished my Ethan cuz of her anger at me. I ain't forgive her. I ain't forgive none of them. But I got my Ervin. I got to see him turn to a man. I got to laugh with him and eat with him. I got to see him work miracles with his hands and hear other people talk bout my boy in good ways.

What's going on mama? Ervin finally ask me. I thinks he was scared to say nothing. He knowed I been sick for a while.

He see me and feel my thin fingers. Ain't no hiding the truth when it's sitting right in front of ya.

You know how sometimes we wanna do what we wanna do but we can't?

Course mama. Course I knows. That's everyday.

Sometimes it ain't just cause we slaves and ain't got freedom.

Well that's a big reason mama.

Ervin. One day this world gon be different. There's whispers in the wind bout freedom and that slavery is bad and I believes it ain't gon last always. It can't. Even the Israelites got free. God can't forsake us if we all his children. I needs to tell you something Ervin. You gotta do what you can to be as free as you can be whether you a slave or a free man. Not all emancipated men are free and not all slaves are in bondage.

I don't understand mama.

You gotta choose in your mind if you gon be free or in bondage. Then ain't nothing nobody can do to convince you otherwise. You make your money and save it so that you can buy your freedom. You earn your way to freedom. You keep it. In your heart and in your mind. Don't let nobody tell you different that you ain't free. They may own your body but not your soul and not your mind. That's between you and God. Don't nobody else have claims on that.

I unstrapped the sack round my waist. I been carrying it on my body for weeks, scared to leave it in the house case something happened. I put it on the table.

This yours. You hold to it and put it somewhere safe. One day you gon be free and your children gon be free. My grandbabies gon be free, I whispered to my Ervin. That's God's promise.

He pulled that bag across the table and feeled it.

What's this mama?

It's everything I saved up. I ain't got no use for it Ervin. Sometimes our plans ain't the ones God has for us. I ain't wanna say what I knowed was in my heart. But I had to be with my Ervin.

This is yours for you to make my grandbabies free Ervin. You do something that I can't. Keep it safe. Guard it.

Mama. Why you doing this right now? Tell me what's going on?

I looked up at that moon hanging in the sky and then back into my boy's eyes.

Sometimes we gotta do what the lawd wants us to do. I guess the lawd wants me with him. He wants me back home.

What you mean mama? You are home. This is home, round the way at Misses Shelly house. The lawd don't need you.

I hugged Ervin that night. I held him tight as I could for long as my arms would let me. He keep me up hugging me back.

Mama. Just stay here with me. You'll be alright and we can be free together.

My son done got so strong. I seed my mama. She put down the tomatoes she holding and put her hand out to me. Daddy standing by her. She say it's okay to come on home cuz my Ervin gon be okay and I'm gon be okay. She sayed it's time. It's time to rest and my heart need to rest and my body and my soul. I heard her voice, It's okay. It's okay. I wanna reach out to her too but that mean I can't hold to Ervin no more. But I feels my arms loosen round Ervin and I see a glow and mama and daddy standing inside it they arms out for me to come with them. I reach my hand to them and feels my spirit leaving and know God pulling me back to him. Ain't no more pain. Nowhere. Ain't no more pain.

Freedom

It was a Saturday night when mama gone on to God. She wasn't but maybe 90 pounds when she went to sleep in my arms. She looked happy. At peace. I falled to the ground holding her and Master John and Misses Shelly run over. I couldn't speak. There ain't no words for a time like this. I lost other people, but not like this. I could hardly breathe. My body shaking. My everything. She finally had the freedom we was promised.

Not a word crossed my lips for days. Not to Master John or Misses Charlotte. All I could do was work on mama's casket. I spent every waking moment on it. Master John ain't sayed nothing bout it. He let me be. I ain't get nothin else done for nobody else. He did that himself and let me take care of mama's final resting place. He asked me if I wanted her there or the negro graveyard back of the church. I sayed I want her with me, that's what she woulda wanted. We had a small service with friends and even some of the women mama sewed for come by to pay they respects. I looked at mama laid up in that casket I made for her and stained a pretty cherry color. I done a beautiful trim and it looked nice as one somebody woulda paid a hundred or two hundred dollars for. Ain't nobody sayed nothing bout it cuz they knowed I made it with my own hands. I couldn't speak still and after everybody gone I went to my room and cried that whole day.

I ain't play the fiddle for near a month after mama died. I worked in the workshop in silence. Master John passing work over but letting me be in my quiet.

Master John and me was playing on a Friday night in October for the gentleman's club. It was always too smoky in there but it paid well and consistent. They paid us that same night and Master John never hold onto it. He give me my cut when it was done cuz I earned it. I had the sack mama give me. I added my money to it and put it inside my fiddle case. This was our first gig since mama died. My fingers ain't even plucked a string since the night mama passed in my arms. Master John asked me if I was ready to play and I told him I could.

I played next to Master John that night. We played the songs we been playing together for so long and I smiled cuz he done teached me to play that fiddle and do carpentry.

Freedom. Mama was free. Finally. I wasn't. But there was places I could be. Places I could make good money with my trade. Places where a black man could have his own things.

When I got set to play that evening I wore my boots and both of my pants and shirts. My fiddle case had smoked pork wrapped up in a cloth and three apples. I stuffed bread inside my jacket pocket. I told Misses Charlotte bye cuz we was going to play. She sayed to have a good time and take off our clothes at the door cuz she ain't want the cigar smoke in her house. I sayed yes ma'am fore I come out the back and climbed in the carriage beside Master John. I look back at that house remembering all them years ago I first come there.

It was late September when I decided I deserved freedom like any other man. I been there with Master John and Misses Charlotte bout ten years. I knowed Master John would be more sad than mad and Misses Charlotte, well I ain't knowed how she might feel. I think she don't let herself feel much no way. But mama was there in them woods. Not far from Misses Charlotte's babies. She was closer up though so nobody would disturb those babies. If I was to go I'd be leaving mama. No. I figured I can't leave her cept the body that broke down on her. She be with me like she always been. I had enough to get away if I could get on the other side of town.

I ain't wanna hurt him. I know how he feeled bout me. He gon feel kinda like when somebody take something from you that you ain't knowed you even wanted, til it's gone. But I had to try. The men in that room knowed me and my work. I'd leave there and start all over. Nobody would know me or what

I could do. But maybe nobody would know I been a slave either. Maybe they figured with what I knowed how to do I must be free.

He was there. The minister's son Matthew. Standing in the back like he been outta place. But he was there like he promised so I can see him. I was scared. I ain't knowed what would happen if they catched me. They ain't take well to slaves running away. I had to get out though. Freedom. This was my chance. Matthew was starting a church in Virginia. I was scared a Virginia but if I could get to Virginia I could get past it. He was going with his wife and baby girl. They ain't believe in slavery but they seemed to be one of the few who wasn't okay with it. Everybody else seemed to excuse it as just the way things was. Ain't no reason for it to be the way it was. Wasn't Godly. Just evil and greedy. I thinks of Master John. He wasn't evil or greedy but he went along with it still. So I blamed him too. He could make me free but I thinks Misses Charlotte wouldn't. And mama always sayed it's the women that rule the house.

When we was finished Master John gave me my coins and I went to the back to relieve myself. I sneaked to Matthew's carriage and crawled under the tarp. It smell like hay and pigs but aint been but two chickens back with me. Matthew sayed the hay and that tarp he let the pigs use all week was to cover my smell. I bout vomit in the back when he cover me up. The chickens making a racket in they crate wasn't helping neither. Specially with all the bumping. I prayed then and there that God would let me go. That my suffering and bondage was over. I prayed that he'd see me through to Philadelphia.

We slowed down and I wondered if it was cuz somebody was stopping us to look for me. I ain't sleep none the whole night. I peak out the back and it was dark but the moon was full and high. I laid back there, scared the whole time. The baby cried off and on and Matthew's wife sang lullabies to quiet her. Mama used to sing to me. When we stopped I got out and stretched and relieved myself and ate a strip of bacon and an apple.

Matthew come running back from the woods and speaking in a whisper yelling and waving his arms all wild. I's trying to figure if he need help then I hear him tell me to get back in under the tarp. He tell his wife to ger back in cuz we gotta go.

I look at him trying to see if he true.

You wanna get caught or get back in? He look at me and jump in the carriage.

I took a deep breath of fresh air trying to hold onto some of it fore I got in and crawled under the hay and pulled the tarp over. Wasn't a minute later I heard a dog barking. Matthew start moving but he wasn't going too fast. I tried to hear what he was telling his misses but the sound ain't come through good. Something bout catchers and that been all I need to hear. I wiggled to the back and push them chickens to the edge with they luggage. All gon smell like shit and pigs.

Dog got louder and close enough for me to hear a horse and somebody shouting in our direction. I lay there still as the night sky trying to listen, trying not to be scared and failing both ways. Matthew slow down and we hear the dog barking all the way. I lift up the wood plank he put back there. Just in case, he sayed. This was the case. I lay flat against the back of the wagon and hold that board up. I heard them talking and the dog barking. That dog scaring the chickens and they hollering in they way.

Like I sayed just a couple chickens, our luggage, and some household items. We're moving to start a church.

I ain't hear nothing back and then Matthew ask that catcher if he wanna take a look. He put his hand down on the tarp and tap it twice like it been all on the right.

Yeah. Then I can move on. I heard a negro male late teens may have escaped this way last night.

You got hired to catch him?

Not exactly. I work on speculation. Nothing official but they sayed he mighta come this way.

Well you're on it fast. I can let you have a look if you want. Mind if I pray for you too, and leave you with the good Lord's words? We have some bibles back here. Never know when someone will be in need of the word.

Where you heading you say?

Virginia. Me, my wife and infant daughter.

He sayed infant daughter and that baby start crying like her mama done pinch her. The chickens still carrying on and it smell like pigs and his dog barking at the back.

The baby's hungry. I need to feed her. Is this gonna be long? Matthew wife called back.

Umm. Mind if I just take a quick peak? Then you can be on your way.

Sure. Take a look and get a bible at the same time.

Matthew lift the tarp over the chicken crate to the start of the luggage and then open up a crate he pack with bibles.

It smells awful. That's okay. I don't need to be carrying around anything smell like that. It'll throw my hunting off. Go head and get outta here. I got a nigger to catch.

You gotta name in case we come across him?

Goes by Luke. Bout yay high and a mulatto. Almost passing which is why I need to find him fore he slip outta these parts.

Well we'll keep an eye out for anybody look like that.

Matthew covered the luggage and pulled the tarp back over the top of the chicken crate. He got back in and we start moving again. I feeled the air finally leave my lungs.

By time night broke we was far enough that I could sit in the back and pretend that I was they slave. I was still scared since we selled our work far cross South Carolina and was still in South Carolina. Somebody might recognize me. Matthew's wife sayed I should take off the top clothes and put them away. They was too nice to be wearing on this type of trip and would draw attention. She was kind and soft spoken like she ain't wanna disturb nothing.

We rode through the rest of South Carolina, bumping up and down. When it got dark this time we stopped cuz Matthew ain't knowed these woods and ways like closer to home. He says we gotta be careful cuz they might be looking for me too. Even if Master John thinked I'd sneaked off to be with some girl I should be back by now and he'd be worried.

My eyes was looking for anybody coming after us. They wouldn't know yet where I was or where I was going. I reckon after asking questions they'd think I stowed away in Matthew's carriage. Think he ain't got nothing to do with it. That's how it was spose to be. We had so far to go. Weeks to go. Time in this carriage worrying bout getting caught and taked back. The moon was getting smaller little by little. I wondered if Master John looking for me. I wondered if he sent a letter to the church in Virginia cuz he knowed that's where Matthew been going. I wondered if he thinked I hate him. I hopes he know I ain't hate him. I hated being a slave. If I was a free man like him it'd be different. But I wasn't. Wasn't no going and coming like I please. Like it been for him or Matthew. And it'd take me another ten or fifteen years to buy my freedom.

I wanted to be free when I meet the woman I was gon marry and who was gon have my babies. I wanted them to be free from the beginning and not have to die to be free. Those girls in town was nice enough but they wasn't free. Not in no way. They minds, they spirits or they bodies. They ain't understand that I wanted freedom and even if they body wasn't free they mind could be. Mama's grandbabies was gon be free. My babies was gon be free or else I ain't want them. I'd keep my seed to myself and let it die inside me.

Bout two weeks past by time we finally gots to Virginia. The moon was half full. We stopped to sleep along the way. I sleeped in barns and workshops and they sleeped inside. We got food and water from people who was part of Matthew's church. The big one, not the one he was starting. We finally got to Richmond and Matthew collected papers and other things from the big church. I helped him carry extra bibles and hymn books to the carriage. We had another fifty miles north to go fore we reached where they'd be stopping. He sayed there was help there to get me to the next stop and soon he'd be part of a network to help people get free. He smiled and sayed, I guess I already am.

I still wasn't free. The church ain't give Matthew no letters bout me but my nerves was still jumpy. We was still in Virginia and Master John was likely looking for me. We got to Matthew's church three days later. I helped him take out the bibles and the hymn books. We was setting up inside when a man walked up and came thru the door.

Matthew stop what he doing and walk up to shake his hand. Hi. Welcome. I'm Reverend Matthew Clark. How can I help you. He smiled and look at the man then me.

Welcome Reverend. I'm Mickel Anderson from about a half mile down the road. We're glad you're here and I'm pleased to meet you and be first to welcome you. Am I the first to welcome you?

You are. It's nice to make your acquaintance Mr. Anderson. Thank you.

My wife made you some cornbread here and I come bearing this letter we've been holding for you. Arrived two days past.

He handed Matthew a dingy envelope. I was scared to know what was in it.

Thanks for delivering it. Mickel look like he was waiting on something or for Matthew to open it up right then.

Stead of that Matthew nodded and invited him to church the next Sunday. We need this week to get things together, he sayed.

I'll be here with the family, Mickel sayed, looking at that envelope again. I look forward to building community with a good church close by. Have a good day Pastor.

You too Mr. Anderson. God bless you. Matthew close the door behind him and put the lock on.

That man ain't looked at me once, like I ain't exist. It wasn't like back home where people looked at me. Maybe not in the eye but they looked at me. They knowed who I was and what I could do. With that man I was like nothing. But I'd be something when I got to where I was going.

We finished unloading the church stuff then went round back to unload the house stuff. They house was right behind the church. It looked like it was attached from the front but there was a few feet between. I'd be there with them til it was time to go a little further. Matthew reckoned it might take weeks for me to get far enough to be free. I told him it ain't matter how long it take. Only thing mattered was me being free in the end.

He ain't make me eat separate at no table like Misses Charlotte. Stead we eat at the same table like when me and Master John eat outside. Like there was no difference. Baby was there too but not at the table. She a sweet baby I guess. Don't seem to cry all that much. She gon look like her daddy, at least she do right now, but her hair the color of her mamas. Dark brown. I wondered if she gon grow up kind or be like some folk I know who ain't. I wondered if she gon help other people get free like her mama and daddy or if she gon try to keep them slaves. I wondered if her mama and daddy gon tell her this story when she get older. Bout how we leaved South Carolina and they helped a man name Ervin get free. It wouldn't be much longer and I'd have papers and a name.

After we eat Matthew pulled me to the front of the house. We sit in two chairs we take with us outside while his wife feed the baby. He pulled out the letter he get from that man and sayed, This is about you, Ervin.

I can't read so I looked at it in his hand. He unfolded it and started reading the letter.

> *Dear Matthew Clarke,*
>
> *It has come to my attention that there may be a slave that bears the name Ervin in your possession. It is believed that Ervin escaped on the eve of October 28 from the area around where we gathered for our monthly gentleman's evening. We played at the event after which Ervin excused himself and did not return. I was later told that you were beginning your journey to Virginia to begin your new church and learned that Ervin may have been aware of your plans and chosen this opportunity to leave.*
>
> *I do not believe Ervin to be dangerous. Do not fear. I would simply like him to be returned to me in haste and am willing to compensate you for his return by train or boat. Please keep him in your stead if he has indeed gone off with you and you have found him. Please let him know that I am not angry and he will not be harshly punished. I am concerned for him and what they might do to him if he is not*

returned. Please write back to inform me of whether he is with you or is not with you.
I eagerly await your response.

Sincerely,
John James

    I listened to him read that letter and my stomach was in balls. I couldn't hardly breathe. Feeled like my supper wasn't gon stay put. I walked away and leaned up next to the church. Maybe God could help me. I knowed this might happen but that don't make it no easier. He wasn't gon just let me go like that. I wondered who he had to write that letter. Master John ain't never talked like that. Probably that man at the leather shop helped him write it. I wonder did Misses Charlotte even know. She coulda written a letter even if it ain't been as fancy as this one. She read a little but Master John don't read more than letters and numbers, enough to make a note and make sure he get paid.
    What do you wanna do Ervin? Matthew asked me after a while.
    I wanna be free. I wanna keep going til I'm free. I ain't tryin to hurt nobody. It ain't bout nobody else right now. They gots they freedom. I want mine.
    Alright then. We help you get free Ervin. All God's children deserve to see the promised land.
    Matthew folded the letter up and put it in his pocket. I knowed he had to answer it or else them other folks be wondering what he hiding. His daddy would be getting questions. I could see it cross his face. Matthew thinked bout what it mean for the first time. He ain't never help nobody escape. It weighed on him like it weighed on me. He couldn't let nobody think he knowed nothing or else all that nothing would go right for him or his family.
    Thank you, suh. I know it ain't easy so thank you.
    Matthew look at his hands so I look too wondering if I was spose to see something.

This is God's work, Ervin. Many men won't understand it now but one day they will. The Egyptians didn't want the Israelites to be free. They wanted them captive and serving them as slaves. It was how it had been long as anyone could remember. But God made a promise and it took faith to bring the promise to life Ervin. I have faith that what I'm doing, what we're doing is right. In the end, God will show it is right and his blessings will fall on those who serve him and all his children.

He sayed it but he looked sad and a little scared. I ain't never been too much for church. Seem like it was always trying to remind us how it was God who wanted us to be happy as slaves and wait for a promised land after we dead. But Matthew talk bout a promised land like the ones the Israelites had - when they was still alive. I like that promise land more.

When I leaved Virginia and Matthew and his wife and baby I was scared again. Matthew wrote a letter back splaining that if I had caught a ride somehow I musta jumped out when they slept for the night cuz he ain't seed me and don't know where I mighta got out. He sayed he was sorry bout the loss and how he couldn't be more help. He read the letter to me and I smiled. I asked him if he could write something bout he sure I ain't escape cuz a bad treatment or cuz I ain't like them. Matthew sayed he shouldn't add that cuz it might give something away.

I only wanted Master John to know it ain't had nothing to do with him. It been bout me but he just gon have to know it in his heart.

John

Like it wasn't anything he was gone. One minute we're playing like we always do and the next he wasn't anywhere to be found. I was scared to make a scene because I didn't want anyone alarmed. If somebody caught him they'd expect me to hurt him or they'd hurt him. Either way I couldn't do that. I never laid a hand on him in anger all these years and didn't plan to start.

His mama changed things for him. When we put her in that casket and lowered her into the ground I knew I was losing him, one way or another. I just didn't expect it to happen so fast. I didn't get to send him off or wish him well or tell him anything else about the world out there. All our talks, our jokes, my terrible ones he'd laugh at only because they were too stupid not too. All the times carving those little trinkets we gave to Charlotte to sell to her piano students families. They are both so smart.

Charlotte tried to tell me not to worry. Whatever's meant to be will be. But it's different. She says he'll be back most likely. She doesn't really know, she just doesn't want me worrying. I am though. She says it'll be okay because President Monroe is against the slave trade but even then he didn't get the senate to approve his agreement. That tells me there isn't much changed. Not yet. At least he did something but who knows if he'll get more time with four in the race. And if that Jackson wins it'll be all over and I hope he'll know he should come straight back.

I know he's a young man now but he's not grown. Barely eighteen. And I didn't do enough. I wish I could've done more but it's done. He's gone.

Charlotte

He worries about that boy like he was his own. Fretting and fussing over how far he got, where he was heading, if he's okay, who's helping and a hundred other things. Worrying won't help a thing. Not a single thing, and I know because I've worried and it got me nothing.

I can't tell John he's okay like he wants me to. Only that he did what he felt he needed to do. I wonder why though. He had everything he could need right here. Food, roof over his head, earning money to buy his freedom, though John thinks he shouldn't have to. And we need the money. We finally paid off our debt for him three years ago and now the investment walked right outta Georgetown.

We just have to keep going. I have to keep up my lessons, and John his work. E didn't leave us like he could've with a field full. Thank God for that. He helped us bring in the crops, helped John finish up two pieces we were counting on. Didn't leave us flat.

I didn't want him at first. I didn't. I do wonder where he's gone, and if he's getting enough good food. He grew strong here. I imagine I don't have any right to thinking he belongs here but I do. Plain and simple, E belongs with me and John, and him leaving us like that tore another hole through me. Makes me want to put out another stone. It'd be ridiculous but, if he doesn't come back and we don't get word from the letter we sent, I will. It would be the decent thing to do.

Philadelphia

I ain't knowed the other people Matthew dropped me off to bout a week later, fore they had church on Sunday. I was scared they'd take me and sell me back someplace else. Worser than anything I could imagine. One of them big plantations and I'd be back in the field like the place I was when I was young. I ain't never wanna go back no place like that. I was scared a Virginia too. That place took my daddy, sister, brother and more family and friends then I can count. I was glad to be outta there but I was still scared.

I ain't had to hide in the back of a wagon since we crossed into Pennsylvania or act like I was somebody's slave. I sometimes sat right up beside whoever was taking me on that part of my journey to freedom and sometimes in the back, looking out at where I was leaving. So much I was leaving. So much behind me.

I don't know if anyplace could smell so sweet and stink at the same time. We got to the city and it was people everywhere. Black people. White people. Brown people. People doing stuff and working. Black people walking round with nobody. They wasn't walking behind, side, or front a no white woman or man. They was walking like they had they own business to tend to. I imagined myself making furniture and playing fiddle and walking round like I was a man with my own business to tend to like they was. People loving my work and talking bout it. I wondered if I could be the best like Master John. I gots sad right then cuz I missed him. I wasn't spose to but I did when I thinked back on us being in the workshop and how he showed me exactly how to cut something so that it bent right. That the curves lined up. How he showed me how to put marks in my work table so that I ain't had to measure over and over. We made our table and chairs together and that been where we take our midday break and Misses Charlotte would bring out food. We talk on the work we had to do and how the leather was rougher or softer this year cuz of the feed. Or how he wanted to get some new equipment or sell down the river further. He talked bout getting a place in town one day to have stuff in the window to sell but then sayed it cost so much. I telled him he ain't need it cuz everybody knowed him and he did the best work.

He showed me how to play that fiddle and put his fingers on mine to place them the right way. I remember how proud he been when I played my first song. He called Misses Charlotte out to hear and she listened. Sayed it was good and went back in the house. I keeped my fiddle on me the whole time we was riding cuz I ain't had much else I cared for. Clothes on my back and the pouch round my waist. I sayed a thanks prayer to God for keeping me this far and for putting me under the care of Master John and not somebody else like the other masters I done meet. I asked God to make it easy for Master John and to put it in his heart that I ain't had nothing much against him.

We stopped in front of a dark brick building and a tall thin black man come to the wagon. He nodded to the man driving who tipped his hat then telled me, This is your stop young man. Good luck.

The driver already welcome me to Philadelphia when we got to the city. He laughed cuz my nose turned up at the same time I smiled. Smelled like horse manure and urine. I thanked him and jumped out. It was November and the moon was full again in the sky at night. I wish I had a coat but freedom is warm to the soul. I still needed my papers though.

The tall man shook my hand. Name's Marcus Freeman. Born free right here in Philadelphia to parents who got they freedom like you did. He looked proud. I ain't never seed a black man in public looking proud. Nobody coming over to see what we talking bout or what we was doing.

I'm Ervin. I ain't tell him no last name cuz I ain't had a last name.

Follow me. He start walking to a building with gold letters on the window.

We walked through the door and Marcus nodded or smiled at the people inside fore we went through another door and down a hall and down some stairs to what seem like a cellar. A black man come out from another room. He looked like he was working on something with fire since he had on one of those thick black aprons and thick gloves. He look at me a few seconds fore saying, Come round back.

I followed him and Marcus and then there was another door that went outside. He had a metalshop and was making horseshoes and other stuff. He took off his gloves and sat down at a wood table that sat up on two horses like we had back in our workshop. He pulled out a box and set it on the table. He took out a big ledger book like Master John keep, long with another sheet a paper, a pen and ink well.

Welcome to Philadelphia. Welcome to freedom.

He smiled at me and I couldn't help but smile back. He had a happy face. Content with life. He missed some teeth but his smile still made me wanna smile. Jeffrey back home helped in a workshop like this. What he'd think to see this man having his own metalshop and being free? He'd never believe me.

I go by William Smith. What are you gonna go by young man?

I looked at William and Marcus. They was both free longer than I'd even lived. I ain't never had a choice bout nothing and now I spose to choose a name. I spose to say what I'd be called. I knowed my first name was gon be Ervin cuz mama gave me that name. Mama ain't never had her own name either. On her headstone they carved Ellie Bowers cuz her owners was named Bowers.

I ain't knowed what I should say.

You wanna pick a new name altogether? William asked me. It's okay. I know this is all brand new. Freedom is heavy.

I ain't sayed nothing. I was thinking bout mama and my name and Master John and my daddy and Greta and Ethan. I wanted to honor all of them with my name. And I ain't had one cept one I been given. I was mad I ain't already had that figured out by time I got there but I ain't believed it was real til we pulled into Philadelphia. Til I seed them black folks walking round free. I was scared to curse it with going too far too fast. Like Matthew told me - one step at a time, one stop at a time. Now I was here and it was time. Daddy ain't had no last name that I knowed and I never knowed him. I wasn't naming myself after the place I done got away from or the place I was. I pondered on it a long time and they was patient. I guess I ain't been the first to get stopped up by that question. I was gon set up shop and play fiddle. I was gon do what I learned how to do from the one person who teached me everything and cuz a him I had a chance to be free and, long with mama, to have money in that pouch. Cuz a him I could keep making money. He telled me men deserved to be able to make money and I would cuz he teach me how - from making furniture and playing the fiddle to doing business.

Ervin James, I sayed.

You sure? William asked. He held the pen in the air and the white feathers moved in the breeze that come through the barn looking doors in the back.

Yes suh. I'm sure.

Was James ya daddy? William ask me.

I ain't knowed how to answer that. I started to say something but then closed my lips and ain't sayed nothing. He finally wrote in Ervin James on the paper saying it out loud as he wrote. How old are you Ervin?

Eighteen.

And when's your birthday?

Not sure, suh. Sometime in the fall. I thinks I just turn eighteen or fixing to.

Do you want today to be your birthday?

I smiled and nodded, Yes, suh. That be fine.

Alright then. November 25, 1807. He wrote it on that paper too with some other stuff. Telled me to stand by the opening of the workshop door and sayed, What you think Marcus? About five feet nine?

Marcus standed beside me. He looked at the markings on the door. Yeah, that sound about right.

What kinda marks you have Ervin? William turn back to me and my mind went through my body starting at my head.

I got a birthmark shape like a crooked little worm on my ribs right here. I pointed to my right side.

Anything folks can see without taking off your clothes?

Marcus looked at my face. He got a mole under his left eye.

I ain't knowed my face that well. William copied all that into the big old book he had and then blew on it to make the ink dry. He blew on the piece of paper too. After a minute he put the book back in the box.

He held the paper in his hand. You wanna see? I just looked at it in his hand. It looked important but I couldn't read nothing. These are your papers, Ervin. You protect this with your life. Keep it on you all the time. It tells your name, your birthdate, your marks. Says you are from here in Philadelphia, Pennsylvania by way of New York. Now, you gotta get set up in a place to stay while you get settled. Marcus will take you to the Shepherds' house. They'll take good care of you. Get you a bath and some fresh clean clothes. You can't be here a free man and looking like you escaped. That's a sure sign. And you gotta act free, cuz that's what you is now.

Marcus walk and I follow behind him out the barn door from the blacksmith's shop. William wished me luck again and sayed he'd see me around. Keep your head up, young man.

Marcus sayed the same thing. I ain't never been able to do that round white folk without fear of getting asked what I'm looking at or why. Cept with Master John. I could put my head up and be proud of what I can do with him. That's it.

We walked bout a half mile passing all manner of folk. Some smiled at me. Some ignored me. Some looked at me curious like. I was embarrassed by my clothes. I did look like I just escaped. I figured some a them knowed. We came up on this white house with black round the windows. Flowers in autumn orange and rust red was all round the outside in the ground and it smelt like cinnamon when we got to the door. Marcus knocked and then looked at me with a little smile.

Who is it? A woman's voice sayed from the other side of the door.

Marcus. I've got a friend Misses Shepherd.

The door opened.

Oh Lilly. Your mama home?
Lilly. She look like a flower.

Found Sheep

Lilly seem like she look right past me. No she ain't home right now. But she said to be expecting you. My brother's home.

She smiled, glanced at me and then away. She was the prettiest thing I ever did see. I couldn't look at her and couldn't not look at her at the same time. I ain't knowed what to do with my eyes or my hands.

Come on in, Lilly sayed and opened the door wider.

I looked at Marcus.

Go on inside, he sayed then he come behind me and shut the door.

I ain't move more than a couple feet from it. I couldn't believe this was they house. They had they own house. I wondered if they owned it like white folks own stuff but was scared to ask. Scared to say something in front of Lilly. I ain't talk like she do or William or Marcus. I was dirty and my clothes worn, even the good pair I wore on the outside. I knowed I stunk awful and ain't wanna get too close to her. She was clean and pretty.

Lilly this is Ervin James. He just got to town. I'm sure he's hungry. Maybe he can wash up and eat something while we wait on your mama.

Yes. Of course. Lilly leaved come back a few minutes later. She was holding clothes folded up. There's a washroom you can use back here. Just close the doors good. Rag and everything you need is there. When you done I can clean up your hair and shave you.

She say all this without looking at me straight. I wondered if I was that ugly or smelly or both. I took the clothes when she held them out to me and looked at Marcus.

It's okay. Go head and get cleaned up.

Lilly showed me to a room with a big wash tub. It was big enough for me to fit inside with my legs stretch out some. I ain't never seed one inside a house or been in one myself. I wondered if Master James and Misses Charlotte had one. I shut the door then tested it to make sure it was shut good like Lilly sayed.

I taked off the white long sleeve shirt and then my old work shirt underneath and my long shirt under that. I held the last one to my nose and smelled it. Almost knock my own self out. No wonder she hold her arm out so far to give me the clothes. I slide out of my two pants and socks and my boots all the while looking round. I ain't wanna smell nothing else.

There was a table in the room looked like somebody knowed what they was doing made it. It had curved legs and clawfeet with four toes like me and Master John did. Inside was two types of wood. I looked at it. It was smooth and they got the woods to line up good without gaps. The outside and legs was a pretty oak and in the inside look like birch. I liked how the grains was going opposite coming together like a crossing. It was a small table but it was pretty. An oil lamp sat on the corner of it. There was a wooden rocking chair in there with a blue pillow cushion on it and a cabinet that stretch almost to the ceiling. It was simple but I could tell it was made well. I wanted to knock on it but I ain't want them to know. I could hardly believe this was all they stuff. That they had a room like this in a house like this.

One day I's gon have some furniture like this in my own house. A little bronze bell sat on the window sill. I picked it up and it made a sound and I put it down quick.

Everything okay? Lilly asked through the door.

Yes. I listened for her to leave fore I got into the water. I ain't never been in water like that. I was a little bit scared. I put my hand in it and it feeled nice and warm like they knowed I was coming but I ain't knowed how they got the water warm. Then I seed it. The fireplace on the wall had a metal thing sitting in front of it to blow some of the heat to the metal tub. I put my hand on that side of the tub and it was warmer. I moved the water around fore putting in one foot then the other and sitting down. When my back hit the water I slid down further. My knees was folded and I let my shoulders go into the water. I cried. Couldn't nobody see me.

I let my tears slide into the water too. I sat there like that for a while feeling the water on my body. Only times I ever feeled the water on my body was in the barrel in the yard during summer or when I got in the river on the way to Charleston. But then I was in my shorts and shirt and it was hot as summers in South Carolina likes to get. In that barrel Misses Charlotte tell me to scrub good when I was young. By time I leaved, the barrel come to my waist but I still got in and the water been good relief in the heat. Master John and me going to Charleston like to cool off in the river when the horses was catching a break. Then dry off by the shore fore putting clothes back on. Master John would always find some place we wouldn't be bothered with nobody asking why he was in the water with me.

That was the only times and never long as I could remember did my whole body feel the water naked at once. I bet Master John would love this too. Mama would love this. She'd say she got a headache and need to stay a while longer. Mama. I made it mama. I'm in Philadelphia. I'm free. My babies gon be free one day. Your grandbabies gon be born free. She still been in South Carolina but maybe the part a her that matter made the trip with me too. Her body was in those woods behind Master John's house cuz I asked them to bury her near me and then I leaved. She was with me. I could feel her. Specially at night when it was dark like when we would talk at Misses Shelly's house after a long day. I swore I sometimes heard her laugh when she cross my mind. A laugh that was almost scared to laugh cuz any minute somebody might come take away her reason for laughing. She'd let a laugh out, look around and press her lips together like if she hid it they can't steal it. I loved it. She ain't laugh with most people. She laugh with me though. I imagine she laughing now and smiling. And she ain't gotta hide her happiness cuz ain't nobody taking it away no more.

Nobody taking mine away no more neither.

Lilly was in the front room when I come back out. Marcus was sitting there talking to some boy a few years younger then me. Musta been Lilly's brother. Lilly look bout my age.

He and Marcus got cups and little plates with biscuits. My stomach made a loud noise. I ain't eat since the day before but with all the excitement I ain't paid hunger no mind til then.

You wanna eat before you get your hair cleaned up and shaved? You must be hungry. Her voice was so kind. Soft but not quiet. I wanted her to say something else so I could hear her talk.

Marcus and her brother ain't seed me fore she sayed that. You look refreshed, Marcus sayed. And smell refreshed. This is Lilly's brother Adam. Adam this is Ervin James.

Adam standed up and take my hand and shaked it like he was testing if I was strong. Nice to meet you Ervin.

I shaked his hand back. Nice to meet you too.

Ervin. Sit down. Go head and eat. Marcus deep voice wasn't nothing like hers and took away her chance to say something else to me. I wondered if she thinked that too.

Lilly ain't wait for me to answer bout eating. She was gone to the kitchen for I knowed it and come back with a plate of food. It wasn't like what Misses Charlotte made but the plate was full and I was hungry. A table for four people was on the side of the room we was in and she put it down there. I was still standing like I ain't know what to do.

You can sit down and eat, Lilly sayed. She disappeared again to got some water and bring it to me fore she gone again. This time she come back with a plate of biscuits and honey.

Lilly sayed, Adam and Mister Freeman yall can have some biscuits while we wait on mama. She'll be back directly. She went to go see somebody bout some work.

Adam and Marcus come to the table and sat down while Lilly bringed more water.

So what kind of work do you do? Adam asked me. My mouth was full of food so I ain't answer quick. I'm a carpenter and play the fiddle. I tapped the box that was beside me.

89

You play the fiddle? When you finish can I hear it? He looked excited.

Now he just got in town. Been traveling a long time. Let the man rest. Don't bother him about playing no fiddle, Marcus chided.

Ain't no bother to me, I sayed and keeped eating. Lilly came back in and sit down.

How was your trip? She looked at me now. I guess maybe I wasn't so bad looking. Least I ain't smell like I did.

It wasn't bad as I expected. Mostly wagons. Sometimes I hads to pretend I was they slave or lent out to them. Sometimes I hid in the back. It really ain't nothing when it mean getting to be here.

Were there alot of slaves where you was? Adam asked.

Let's leave the man alone. He needs to settle in without having to answer a bunch of questions, Marcus sayed fore eating another biscuit.

The food was good. Rice with boiled chicken and chicken juice. Corn and biscuits. Mama made the best biscuits. Misses Charlotte's always came out flat but sometimes she got it right and then she'd keep asking me and Master John if we want more. These was pretty good. Not like mama's but pretty good.

I finished my plate and Lilly carry it to the kitchen fore telling me, Come on.

She walk to the back door and I followed. There was a little porch and a chair. She brought out a piece of leather with a comb, scissors and a blade. I ain't had someone else shave me since Master John showed me how to do it myself. I was scared she might cut my throat and my neck was stiff in the chair.

She ran her fingers over my head, feeling my hair. It was still damp from the bath. She got some oil and put it in my hair fore she started combing it.

It hurt, girl. You pulling too hard. I ain't never combed my hair with nothing but my fingers and there was knots and snarls.

We can cut it short and start fresh, she said. Then you can start taking care of it.

I ain't cared nothing bout hair no way. Just something that growed out your head to keep you warm.

I just need enough to stay warm.

You talk kinda funny, she sayed and smile at me. I never met a slave from South Carolina before.

Well I'm free now.

Hold still. She pick up the scissors and start cutting round my head. Her fingers was slim and smooth like she ain't never been in a field. She was pretty and dark brown like mama. She come to the front to cut and I could smell her. She smelled like honey and cinnamon. I closed my eyes so she could cut without me being scared she might miss and cut me. I leaned my head back and took in her scent. She took the comb again and combed through my hair. This time it was easy. I opened my eyes in time to catch her smiling at her work fore getting the blade and running it over the leather to sharpen it. She took some more oil and ran it over my face and my neck.

Her hands was soft like grass in the morning. I closed my eyes again so she ain't catch me staring at her. She had long pretty black lashes over her pretty dark brown eyes. They almost look like coal til the sun catch them and I see some flecks. Her eyebrows was full and thick like her hair. She had it tied up into a big ball that sat in the back. I wanted to touch it but I kept my hands in my lap, embarrassed. Trying to cover myself and hoping she ain't notice. She moved behind me and telled me to lean my head back and stay still. She was gentle and unhurried. She moved that blade up from the middle of my neck to my jawline and then jawline to where the hair stopped. She did this over and over rinsing it off in the small bowl on the wooden stool beside her. Every once in a while she added a little oil to my face.

She patted my face. Go head and sit up, she whispered fore walking round the front to see. She lift my chin in her hand and turned my face from one side to the other and then lifted my chin. She went back and put some oil under my chin grabbed the blade and cleaned up that spot. Then she put it back down again.

All done. You look good. It looks good. You're all cleaned up.

I looked at her wondering if she meant I looks good or that her shaving looks good. But she ain't say nothing else. She dumped out the water bowl in the flower bed on the side and grabbed the shaving and cutting stuff and told me we can go back inside and wait in the room we had started in. She went someplace else with the stuff she been carrying.

You look like a new man, Marcus sayed.

I feels like one. I smiled like I was allowed to without worrying bout nothing.

You should let me take you into town, Adam sayed.

Marcus shook his head and sayed, I don't think so. We gon wait on Misses Shepherd cuz she gon let you know where you'll be staying to start. She out talking to Jonathan Greenland. He got that woodshop on the edge of town.

Maybe tomorrow then, Adam sayed. He looked disappointed.

We was sitting there a little while longer when the door opened. A pretty woman come in a little younger than my mama's age when she gone to God. She looked like Lilly. Same thick full eyebrows and long dark lashes.

She smiled at me. You must be our new arrival.

I standed up, feeling less embarrassed. Yes, ma'am. Ervin James from South Carolina.

She looked at me and nodded. Welcome. I trust you've eaten. She looked at the table behind us and nodded again. Looks like you're all cleaned up and got on fresh clothes. Now I been talking to Jonathan Greenland. He's a carpenter too, since I heard you do carpentry. Heard you're pretty good. He could use a hand there. He doesn't have an overflow of work but maybe he can do more with another set of hands. He's got an extra room too. Now he's the only carpenter in town and he's okay with having negro help.

I ain't have much choice less I wanna keep going further north. I ain't knowed nowhere else to go or nobody to help me get there. I ain't wanna work for no other carpenter. I wanted to work for myself. She musta seed my face twisted a lil bit cuz she asks me what's wrong.

Nothin' ma'am, I sayed back cuz I knowed I should be thankful. But I was free now and if I works for him I'll get paid but it seem a lot like what I leaved. Cept for not being a slave.

I looked at Lilly standing there with a broom in her hand and wonder if she spoken for already. I ain't had nothing to offer her. Not yet. A man sposed to take care of his family and I ain't got no way to provide for a wife yet. I hardly got a way to provide for myself. Til I do I ain't hardly no man.

Misses Shepherd telled Lilly to wrap up some of that chicken to go and some biscuits too. She come back with some cloth and put three pieces of chicken in and three biscuits. She ask me if that's enough. I wants more cuz that chicken was good but I ain't wanna seem greedy so I sayed, Yes, it's plenty.

She tie up the cloth and hand it to me. My finger touched hers a little bit and I find something else to look at outside the window. I can't be with no girl like her. I ain't had nothing and she had all that.

Alright then, Marcus sighed. We best get on to Mister Greenland's.

Yes. He's waiting on you. Wants to meet you, show you round and get you settled in so by morning y'all two can get to work, Misses Shepherd sayed as she start walking to the door.

I sighed to myself. I can't remember if I ever imagined what freedom would be like or feel like. I wanted to be like them. Like Misses Shepherd or William or Marcus. They looked nice and Misses Shepherd had that nice house. Marcus telled me she gets money for keeping guests come from out of town. They stays a night or two, sometimes longer and she and Lilly cooks for them and Lilly clean them up sometimes, like she did me. But they paying guests. I spose she can't afford to keep non-paying guests if she don't have to.

I wanted to see Lilly again but I ain't say nothing. I needed to make some money and be able to show I got something going for myself first. Once she see what I can do with my hands or hear me play my fiddle, I might have a chance. I looked at Adam. I ain't never played it for him but now ain't the time. Besides I ain't care bout playing for him then and Lilly disappeared again.

Thank you, Misses Shepherd, I sayed, trying to smile.

Marcus looked at me and opened the door. We'll see you around, Misses Shepherd.

I hoped Marcus was right. We got outside and Misses Shepherd closed the door. Marcus turned to me fore we started walking. He sayed, Lilly is a special girl. Don't think I didn't see how you was looking at her. She comes from a good family and her parents expect her to marry a good hardworking man. You understand. Don't try courting her in your current position. The town won't take well to you coming in with nothing and stealing a jewel.

I looked at him confused. I ain't gon steal a jewel or her. I ain't no thief, I argued.

You could steal her heart, he sayed back to me. You get a heart like that you better plan on keeping it and keeping it well.

Yessuh, I mumbled and walked beside him all the way to Mister Greenland's house.

Greenland

A sign hanged up over the barn door. It looked like it was made by Mister Greenland himself.

Greenland's Fine Furniture and Things

Marcus walked to the open door and looked inside. An old white man was in the corner hunched over a table, back to us. He knocked lightly on the door then sayed, Mister Greenland?

The old man turned around. He wasn't as old in the face but his hair was all gray. He looked maybe ten years past Master John's age in the face.

Marcus. Good to see you. I see you brought the boy around. Good. I'm looking forward to having some good help around here. Hard to find nowadays. I heard you was trained real good by a master carpenter. Is that true boy?

I looked at Marcus. I wasn't sure I should answer him directly and wondered why he called me boy.

Go head and tell him Ervin.

Yessuh. I was trained by a master carpenter for nearly ten years.

Ten years. You don't look a day over twenty.

Suh I'm eighteen years old now. A man. Trained and I can do most anything in this here shop. I looked back down then cuz I was scared I went too far and sayed too much.

Well we'll see about that. You ate already? I'm sure if you was at Misses Shepherd's you got fed. Lord knows that woman will feed you.

Let me show you round the shop, but I reckon you already know everything so not much explaining is needed. He looked up at me to see if I'd say something.

Marcus looked at me too but I ain't say nothing. Just nodded and let him show me the equipment and tools and his leather stretching rack. It looked nicer than the one we had but it work just the same. His tools was newer but they gon work just the same. That Mister Greenland wanted me to be impressed but it ain't the tools that make the shop. It's the man using the tools.

I looked at some of his pieces he had going. He showed me a dining set he was working on that I was gon help him finish. I wondered if he was really a master carpenter. He sayed they ready for staining and I'm thinking they need another round a sanding and maybe the legs need evening out a tiny bit. I could see without picking them up that the curve on the top of the legs ain't the same on all of them. Not by just a tiny bit either.

I wondered how much they paying him for this. I wondered what Master John would say if he seed this. I knowed what he'd say, to me in private. That you gotta pay attention to the details E. You gotta pay attention and look like it ain't your work, but that you looking through somebody else eyes. That's why we always switched up and check each other or come back a few hours later to check it so we gots new eyes. He must not have new eyes or that's why he need me.

Alright boy, what they call you? Ervin right? You gotta nickname?

No suh. Ervin is my name.

Alright then. Martha bout done with supper now but since you already ate I can show you where you'll be sleeping and you can get some rest. I imagine you had a long day.

That was the truth.

He took me to the other side of the shed and in the back was stairs leading up above the workshop. It was a low roof, not quite high enough to stand full on except in the middle. He sayed we work everyday cept Sunday and I get a dollar a week to start to see how I do. He sayed after that I get a part a every piece I help make that sells. A dollar a week is bout the same as I was getting with Master John. But then Mister Greenland say, Room and board is only thirty cents a week. Don't worry about that though. It'll come out your pay so you don't have to worry about spending it.

I looked back up at the room above the workshop and I ain't even seed the food. I looked at Marcus.

Ain't nothin free when you free, Mister Greenland smirked. You work hard and you earn your keep. You earn a wage and eventually you'll earn more but I can't pay you more without knowing exactly what I got.

Now let me show you where you can eat and bathe and all of that.

We leaved the workshop and walked across a patch of grass twenty feet to the back door of a house that reminded me of Lilly's house. He pointed out the outhouse while we walk to the back door. He sayed Misses Greenland would put water out for me at night with supper so I could wash up. We went in the back door and there was a little room to the left with a table and two chairs and a small cabinet.

You can use this space. This where we have folks who use the spare room in the workshop dine. You got your own private space but you can't be entertaining guests after dark. Besides it's best if you're not out past dark without a good reason. That's for your general safety, of course. He pointed out the fireplace and stove against the far left wall. There was a pot hanging on it already but wasn't nothing in it. He opened the cabinet doors and showed me there was flour and butter and water and rice. That Misses Greenland would usually have some extra eggs or bacon in the morning to add to what I made for myself. Sayed I'd have to get more when it run out but that dinner and the eggs or bacon was included in my board. I wondered how much I could save if I was getting a dollar and already down thirty cents plus whatever extra food and anything else I need. I wondered how good business was for him and who he had to sell to. Master John selled to everybody from the churches to teachers and politicians and anybody else.

Got any questions?

I can go and come as I please?

Well yes. Except you gotta be at work when you supposed to be at work and we won't have anyone living under our roof who suffers from an immoral character. If I or my wife hear that you're out doing anything that is displeasing in God's eyes then we can't have you here. You understand that don't you Ervin?

Yessuh.

But I ain't really understand what might be displeasing to God. Where I come from there was so much we wasn't allowed to do. I could go and come as I please. See who I want to and be where I wanna be. Work hard but then I was free. Free to do whatever I wanted.

Marcus waited in the workshop, chewing on something. Mister Greenland walked with me back there. I looked at the steps and asked Mister Greenland whether there was a door to keep the air out and he sayed, At night we close up the workshop but there's no extra door for you.

Follow me. Only other thing I need to show you is the tub around the side here for you to use to wash your clothes. You can wash your body in it too but I say to pull it into the workshop for that. Empty of course.

Wasn't no way to tell if he liked me or not, or ain't care neither way. I was help and that's the only thing mattered. I ain't want Marcus to leave me there. I ain't knowed my way back to the blacksmith William and we taked so many turns since Lilly's I ain't had no way to find myself back there.

I'm gonna head inside and you probably better be getting home Marcus. It's getting late. I looked at the sky and it was still light but dusk was coming and Marcus was on foot.

Yessuh I'll be leaving shortly, Marcus nodded.

Mister Greenland told me he'd see me in the morning and then went back to the house and inside. The door slammed and bounced and he pulled it again.

You look scared, Marcus sayed.

Nah. Just different. Guess I gotta get used to it.

Truth be I was scared. He was gon leave me at that house in that workshop by myself. I ain't knowed that man and I wasn't sure I was gon like him. Seemed like Master John would say he might be trying to get the goose and the egg bout him.

Is that normal? I asked Marcus. He say he gon pay me a dollar a week to start and then take thirty cent back for room and I gotta pay some still for food.

Everybody is different. Being a carpenter mean you making and selling like everybody else. You gotta earn it and it ain't no easier here than where you came from. Especially with what you told me. If it wasn't for being a slave, well, sound like you ain't have it so bad. I look at Marcus for a bit then round that workshop. Being a slave is bad enough, I told him.

He sayed, It is. You gotta know being free ain't easy. Not here when you still treated different, can't do all the things white folks can do, and sometimes they don't want you doing too well. Be careful Ervin. You can't show up your boss, not here. You need this job, this place. Mister Greenland can use your help but he don't need it. He'll stay getting by. You understand the difference?

I nodded my head. I wondered how far I gotta go north to be free really.

I know that look. I've seen it before Ervin. Don't press your good fortune to have made it this far. Folks think you just transplanting here looking for better work as a carpenter. White folks don't know you was a slave and don't need to know. You understand that. You go further north like Boston and they just as likely catch you and sell you to the highest bidder.

I understand what he sayed but that don't mean I gotta like it. I wanted freedom. This so far with Mister Greenland ain't feel much like freedom.

Lilly

Lilly

I liked him. I did. He was new and different. A slave but with a trade. But he was so dirty and raggedy looking when he came to the house. I'm glad I got him cleaned up before mama saw him cuz that woulda been all she remembered. I wonder what he left behind. A wife or children? I figure I'll make a good wife when the time come and have lots of children but not too many. Mama say be careful cuz every baby is a mouth to feed. She had five and says that was plenty. Now it's just me and my little brother. And I'm bout grown so she looking for me a husband. Til then I'll be keeping house.

He's at that carpenter's house. He and his wife can be some kinda difficult. I'm surprised mama got him to accept Ervin for help. I wonder if Ervin knows it ain't gonna be no easier here based on what he was used to.

If I'd known he was gonna be like he was, I woulda put on my nicer dress but then mama and Adam woulda been asking me why I was all dressed up so I guess it's better I didn't bother. No matter. I'ma see him again and be ready. Specially since it'll be Sunday and I'll have a reason. I keep thinking bout him. His smile and those eyes. I know he was looking at me but I hope he ain't too shy to speak to me when the time come. Guess I should wait to see how he work out at Mister Greenland's before I get too excited. He might not be cut out for freedom. Still I wanna see him again.

Ervin

I couldn't hardly sleep. Mister Greenland's mat up there was cloth stuffed with hay and my nose seem to run all night. The air been dank and smell all the way like sawdust. I pulled the blanket to my ears cuz a the cold and I ain't had no heat. I wondered how I'm spose to stay warm in there. I figured I'd ask the next day cuz I ain't wanna set myself on fire. Closing them doors might keep the heat in but what if there ain't no heat to keep in?

Lilly could keep me warm. If I coulda win her it might make this place more bearable but I wasn't gon bring her here not when she been living like she was. I had to wonder if she like me at all. I wonder if I'ma see her Sunday. I figure I will since Marcus sayed all the free blacks get together for church and meeting. Sayed we gotta stick together cuz they don't much like blacks anywhere, free or slave. That ain't cross my mind before then. Folks I meet on my way coming here musta been different. They was mostly kind and good. They ain't act like I was less than they was. But Mister Greenland seemed to be like some of those men back home. Cept he had to pay me and then I had to pay him.

I wondered if Lilly would consider me. When I started working I'd be a man and making a wage. That be just the next day. She been a woman already. I seed her brown skin and pretty smile she tried to hide from me. But I seed it anyway. I wanted to know her. Feel her fingers again. Touch her skin that look so soft and smooth. Mama woulda like her and Master John would likely had approve too. She'd make a good wife if I could make a good husband. But I had to be able to provide fore I even think that far ahead. Right then wasn't nothing I could do sides lay on hay.

May Day

Bishop Allen been in the pulpit again that Sunday. I got there late but I still seed Lilly from where I sit. I knowed she been looking for me cuz she turned and seed me and start smiling from where she sit with her mama and her daddy and brother near the front. I smiled back. I been looking to this day for a month.

May Day. I bringed Lilly a gift and when church let out I planned to give it to her. The whole place smelled good. Like the kitchen when mama would cook for Misses Charlotte and everybody would eat. I know my Lilly brought those biscuits and they had that fried chicken. I could smell cherry pie too. I'm sure pastor's wife brought her green beans with ham hock and Misses Sherry had her rice and chicken. She always leave them gizzards in which I pick through cuz they taste like slime. I wondered who bringed the lemonade. If Misses Jessie bringed it I ain't want none. She ain't never make it sweet enough.

Bishop Allen talked bout our dominion over the earth and our responsibility to care for that which is under our care. Power doesn't come without responsibility, he sayed. He sayed that no man can truly have dominion over any other living thing without first taking right responsibility for it that it thrives.

We all finally sayed, Amen. I walked quick over to see Lilly since I knowed I wasn't gone have much time. I sayed hi to Misses Shepherd and ask Adam bout his apprenticeship. He pulled me over some and speak low so Mister and Misses Shepherd can't hear. Then he told me he hated it but ain't really had no other options. I understood what he mean. Before I come to this city I loved being a carpenter, working with my hands and making things that was beautiful. Wasn't no joy in it no more. I followed Lilly outside with her two pans of biscuits. She held the silver honey bottle William the blacksmith made.

The May pole seem to touch the sky behind the church. It was almost tall as the church and two metal loops was fastened to the top. Bishop Allen bringed the church ribbons out with his wife. Every family had a ribbon. I was glad Bishop been there. Most times he was traveling but he made it back through to celebrate with the church since he the one started it. He was proud of us, the first black Methodist church in all the country. Woulda been first black church but his friend beat him to it just down the street. Episcopalians. I figured I'd go wherever Lilly was if I could help it. She came here so I came too. Wasn't as big as the other but far as I could tell we have more fun.

I ain't have a ribbon but I been gathering wild flowers the past couple days. I went back into the church and got my fiddle and basket while Lilly help set up the food. Her hair was pulled back and she had that white bonnet on, covering the back where she had it in a ball. I knowed she'd be wearing that today so I had to get smart bout my gift.

I keeped hold of my fiddle in the box with one hand and set down the basket with the other. I taked out her gift and walked up beside my Lilly and put it round her neck. The flowers was white and pink and red and yellow. She made them look even prettier. She turned to look at me with those big brown eyes and then held up her necklace. It's so pretty Ervin. I love it. She grabbed my hand and squeeze it gentle while touching the necklace with the other hand.

Where you gonna set up to play? she asked, smiling.

I looked for a place that I could play and went back into the church and brought out a chair to sit in. I telled Lilly, Make sure I get a plate. Last time I played and wasn't nothing worth eating after I finished. She right then fixed me a plate and sayed to eat before I played. I did. Then she gave me an extra biscuit with honey.

Bishop Allen been here fore I was born. Even sued to get this church started, twice. A free man. He ain't had to steal away cuz his master let him buy his freedom. I see him and thinks bout Master John. I sometimes wonder if I coulda bought my freedom. But he was from Delaware not Virginia or South Carolina, the devil's crater. Anybody black in South Carolina was assumed a slave and they'd just as soon steal your papers as let you be free and your own man.

Wasn't even worth thinking bout. Lilly take my plate and I sit down and got to playing something slow while Bishop Allen and Misses Allen start wrapping they ribbons round the pole. Then the other families joined in. Once they was all in a circle I started playing faster and they danced round the maypole laughing. When they had it all wrapped and folks wanted to eat, I played regular again off and on. Lilly finally sat down next to me after serving folks food and we talked and I played. I asked her if she thought bout what I asked her the week before. She looked everywhere but at me. Sayed she ain't never consider living no place else. Scared somebody might make her a slave. Scared she ain't gon survive and they might separate us. Scared of a lot a things. I told her we can make it together. That someplace gotta be more free than this. I already knowed wasn't no way I ever have my own shop. Not with Greenland alive and he wasn't old enough to be dying no time soon.

She know it too. Say I do better than most of the free blacks even if it ain't what I hope for. I told her I wanna give her the kinda life she got now without having to worry, but she got it good. I knowed it and she knowed it too. I been the one who ain't have it good. Still living in hay and breathing in sawdust in my sleep. I wanted to get away but I loved her like I never loved nobody cept mama. It been a different love but I knowed she done got in my soul. Done stole my heart while I still been trying to all the way steal hers. Ain't nowhere I wanna be if she wasn't with me so til she decided I can give her all a what she need only place I could be was right where I was.

From the first time she let me kiss her soft lips and pull her in close on the back porch of her mama's house, after she shaved me smooth I wanted her. In every way. But wasn't having her. Wasn't no having her like that cuz if I did I gotta be man enough to keep her and I ain't had nothing. Wasn't no kinda man expect a woman to make no family and take care of things at home if he can't make sure they got a home and what they need. And I ain't have neither home or what we needed for it. Fore I could even think of making her mine and having babies she need to know she wasn't gon have to worry bout feeding herself and our baby. Wouldn't be nothing but shame on me, even if nobody sayed it. I'd know.

I think bout what Master John would say bout a man providing. I been trying to be a man but doing what I needed to be a good man ain't happen and way it looked, it might never. Not here. I maked some change playing the fiddle but Master John got a dollar for us to play. I couldn't hardly get but twenty cents playing there. Twenty cents. I made more playing in South Carolina. At least that whole twenty cents is mine and I'm putting it away.

I ain't tell Mister Greenland nothing bout what I make. If he wanna know he can find out from the men who paying me. Still it ain't none of his business. If he knowed I was making something extra he probably woulda try to figure out a way to take some of it. I keeps my business to myself and I figured if I save enough me and Lilly might can catch a train north. Maybe Delaware where Bishop Allen come from. Maybe they more right there.

None a that was gon happen if I ain't first get myself right and prove to her mama and daddy they can trust me with Lilly.

I walked Lilly home. By now I ain't hardly pay Adam no mind walking long with us, a few strides behind so we can have some privacy. We took steps that was short and slow and walk the long way. She played with the flowers round her neck and I talked bout freedom. She ain't really understand where I come from. She always been free and her daddy was freed when he was a little boy. He worked with Bishop Allen and they had that house. But I told her anyway cuz it make me who I been. I let her know bout my brother Ethan and my sister Greta and bout my daddy and my mama and Misses Charlotte and Master John. I told her what I used to do in South Carolina. Ain't nobody heard all this before. Fore her I ain't speak it to nobody. But if we was gon be something more she need to know bout me. And we on May Day. That's sposed to be the start of new things and I wanted something new with Lilly.

I ask her what she want. She shrug up her shoulders like she ain't never thinked bout it before that. I knowed she done think bout it. Every girl her age done thinked about it. She just ain't thinked she could have it so she ain't say nothing.

What you want Lilly? I asked again and she look down the road like it just got there and she was seeing it for the first time that very minute. It ain't been new since it's where she lived. The dirt covered our shoes after we done walk that far.

She sayed, What if this is all there is Ervin? This right here is what we need to want so we can be happy? What if we need to be satisfied with what God already give us? You ain't satisfied. You got free, all the way from South Carolina and you got me and a job and you make money playing the fiddle and you ain't satisfied still? What's gonna make you happy Ervin? I want to be happy and it don't take as much as you think it do. I'm happy right here with my family, my friends, my church. You. Can't you be happy with that too?

She look all huffy but still staring at something I can't see.

I ain't got no family Lilly. These your friends and I'm trying to fit into a world- into this town where I don't fit. I wanna be happy. I wanna be satisfied but I ain't escape slavery just to work in somebody's shop who can't do work as good as I can and he paying me less than I was making when I wasn't free.

Adam looking like he trying not to listen but can't help it. Lilly shaked her head side to side and start walking again. Her head looking at the dirt in front of her and her fingers twirling around the flowers. I knowed I upset her but what I sayed is true. She got family and friends. Ain't nowhere I got either. We walked quiet the rest of the way to her house. She stepped on the porch before finally looking at me again. It was like pity and sad all in one. She sayed she gotta think through some stuff and maybe I should too and she talk to me later. I likely wasn't gon see her for a couple days so that meant she had all that time to think a what was wrong with us. I grab her hand cuz she think too much on it and she probably think herself right outta my life.

Adam step up next to Lilly. It's okay Adam, I'll be right in. He looked at me once he went in and shrugged his shoulders, leaving the door open so he could see.

Look Lilly. I knowed what you sayed. I understands you gots people here. I love you and I want to be with you. Here? Here ain't what I thinked it would be for me. I ain't got what you got but maybe we can make something together somewhere else.

I gotta figure some things out Ervin. Good night.

She drop my hand and turned herself round. She ain't even look back going inside fore she close the door. And that was it. I backed up from the porch and start walking home. I ain't like talking to lots of folks so I ain't knowed a lot more than the ones I done meet early on when I got there. It was hard to make friends and how I was going it was gon be harder to make family.

A Year

I keeped trying with Lilly for another six months. A year done gone by. She sayed I had to show I could take care of her before she might think bout going anywhere with me, marrying me, or anything else. I asked Marcus what he thought bout me marrying Lilly cuz he warned me bout her the day I been at her house and she touch my skin. He shaked his head like I ain't knowed what I was doing.

She come from one of the best families here and what you got Ervin? What you got to offer her? Can you even get a little place to live with her? And what if you have kids? Can you feed them and her and you?

I'm a man, I sayed to him. I will take care of my family. That's what a man does.

You playing that sad music on that fiddle like it gon do something. I'm asking you how. How you gonna give her what she deserves?

She loves me. I pulled across the top string. She don't need all that if she loves me.

Well she might feel different if her babies ain't got what they need. If she sitting up taking care of your house and babies and her stomach empty. Ain't no decent woman gon stand for that. Not if they care bout themselves, they babies. Not if they worth anything. And that one. That Lilly. I'm a tell ya right now, she worth something. She worth doing right by and she ain't gon settle. Don't need to. Shouldn't have to. If you can't do right by her, Ervin, leave her be so somebody else can.

Well damn Marcus. I thought you was my friend.

I am. That's why I'm telling you the truth. You can't get a good woman, a good wife if you ain't ready to keep her that way. So you gotta choice. You get yourself in a way to keep her right and be able to take care a your family like a real man should or you leave her alone. That's it.

I sat on the chair behind the workshop and Marcus sat beside me chewing on a piece of sugar cane.

You don't get it Marcus.

What? This shite you been complaining about with Philadelphia?

It ain't shite.

What's wrong with what's here Ervin?

I can't get nowhere here. I can't give her what she deserve here and she ain't going nowhere.

You can do it here just as good as anywhere else.

No. I can't. My hands is tied. I can't get nothing more than what I got. This. This don't feel like free.

It don't feel like free? How you know what free supposed to feel like? You been free a year. It's real. Marcus look at me in the dark and I see the whites in his eyes waiting cuz he ain't never knowed nothing bout being a slave or cuz he figured I'd shut up.

I don't wanna be scared that they gon take away the people I love. My family. I don't wanna have to worry bout somebody stealing my babies or my wife and selling them away from me. My brother, sister, daddy, friends. They all gone. If I gotta worry bout that I don't want it. If I gotta think bout somebody taking my babies I don't want none. They won't be slaves.

You're not a slave anymore Ervin. You are free. You got papers, Marcus sayed looking like I still ain't understand.

What I understand is that I got papers but they ain't legal cuz in South Carolina I'm a runaway slave owned on paper by a Master John James, carpenter of Georgetown County. I still fall asleep at night scared I'ma wake up to getting dragged out of that hay bed and down the steps and carted off in chains. I might wind up with him or somewhere else.

That's what you worried about? Marcus asked and start chewing on that stick again.

I don't wanna be close enough for them to get me Marcus.

If that's what you really worried for ain't no place safe in all these states. At least people know you here now. There's a community and we stick together. That's how we making it. It ain't like that everywhere. Some places free blacks still can't come together. Even further north. There ain't no perfect place Ervin. Ain't no place they gon treat you like you equal. Least not before you die. And have them tell it you still won't be equal then.

I smirked cuz he was right. You got a point. I laughed. I can't say I like it but you got a point.

I'd been there a year already and saving was slow, Lilly was slow, and there wasn't much to look forward to without knowing what I was doing and who I was gon do it with. I had at least another year fore I could rent a place for us unless I started playing more. I had to get in with the white folks better. Twenty cents to play a few hours add up if you got regular work. But by myself it was hard. Master John got the door open and helped me walk through. There wasn't nobody opening no doors and starting no conversations. I remembered what mama sayed bout how white men only listen to white men. Only way round that was to get them to listen in the white man space they was already in.

Mister Greenland still wasn't paying me but a dollar a week but he sayed it would change since I been working for him a year and finally proved myself. I was mad but wasn't nothing I could do. He had the workshop. I swore he'd keep it going forever if I ain't sayed nothing every few months. When we got started he figured I ain't knowed my money. I might not could read but I knowed my money. He tried to give me sixty cents or sixty-five cents at the week instead of seventy cents sometimes. I made the mistake once and took it and counted it later. From then on I counted it right there when he hand it to me. Every once in a while I had to correct him and he act like it been a mistake. God done make a place for him. He don't like liars and cheats.

It be alright I reckoned. Ain't no other way for it turn out but alright. I ain't had no place to go so I had to make this work best I can. Save up and get my Lilly. I prayed that God help me with it and give me some favor cuz he done took so much, it seem due. And he promised mama and this ain't seem like what he promised. She sayed some free people ain't free. I think I been one of them. I was freer when I was a slave. Don't make no sense. Some days I wondered if I did the right thing. If running been what mama woulda wanted. If that been what she was talking bout when she talked bout freedom?

Wasn't no Lilly-like women I'd ever known there though. They couldn't help it but they was broke down cuz they had the life taken from them so they coulda taked being a slave. Lilly ain't never had to have that. Never had to be broken like they break a horse or a dog. She can't see how being free give you something inside being a slave don't. I wondered what those women woulda been like if they hadn't been slaves. If they had a chance to be something else.

Mama coulda been something. She was something. She got freed in her way, best she could. Tried to help some of those other girls but they ain't wanna hear. Couldn't hear or they masters wasn't like Misses Shelly or Master John. She used to say how she thanked God for blessing us like that and I ain't understand then cuz we wasn't free. So many had real bad situations but God gave us bout as good as we could get being black in South Carolina. Being slaves.

I wondered if Master John was still looking for me or if he done give up. I wondered how Misses Charlotte was holding up. Least having to cook for two others gave her some purpose in the house sides teaching piano. And Master John probably been lonely in that workshop. He ain't had many friends cuz he was scared to speak his mind. He sayed we'd all be hungry if he speaked his mind.

Master John the reason I ain't toiling cleaning streets or washing horses and buggies or shining shoes. He deserved to know I been alive but I been scared to tell him. I been gone a year already and ain't nobody come yet looking and I ain't had wanna give no cause for that to change, but still.

I goed to William Smith and ask him to write a letter to Master James for me and have it routed back the way I come so he can't know how it got back. Once it made it to South Carolina they send it to him by post. I sayed,

Dear Master John James,

Thank you for teaching me how to do carpentry like you did. I use this skill now to care for myself. Thank you for teaching me to play the fiddle. I do what we used to do and play sometimes and people pay me. It ain't the same as playing with you. Carpentry ain't the same either.

I want you to know I am alright where I am. I am free and becoming a man so I can do what you always said and take care of myself and my family. All men deserve to be free and are equal in God's eyes. I wish they knew that in South Carolina. May God keep you and Misses Charlotte.

In freedom,
E

Marcus and William asked me bout ten times if I was sure I wanted to send that letter and I telled them yes for the tenth time and shut them up. William put it in an envelope and stamped red on the back to close it. Then he hold the letter in his hand waving and ask me why I leaved if I ain't really wanna be free.

I telled him cuz I wasn't free. He held the envelope and looked at me and sayed, Ervin ain't nobody like us really free. A lot gonna have to change before we really become free. And then a lot more gonna have to change before the white man recognize it. Who knows when that'll be.

When early March come round I knowed I could finally pay for a place that Lilly might be okay with. I asked her daddy if I could marry her and he asked me question after question. Sayed I better do right by her and take care of her or else he'd take her back. I swore I would do my best and give her everything I could. I couldn't promise I'd give her what he could cuz I ain't had no means for doing that. He asked me if I planned on getting means. I telled him I wasn't never gon stop trying to do right by my wife and my family.

We got married after church on a Sunday and moved into our new place at the start of April 1827. I couldn't wait no longer. She was as sweet and smooth as I imagined. Her skin soft and willing. By the time we realized how strong our love was Lilly was at least three months with child.

We spent the summer trying to plant a garden in the patch of grass behind our little house. It was shady on account of a big pecan tree sitting between our house and Henry's. It drop pecans like rain but Lilly pick them up and we'd snack on them or she make us pecan pie. We'd sit out there when the stars lit the sky and talk bout baby names while I pluck on the fiddle.

She been the prettiest woman I ever seed carry a child. She ain't like to go nowhere out where folks ain't know her unless we was together. Even though we was married, folks still look at her funny. She ain't done nothing wrong. I ain't mind cuz it gave me reason to watch out for her and make sure she alright.

By time winter come we settled on a couple possible names but Lilly sayed she wanna wait to look in our baby eyes and face fore we name it. I done learned months ago it ain't worth arguing with her bout nothing right now.

The new year come with all kinds a cold and snow and then so did our baby girl. We named her Ellie after mama and Lilly was happy with that. She sayed she don't wanna rush making babies and I agreed. Ellie enough with winter being so cold and trying to keep our house warm enough.

Lilly a good mama. That baby spoiled more than me. Lilly sayed, You a man. Right now you can take care of yourself. Baby Ellie can't.

Doctor say Ellie mostly healthy but sometimes I don't know. She got the cold in her chest and it mostly gon but she don't seem to breathe like she should. Sometimes she be napping and I go shake her or Lilly shake her cuz she ain't seem like she been breathing. We ain't hardly sleeped cuz we been scared she ain't gon wake up. I been so scared but I ain't wanna let Lilly know cuz then she be more scared. We taked Ellie to church and had them pray over her and we waited on God to make her breathing okay. The doctor don't seem worried but they ain't seem worried bout mama either. Like they wasn't important. Mama ain't here cuz they ain't bothered to figure out what was wrong with her. And now my baby by her name can't breathe right and don't nobody care to figure out why or how to fix it.

I wanted to tell Master John bout Lilly and Ellie. That I got married and got a little girl too but I been scared by time he get the letter something bad mighta happen. I been scared to say or do too much with her cuz God like taking away things I love. I done got two things I love so I had to hold on for all my life.

I know Master John ain't mad cuz I got a letter back last year in the summer after we knowed Lilly was having a baby. William told me and read it for me. It was strange cuz he ain't address it to me. He addressed the outside to William Smith but the letter inside was to me. But the letter was strange too.

> Dear E,
>
> Blessings to you. I am resigned that you are not returning soon but pleased that you are well on your assignment. While the terms remain open, subject to an agreeable return we would welcome your return should the assignment end. Our community would welcome you as well as they miss your talent and are jealous another owner far away is paying me to benefit from them.
>
> I hope that all you have learned is valued where you are and that you believe I have done my best in regards to you. Should you wish to return at any time I am happy to end the current arrangement for your present assignment and make arrangements for your safe return.
>
> Kindly,
> John James

I thinked bout what he sayed in that letter but ain't write back. He ain't turned me in. He ain't send nobody after me. He was scared a what might happen to me if he did. He let me go and sayed I can come back if I want to. But it's South Carolina. I think that place the worst place to be a slave. They hates us like no place else. Cept some folks like Master John. God made some folks good.

Don't You Got Enough?

She was screaming and hollering and startle me out my sleep. She calling, Ervin! Ervin! Make her wake up Ervin! Make Ellie wake up! She ain't breathing Ervin! I can't get her to breathe. Breathe Ellie. Breathe.

She talking bout mama and then I knowed I ain't dreaming and she screaming cuz of the baby. I crawled over to her where she holding Ellie in her arms and patting on her back hard trying to get her to cry. She put her on her lap and bouncing trying to force air in her lungs. We ain't sleep in six months and we'd been up late and let ourselves sleep too hard. She was crying so hard she couldn't see and I was scared.

I took the baby from her lap and went to the wash bowl. I put water on her face and rocked her. Her head was limp. I felt her in my arms and she ain't feel warm. I listened to her chest and I ain't heard no thump.

God give her back! I screamed over and over. Give her back. You goddamned son of a bitch. You give me back my baby now! You give her back! You can't take her. You got enough in heaven. Ain't you satisfied yet? Can't I keep something! Damnit! Give her back!

I pushed on her little chest trying to force air in and cursed God at the same time. He promised me. He promised me and he couldn't do this. I leaned against the wall rocking her. She wasn't moving. Wasn't breathing. Lilly hollered and screamed. She got on her knees in front of me rubbing Ellie's head and crying and screaming.

There been a banging on the front door and then somebody come in. Our neighbor Henry sayed he heard all the screaming. Nobody answer the door so he come in. He seed us

116

like we was, a screaming mess in the corner by the wash bowl. The three of us balled up together. He asked what was wrong. Wouldn't nothing come out my throat and Lilly been talking but wasn't making no sense but he figured it out fast enough. He touched the baby on her chest and her neck. I wanted him to find something we ain't find. Life. I wanted Henry to say she's okay, she gon be okay. I wanted him to say something like that like when the flowers in the garden died and he told us how to save some a them by moving them to where they could get a little more sun each day. But he ain't sayed nothing like that.

Stead he drop his head. I'm sorry.

Lilly falled on the floor. Like hearing it from him made it real. I stayed rocking Ellie like maybe it might make her wake up. I ain't wanna let her go. I keeped holding her like that for a while and reached out for Lilly's hand to hold her too. They's the only things I got in this world and God done took one. Greedy son of a bitch.

* * *

Mister Greenland let me make my baby a casket but I had to pay for the wood. It ain't matter. She was gon have a beautiful casket and be buried at the church. Both my Ellie's in the ground and my Lilly ain't been the same. She ain't have no strength. The life been taked out of her too. Her mama sayed to me and her that Lilly need to come home for a bit. Her home with me now and I need her cuz I ain't got nobody cept my wife.

Sometimes I still waked up to check on her, make sure she breathing but then ain't nobody there cept for me. Then I dream a her and Lilly, if I do wind up getting back to sleep at all. I hoped Lilly gon be okay. I visited her everyday and sit with her in the back, looking at that tree at her mama's house. I hoped she might come back to me soon. Her mama sayed, Give her time.

They look at me like they pity me. They knowed God took half of what I had like it ain't even matter. I ain't had no words for him. Wasn't no need to speak. I still had that old bible Misses Charlotte gave me but it ain't done me no good. A bunch a black ink stained across white space like we was in this place that didn't want us but needed us. Didn't care for us cept for

117

what we could do for them. I ain't need them pages to tell me what I already knowed from God. He wasn't our God just like that book wasn't our book and this land wasn't our land. Wasn't never meant for us but somebody try to fool us and say it was. They let my mama and baby die cuz wasn't no love in they heart for them, for us. I can't see how any God they serve is the same God spose to be helping me.

Two months done went by and some nights I sit up thinking and wondering what I did wrong for her to die. I wondered if it was the heat of the summer that made it harder for her to breathe after she been sick in the winter and struggling in the spring. Or did she realize in some way she ain't want this life. That it ain't been what she planned and we wasn't the parents she wanted. I wasn't the daddy she wanted and couldn't give her the life she deserved. I wondered if she been up there with mama and mama holding her grandbaby born free and now they really free together. I wondered if she talked to God bout stealing her away from me cuz it wasn't right to take her from me. From Lilly. I wondered if mama mad at God too cuz he breaking promises he made.

Second Chances

I came over to see Lilly after church but I ain't go myself. I knowed she been there. Praying to God even though God the one made it so she need to pray to him. We spend all afternoon together. When the sun start dipping behind the trees she telled me she ready to come home. Back to me. She say it but she ain't the same. I don't imagine she ever gon be the same. Neither of us. Something bout losing a baby, your child change you. Ain't nothing you can do. But we been husband and wife and we made a promise fore all her family and half the church so we gon make it through this.

Mama Shepherd send me with her bag and Lilly and me walk side by side all the way home. It was still nice. October. Seemed like the time had flown by since we gots married and had a baby and lost it. Lilly so quiet her steps got slower and slower the closer we got to our house. Wasn't nothing I might tell her that make her feel better that I ain't already sayed. I wondered do she love me still or if she thinked maybe I been cursed too. I ain't wanna press. Mama Shepherd sayed, Give her some space. Losing a child ain't easy and this her first baby.

That baby girl Ellie been mine too. We lost a baby together. But she carried her and I spose that make it different. Ellie was gone now but I wanted her back. I wanted her back for me and Lilly and then I wanted Lilly back for me. She look like she ain't hardly eat but still she ain't skinny round the waist. Her eyes still ain't hold no light and I ain't seed her smile in so long I almost forget what she look like with her lips turned to heaven.

I cooked for her what I could and try hard as I could to get her to eat. She throwed it up and sayed it tastes funny.

It don't. I made it like my mama did, I sayed. But she ain't want it. She ain't want nothing. Stead she sit in the chair and rock holding that pillow or the blanket Mama Shepherd made for Ellie. I told her we gotta try and talk and she nod like she knowed I been right but she ain't say much. I ain't never been so lonely in my life.

Sometimes I wished I was back in South Carolina. Wished mama was there for me to sit up with after dinner and talk to. I thinked bout how I'd go to see her and then come back and play on the fiddle with Master John. Least that was how we did most nights. Wasn't nobody I could tell how I feel cuz it wouldn't make no sense that I was happier then. Not cuz I was a slave, that ain't it. But cuz the man who raised me is there and I was of the good fortune to be taken in by someone who was good. Mostly good. He still gotta answer to God for his part but I figure God got some answering to do too. And Master John ain't taked nothing away from me worse than God did.

More than a month done pass since Lilly come back home. I been scared a what mighta been wrong with her. I telled God I ain't want no more pain. That if he wanna keep taking what I love he could just keep it in the first place. God don't listen. He just do whatever he wanna do and the rest of us gotta live with it. God must be white cuz that's how the white man do too. I ain't doing nothing but what I want. Least that's what I planned til now.

The midwife looked at Lilly and sayed, Looks like you all of three months maybe four.

That mean she been with child fore we lost Ellie. Lilly been keeping her food down for a few weeks but she still ain't wanna eat. I been scared they wasn't gon- I ain't wanna even think it, even now. She needed to eat and take care of that baby inside her. She been so weak all that time but life been growing in her again.

Lilly sayed, Ervin what if we don't? I'm scared. I ain't ask for this. I don't want this. Not yet.

I'll be here for you and our baby Lilly. Ain't nothing gon happen again. God made a promise on my life. We gon be fine. Our baby gon be fine. I promise you.

I ain't ready so soon, Ervin. It's too soon. I ain't a mama. I can't be.

Yes you is. You a good mama. You gon see. You gon be the best mama for our baby.

She sayed, Things in Philadelphia getting worse. I'm scared it ain't gon be safe for blacks here either.

She been making excuses cuz she been scared like me. Ellie was hard enough on her body and now she ain't even strong like before. I begged her to eat and her mama bringed over her favorite foods. It ain't matter if all she eat is collard greens and biscuits and chicken. Long as she eat.

I told her we can leave the city. We can go further north. She sayed tensions was starting there too. She ain't wrong bout that. Those Irish ain't like us much. Sayed we taking they jobs but they ain't no jobs for nobody. We all struggling and I guess they figure we spose to struggle more than they do cuz we black. But we been there working hard for everythings we got. They ain't too much liked by other white folk on account of them being Irish but mostly on account of them being Catholic. I ain't care much for none of the religions. It ain't make no matter to me what you call yourself if you ain't living by nothing like Jesus lived by. And God seem to hate black folk no matter what religion. But the quarrels start and they finish. I scared one day it be worse than what was going on already.

Lilly asked me to wait to make a bed for our baby til she been good and big. I think she been scared she might not carry the baby all the way. I told her, You gon make it all the way and we gon have a healthy baby.

She sayed, I can't use the one we had before cuz it might be cursed.

It ain't cursed but I might be, I told her. I already started that bed for our baby though cuz I needs something to do that I feel in charge of. Everything else in that workshop is for Mister Greenland and his customers. He keeped me out of it so don't nobody see me or know me. Like I been something to hide or be shamed of. He bark orders at me like I ain't got no sense bout what to do, then get mad when my work turn out better than his.

But ain't no other work like it for me in town so I keeped at it and after doing work for him I work on the bed for my new baby. I planned to keep playing my fiddle til I make enough to get us out of this town, if I can get her to go. She got ties where I ain't had nothing. But being I been her husband that should mean something. Even if it ain't seem to mean much then. This baby gon change things and she finally might see herself as a wife and a mama again, like she loved being. I only hoped to see her smile again and for her to be my Lilly again like she used to be.

If there's a God who care bout me at all, Lilly gon be mine again.

I wanted to write to Master John. I wanted to tell him how Mister Greenland was. I wanted to tell him bout my Lilly and the new baby coming and how I played the fiddle every week almost and I charged twenty-five cents instead of twenty cents now. Only reason is cuz there's only one a me and in the couple weeks before then more than a few folks wanted me to play on the same night. So I sayed I can play for you if you give me twenty-five cents instead of twenty. They sayed alright cuz can't nobody fiddle like I fiddle. I wanted to tell him I fiddle so good cuz he teached me good and played with me so much and that if he been there we'd make good money together. I woulda tell him bout the little garden we planted but it died along with Ellie. I hoped to plant it again in the spring and that like our baby, it would grow. I'd ask him if he got good help and how his business doing.

But I ain't send no letters cuz it been better that way. I keeped the one he send me safe in the pouch mama give me. I might not could read it but I knowed what it sayed. I thinked about Mister John and Mister Greenland and how they was so different and backwards for where they was from. That Greenland wasn't worth the hay I used to sleep in.

Mister Greenland done got an order in from the church to build chairs for the ministers. A set of four plus a chair upfront. He got another one in to build some desks for the schoolhouse. Twelve of them and asked me to start working on them. We ain't got enough wood for it all so we headed out for the day to buy wood and bring it back. I telled Lilly I'd be back by dark. I knowed he'd have me stay outside and just load it on and off and watch the horses. Make it look like I was just a driver.

It taked us all day to leave the city which ain't make no sense if we wanna get back fore night. For good wood we gotta go to the Amish. I travel long with Mister Greenland but they ain't much like me coming in though. He could get enough to bring back for a good lot of projects but it costs more cuz he gotta rent two extra horses and a buggy. He taked one and I taked the other.

We ain't had to go all the way to they village so the ride ain't long as it could be. When we finally get there we gotta wait for them cuz ain't nobody send word since Mister Greenland wasn't the best at planning out stuff. He wait to send that letter bout wood til it's too late then we waste a half a day waiting. So now we was stuck there and ain't gon get back til early morning less we ride when it dark. And he knowed I got a wife with child at home. He thinked it alright and ain't no problem but he ain't driving a buggy by himself being black in the black a night. I ain't wanna be one of them stories.

Lilly

Mama say I can come back if I need to. Daddy say it too. I'm trying to stay with him so we can be together like we made a promise. But God. I need answers. I don't know where I'm sposed to be or what I'm sposed to do. So I'm a stay put and try to stay alive. Not for me but for him and this baby and my mama and my daddy. Least I got them. Ervin don't have nobody but me.

I can't hardly look at him. I love him but he remind me of our baby. She had his face and I can hardly look at him without seeing her. I was still nursing her when she left us. My body still giving milk to give her life and she gone. I cursed that milk. It ain't get to dry up and my body doing what it learned to do before. I feels it getting ready and I don't want it. I don't want that kind of pain again. He looks at me like he scared and I'm scared too. He don't say it though. And I don't have words for it. I ain't never lost nobody I loved, not like him. I never felt this kinda way before and I don't wanna feel it again.

He talk about leaving. Going somewhere else but I know what's out there for us. More of this kinda pain. He can't tell me it's gonna be better when the whole world set up against us. He can't tell me he can protect me and take care of me when the whole world wanna make sure he can't. I don't wanna break his heart but I can't lie to him neither. I don't wanna go out there where people expect we slaves cuz of our skin so they treat us worse than they do here. At least here they expect we free. Some of us doing okay. Others struggling and I'm scared if I leave we'll be struggling and alone. No family. No church. No friends.

And this baby. God help me. This baby growing inside me ain't what I need. Not what we need. I can't take it. Sometimes I just wanna take it outta me. But I won't. It's his baby. He done lost everything except me and I don't know what he'd do if he lost another baby.

I sometimes think this life ain't worth it but I know mine's better than most black folk but still ten times worse than the white folks. Even the ones who mad at us now and causing trouble. They the only reason I'd think about leaving here but I figure even they trouble ain't as bad as what's outside this town if somebody find us and snatch us up. Would God hate me if I didn't live? Would God hate me if I chose not to be here?

Night in the Woods

We set out after dusk by a while. My stomach already yelling cuz I ain't had enough to eat. Mister Greenland taked all day talking bout trying to make a deal after they already set a price. These people wasn't gon keep doing business with him he keep that up. Then what was we gon do? Get second grade wood and then we start getting second grade customers. I knowed how that work. I remember we had to find the best wood and keep folks happy and respected. People care bout respect. It don't matter who you are. Everybody wants it. So he trying to take advantage of those Amish men like they ain't knowed what they got. They knowed what they got and that he needed it. They ain't ignorant. If anybody ignorant Mister Greenland is. He ain't got half of what he need figured out. He could be doing twice as good but he either stupid or lazy or maybe a bit a both and too proud to ask or think that maybe I mights know something. So I ain't say nothing. I ain't had no plans to give him no reasons. He wanna take my pay like he earned it. Give me less than I deserve all this time. He get just what he get. Do unto others. That's what his book say.

By time we leaved they little area it was black out.

It ain't safe out here, Mister Greenland, I sayed. We need to stop someplace and stay til light.

But he only hear what he wanna hear and it ain't me. He sayed back, We be alright. Won't nothing happen out here.

I telled him I need to stay up with him but my horses been the older ones and they loaded full up. They had a hard time keeping up with him.

I heard the cloppity clop ahead getting further and further but I ain't wanna call out his name cuz I sound like a black man and sometimes they be waiting in the woods. After a while the sound of the horses was gone. He must not been paying no mind to us behind him. Forgot that we was carrying just as much. I only could make out a little ways ahead at a time but keeped going. Slow like, cuz it ain't been a real road, just a path through the trees. I stopped to light the lantern but then thinked maybe somebody see it and try to find out who in the carriage and ain't nobody white in the carriage and it's the middle of the night and I might not get home to Lilly. So I press on, squinting and looking ahead to see the light when it come through the trees. Least the horses was smart. Old but smart and they been in these woods but it been a long way to remember. For me or them.

I tried to figure how far we got from the little wood farm and reckon me and those old horses been riding right through the middle of nowhere. I could either stop and ride in the morning or keep going. Neither way was good. If I stopped and ride again come morning they see clear I'm black and steal me, the wood, the horses and everything be gone. I keep going it's gon be slow and it's gon take a long time and I still might get snatched.

God damn Greenland. Son of a bitch.

I keeped going. The moon getting higher and higher so I knowed I musta been making good ground. I ain't have no food for me nor those horses and just a bucket of water in the back. They started slowing so I give them water fore they get too parched. I gets back in and we start going again. I heard something in the woods. I wasn't sure whether I should speed up or slow down. If it's a dog, owl, or man. I decided to speed up. It been my intention to get to my Lilly and our baby and wasn't nobody making a widow of my wife tonight. I find the whittling blade I taked with me. It done slid into the corner of the bench. It wasn't much but it might give me a fighting chance.

The sound came closer. I tried to push them horses faster. The sound got faster. But it ain't sound like no dog. Too heavy. Like a horse. Just one though. Damn. I tried to push the horses but they ain't have much to pull all this weight and get ahead from whoever been riding in the woods with me.

Who goes there?

Sound like a grown man. I keeps riding.

I said, who goes there?! Stop and show yourself.

I wasn't stopping for nobody. I was free. If there was one thing bout being free I ain't had to stop in the middle of the woods for no white man to be able to catch me and kill me.

He rode faster and next thing I knowed he up on my side. He holding up a lantern to my face.

Where you going so fast nigger? Where you running to? Slow down your horses.

I keeped going and he stayed side me.

I said slow down nigger and stop!

I'm on my business. Back to where I come from. I ain't causing no trouble and ain't trying to have none.

I slowed down a little bit but I wasn't stopping. Not there in those woods. Wasn't nobody round to hear me or see nothing.

Where you get this wagon boy?

I works for a carpenter in Philadelphia. We buyed some wood back there and taking it to Philadelphia now. He got ahead a me and I'm trying to catch up.

You mean he let his nigger fall behind?

I took a deep breath and picked up the whittling knife.

Suh I ain't looking for no trouble, I -

You a nigger in the middle of the woods in the middle of the night say you on business. You must be looking for trouble cuz you ain't got no business out here.

If I leave the load and go fast as those horses could carry I might could catch up to Greenland. Maybe Greenland finally seed I ain't back behind him and he don't hear no footsteps.

He can't be but a mile ahead and if this white man had a gun he'd a had it out by now. He ain't got nobody out here with him cuz they woulda been circled me by now. Either that or they waiting on a signal and I ain't wanna give him no reason to give it.

Suh, I ain't did nothing wrong. I'm just trying to get back to town and home for the night. We got caught up late buying this wood so we started back late and if we just catch up with Mister Greenland he can clear it up.

Why would I believe a nigger? Probably stole this wood and made up some story so you can get away with it.

I breathed again. Feel it catch in my chest long with red heat cuz I ain't done nothing wrong sides trying to get home to my Lilly.

I'ma keep going suh cuz I can't see no problem. You welcome to follow me. I sayed this as calm as I could. He came closer with that light and next I know his other hand holding a shotgun at me.

You got a smart mouth out here all by yourself at night. Most folks, specially like you, know better. You must not be from around here boy.

I'm not from around here and I'm not a boy. I remember seeing his eyes before something hit me in the head and I woke up with my head on the bench. His shotgun poking my ribs. You ain't dead nigger. You be alright. But you better listen before you won't be.

Yessuh.

Now you say your employer is just ahead? Yet he didn't come back looking for you. Either you aren't very good help or he's not much of an employer. I'll place my bets on the former. That means you're probably a crap employee. He laugh like I ain't have a gash on the side of my head and blood running in my eyes. I took the handkerchief out my pocket to wipe my brow and then tasted the blood on my tongue. I ain't even realize I was biting my lip.

He rode side me quiet. Looking at me in that light. Go head. I'm a stay close. Don't you try nothing boy. These woods ain't for you. Ride on and find your boss.

I loose my grip on the handle of the blade and set it down beside me right up under my leg. My eyes was watering now but I wasn't gon let him see me wipe it away and blinked til it ran down my cheeks long with the blood.

Mister Greenland was a good mile or two ahead waiting in a clearing. He looked like he having a relaxing evening when I come up with that white man.

I found this here nigger lost in the woods. He yours?

Yeah, he mine. What happened to ya?

129

Say this wood he got going back to Philadelphia. That right?

Yes. That's right. What happened to ya face, Ervin?

You don't wanna let your niggers get lost in these woods. It ain't safe for them out here. You understand? Y'all may do it like that in town but not out here. He lucky I found him and not someone else.

Thank ya. We're heading back now. Why don't you ride up in front boy? So you don't get lost again.

I led the horse and carriage in front of his.

You have a safe ride now, that man on the horse sayed. He stayed there til he was just a speck.

Greenland ask me what I was doing back there and why I was taking so long. But he ain't want no answer cuze fore I could tell him what happened he sayed, We gotta get back. They cut the wood so slow, took forever.

I ain't sayed nothing the whole way back to Philadelphia. Wasn't nothing to say.

Pay

The women sayed it's a boy from how Lilly carrying. A son. I'm a have a son. I ain't knowed yet what I was gon call him. Maybe after my brother Ethan or after myself or a name like William or Marcus. I liked William name. He could read. But Marcus my best friend. She been better than she was. Had a little life in her eyes and sometimes she cooked and talked to me. She even looked at me. I missed her eyes. I missed her smile. It wasn't much of a smile but it better than it was. Sometimes she sit up in that rocking chair I made her all day. She be talking to her belly and the sky and her belly and then her mama come by and she talk to her. She talk to me too, but not bout what I wanted to talk bout. It done got too late for that anyway. Wasn't nowhere she could go then. Canada was way too far.

Philadelphia be home at least a year or more. And things wasn't like they was when I come. Them Irish had it in for us. It the truth. They come round like they was mad I worked in that workshop. That I knowed what to do in there. Jackson getting elected likely done stirred up a hornet nest or made lions of mice. He done what he wanna and support who he wanna long as he got what he wanted. Anybody who do what he doing to those Indians can't be good at all and those people all voted for him. Well I ain't and didn't no women so I guess it was only the folks like him what like what he been doing. I know they wasn't gon be no freedom in the south with somebody making money from slaves being President.

Mister Greenland actually paid them Irish mind. Gave his time when I'm doing his work for him. He ain't let them in the house to sit but he talked to them outside. Thinked I ain't hear but voices carry when ain't nothing to stop it. They asked

131

him how much he pay me and he ain't sayed but they sayed how much they'd work for. One sayed he a carpenter too. I knowed one thing. He wasn't no carpenter like me and Mister Greenland knowed it too. That man standing out there. I know he leaning up on the workshop. Come up here with that thing in his mouth, chewing on something. Ain't had the sense to stop while he talking but wanna make it look like I ain't ready to work.

Next thing I knowed he coming in the shop with Mister Greenland. Mister Greenland turn to me and sayed he want me to work side him for a few days and see how he do, show him the project we been working on. Ain't hardly been no 'we'. We coulda been farther along if ole Greenland get off his widening rear and work longer then morning to lunch, but he say his legs give out on him if he stand too long.

I offer to make him a sitting stool with a back and he sayed, Nah that's okay. We be just fine.

We ain't gon be just fine if we don't finish this job for spring come. And spring was gon come right along with my son Marcus. Greenland too lazy to work so he plan to pay this stranger to do his part. Master John woulda talk bout him til Sunday. Couldn't stand no lazy man.

I worked longside that chewing man for a full week and he ain't done half what he needed to and Mister Greenland paid him full, same as me. But his full pay wasn't same as mine and I knowed it. I had to stop what I was doing to tell him things he shoulda known. Then go behind him and fix his work cuz it just wasn't right. I been here more than two years and Greenland got nerve to ask him how I was in the workshop when he knowed that for himself.

I told Lilly bout what he doing cuz I been a little worried. She sayed, Don't worry. God will provide.

She and I seed God different. I watched her belly grow everyday and try to find other places to play my fiddle. It been hard since I ain't able to go no place myself at night and I can't hardly leave this town cuz I can't get back. The white folk round there ride me back at night after I play but I ain't getting outta no place else and back home after dark. I played with the white folks but wasn't never certain I could get back, and I ain't trust none of them to be riding back a long way. If they hungry for money as I is, they like to steal me and sell me on the way. I taked to keeping my papers tucked in my shoe, neath the lining.

I'ma be okay. That's what Lilly sayed. She sayed, We gon be alright Ervin. You gotta trust God. He's faithful.

I sayed, Alright Lilly. Not cuz I trust God but cause she sayed it and I trust her.

She smile at me the way only she could do and she maked my life all warm again so I figure God must not be all bad if he give me her. Maybe he been trying to make up for some of the bad stuff with her. She finally come back to me, mostly. She put her fingers with mine. Hers soft and smooth and mine hard and rough. But she sayed she like my hands like that.

She telled me, All them bumps and lumps and scratches mean you knows how to work hard and ain't afraid of it.

She right bout that. I ain't never been fraid to work or fraid to work hard. Specially for my family, for my wife. That what make me a man. So if my Lilly sayed it alright, it alright by me.

By time a month pass that Irish man still working side me but he talking bout how he can't believe I got this job and how I learned what I know. He sayed he can't believe no nigra better than he at it and I must be some kinda proud. I sayed I ain't proud I just work hard and learned from somebody good. He sayed he can't stand a proud nigra and I ain't sayed nothing back.

I only wondered how Greenland payed both us. And if he had money for that why he ain't pay me more since I been working hard enough for me and him. I knowed why. He ain't thinked we should live better than the poorest white folk so he pay me so I can't hardly live better than they do. But I live better than the poorest white folks cuz I play my fiddle and some of them don't like that neither.

Lilly telled me don't pay them no mind but they got in my head still. Things was happening. They was stirring up trouble where they wasn't none. Complaining bout us having anything just cause they was still trying to get something. We was all looking at the bottoms of the rich folk, sitting in the stink and somebody got them fooled thinking we was the enemy. Meanwhile the ones who gots the pockets was laughing at all us down here fighting each other for they leftovers and scraps. But they either couldn't see it or ain't wanna see it. Rather hate us and blame us just cause we look different. Foolishness. And I seed it then that it wasn't gon fare well for this town if somebody ain't do something. Mayor wasn't much bothered. Wasn't nobody what could do something bout it much bothered. They seem alright with it.

If it been even six months later things mighta been different for me and Lilly, but Greenland knowed our baby was coming. He knowed I need that job. So I can't say I been surprised when he come to me and sayed, Ervin, things are tight around here. I gots two a you to pay and well honestly I can't pay you both what you might be worth. I know you work hard and you do pretty good work but I'ma have to cut your pay - just temporary see - til things pick back up.

I looked at him cuz I figure he bout to say something else bout business. Bout losing some of the work or how he can't collect on something due. But he ain't sayed nothing else. Just stand there his belly big and legs like short tree stumps looking up at me. His fat fingers tucked in his pants like he was pondering something but his mind was already set.

I asked him what he mean cuz I gots a baby and a wife and I need to work and take care of my family.

He sayed, A man is responsible for his own family and that ain't on me.

I'm working, being responsible and he cutting my pay so he can have more for himself and his wife. Meanwhile we eating bread and honey some nights.

He sayed, Ervin if you don't like it, I can't help that. You can always find someplace else but what I say is final.

God damn, I hoped he get to pick cotton next to Jackson in hell.

I told him I can take a pay cut if it's temporary and ask him how long temporary is cuz my baby due early spring. He shrug like he ain't need to give it no thought. Then he sayed to me, Hopefully by then business'll pick back up. Til then I'm a need the same quality outta ya and we gotta get this work done on time. If you think that's too much Patrick can do more and he's got some friends looking for work.

I watched Patrick the rest of winter half doing his work and making much as I did before my pay was cut. I knowed cuz I heard Greenland whispering bout it outside. Just cuz he done lost some of his hearing ain't mean nothing bout mine. Patrick act like he done something good by cheating me out of what I earn. His family wasn't no more important than mine. Maybe if he ain't act like he was too good to talk to me in the shop I'd feel different but long as he work side me he act like he boss and telled me what he need me to do or ask me to do this or that. I knowed my way around the shop and what he make look like what I did five years ago.

Master John woulda turned his head up at Patrick if he seed his work and keeped going like he did when we went looking at other people's work. Then he woulda ask me if I seed what he done and I woulda sayed, Yessuh. Then we woulda laughed bout it. But ain't nobody to laugh with here and Lilly ain't get what I do. She knowed I work hard and make stuff but side from a couple chairs I fixed up for her mama and the door I put on that cabinet she ain't really know how good I been. Don't matter though it was gon be hard enough when the baby come and I hoped Lilly's prayers work and God might give me my full pay back. I figure she gon drop that baby any day. I maked sure somebody know my whereabouts all the time in case Marcus come. They still sayed it's a boy. He was gon be a fine boy. Her belly looked like she was gon burst with a full watermelon. She wasn't that big but all that belly make up for it.

She done make a new blanket for him and a hat cuz it's still cold. She sayed she don't want him out in the cold at all but it sometime get cold inside too so she want him with a hat on since babies heads be bald sometime. I telled her I think Marcus got hair cuz she be burping and her chest hurting all the time.

She was so pretty. Beautiful. Like an angel and I loved her. I ain't think I can ever love nobody like this. She still had nights when she be quiet. When the tree frogs loud and the rest of the night quiet she be quiet too. She lay there in that bed, her back to me so her belly been on the side. I knowed she wasn't sleeping cuz I heard her breathing. I knowed she been thinking then bout our baby Ellie. How Ellie laid next to her. Then I start thinking bout Ellie too. First our baby. Then my mama. Both them together in heaven. Sometimes I reached over and put my arm around her and Marcus and I kissed her neck and the back of her head. She ain't gotta worry bout being alone or feeling that pain by herself. After a while she drift to sleep and I drift off long side her.

Things to Come

In the evenings after I finally get home from working all day me and Lilly would walk down the street. She walk bare feet cuz she ain't need no shoes and her swollen feet wasn't gon fit them no way. I keeped mine off too cuz I like the feel of the earth neath my feet. When we get back I rub her feet after heating up some water and washing them.

We stayed up late talking even though we both knowed we need to sleep fore the baby come but stead we talk and sometimes if she let me, we even make love. She sayed maybe it'll make the baby come. I wasn't really worried bout that part. The baby was gon come either way. She sometimes looked tired cuz she so full with child. But she beautiful as the day I seed her when I got to Philadelphia. She telled me she liked me then but I was so rough and she ain't knowed if I was gon make nothing of myself. I sayed how she maked me wanna make something of myself.

She smiled then and sayed, You better keep making something of yourself so my daddy stop worrying.

I'm a man and takes care of my family. That's what men do, I sayed back.

She too big to help at her mama's now and can barely move round the kitchen without knocking stuff down. I sayed to let me do it but she say I taked care of her before and she wanna take care a me. I ain't gon get in no woman's way. I loves her. She an angel sent by God so I telled God, God thank you for her.

I send Master John a letter fore Lilly was spose to give birth. I put in there bout Mister Greenland cutting my wages and bout my son on the way. I sayed I hoped it was a son and I was

137

calling him Marcus after my friend here. Marcus was smart and tall and the ladies liked him. He done got a wife and two kids and my boy was gon be friends with his. Marcus worked hard too and folks respect him. I wanted my son to be respected too. I ain't wanna tell him nothing else that might give him no bad ideas. Like how we done had these skirmishes or Patrick. He ain't need to be bothered with that and William ain't got time for writing long letters. I talked bout Lilly and sayed that maybe if things change he might meet Marcus and Lilly one day.

The letter got there quicker that time round and he sent me one back quicker. He sayed Misses Charlotte ain't doing so well. She caught some fever in the winter and been sick but they think she gon get better. He sayed he a granddaddy with a granddaughter and hoped that Priscilla have a son too. He say he wouldn't mind meeting Marcus and Lilly and he wouldn't mind seeing me too. Sayed that if I ever wanna come back he'll be right where he was and he gots plenty of work. More than he can handle and still ain't no good help and finding somebody good as me been hard. He ended it with his hope that God keeping me and my wife good and that I stay safe.

I heard William read that letter and it made me smile all the way home. I walk with my chest higher cuz I was good at what I did and he knowed it. Master John ain't know how this place was changing but we trying to stay safe and make our way. This place was changing and maybe the country if folks let it. One day I planned to be free and if they let me I plan to be on my own land like Master John. Someplace safe for me and my kin. Where we can be free and have respect. Lilly think it funny I put away any extra I get that ain't have to go straight to paying rent, buying food, or taking care of needs. I figured it don't hurt to save something case I get a chance I wasn't even looking for. Or the chance come for us to get outta there.

I figured I write Master John again after Marcus born and tell him I got a son. Maybe we could go back but I ain't wanna be no slave again and Lilly don't deserve to be no slave ever. Nobody do. We was gon have to stay and make it work. Mama Shepherd and Mister Shepherd ain't have no plans to go nowhere either. They sayed this they home and they got they life here. The city was swelling with black folk though. And it make the white folk nervous. Seem like everyday more poured in. Looking for work. Happy for freedom. Thinking it gon be different.

Maybe it would for them. Maybe it be a different kinda the same. Depend on where they come from. For most it's better. Others it ain't. I imagine some lay wake like I did when I come. All these hopes of freedom still stuck in they head til they realize they still just a nigger but don't nobody else hold they papers. Like mama sayed being free don't make you free but they figure it out soon enough on they own.

Lilly want me to go to church with her fore Marcus born. He coming any day so I figured I might as well go with her that Sunday on account people talk cuz I don't hardly ever come round. They start asking her if I have the lawd in my life. Seemed like they need to stop worrying bout me and ask the lawd why he been so busy in my life. But I wasn't gon study what he did that Sunday. I was gon go with my Lilly and when they pray over us and this baby, I was gon take it cuz maybe it'll help. Might help with the money too.

That ole Greenland ain't give me back my pay yet. Sayed things turning round soon. In the spring. Just hold on. I ain't seed nothing changed since fall, fore he cut my wage. He ain't cut that Patrick wage. I seed that too. All that time and he making what he was making fore my wage got cut which was more than I was making. Some folks ain't right even when you do right by them.

Fair is fair. That's what I learned and maybe somebody shoulda teached that to Mister Greenland too.

Marcus

Lilly

Our baby coming. That's all I know. I think I peed myself in the bed cuz my bladder been so loose but that was my water that broke. A long night in the making. I wake up Ervin. He sleep like a log but he need to run and tell our neighbor Henry to fetch mama and the midwife. He gon be a daddy again. I gon be a mama. Lawd make it easy.

Ervin

Lilly wake me up and I put my hand down to sit up and it's wet. I looks at her in the dark and she say, It's time Ervin. Marcus coming.

I leaps outta bed cuz I ain't knowed what to do and start running round the room. She say, Run tell Henry to get mama and the midwife.

I grabs my jacket and run out the house to Henry. He seen us lose our first baby but he gon be part of our next one coming to this world.

I gets back and Lilly tell me to get the rags and the water heat up. I takes the water to the fire and let it sit there so it heat up enough to be warm. I ask her what else and she say come sit side her. She say she ain't in pain yet, just her water done broke so the baby coming tonight or soon. I sits down and wait. Holding her hand too tight but scared to let it go. I ask if she want some water and she say she do so I gets her some fore it get too warm. She say it gon be alright and I say I knowed but I still ain't going nowhere else. She drinking the water like she ain't had none in two days.

I ain't knowed how much time passed fore she start breathing heavy and moan like she in some pain but she don't say much bout it. She say it's starting, the cramping to help the baby come out. I tells her to lean back on me and I slide behind her so she rest her head on me and I holds her like that waiting on somebody to get there. She breathing and moaning off and on and squeezing my hand and I trying not to squeeze hers too much cuz I ain't wanna hurt her no more than Marcus already doing.

I tells Lilly to breathe. Tells Lilly to breathe slow. I say, like the midwife sayed. Then I tells Lilly to see our baby in her arms. She already irritable with me. She say to stop talking a while and just hold her cuz she can't focus with me talking and asking her how she doing every other minute. I shuts my mouth and watch the door. I's looking for Mama Shepherd or the midwife to come in and help. Somebody who knows what to do. I's wishing they lived closer and it wasn't the middle of the night when they sleep.

I whispers for Lilly to breathe cuz she done stop breathing through one of those cramps. She start breathing again. I tells her I gotta get the water off the heat and I ease myself from back of her and cross the bed to the fire. The pot is real warm now and ain't nobody here but us.

She scream this time and I bout drop the pot of water. Some spill on my bare feets and I knows for sure it's warmer than it need to be. I ain't say nothing cuz I know it ain't hurting as much as her.

I's getting nervous cuz I can't bring no baby in by myself and it was hard on Lilly last time. She getting on with these cramps like they getting worse and worse. I wishing we coulda lived closer to Mama Shepherd but we can't pay what rent cost over there. And the midwife don't move fast. Sometime neither do Henry but I thinks tonight he moving fast. I wish the other midwife ain't moved a few months back. Sayed it was too much for her.

I hopes don't nobody stop Henry or give him no trouble. I gets back behind Lilly so she can rest up against me some more and she sweating now. I lifts up her hair from her neck and she breathing hard. She screaming what seem like every few minutes now. Some worser than others. I feels her belly and trying to feel if our Marcus is moving but between her squirming and my nerves I can't hardly tell. She don't want me messing with her belly cuz it hurt.

The door slam open after she holler again and it's Mama Shepherd. She run back to us. Where the light? You ain't got no light in here? I sayed it's in the corner on the floor and she find it and light it so she can see. I figure the fire was good enough. She come to Lilly with the lantern and touch her face then feel round her belly.

Mama Shepherd run back to the door and hollered out something bout hurrying up. She come back and ask me where the water and rags is, then she checked what I had. She ask how long Lilly been having those cramps come close together. I say I ain't really know but it been a while. Not too long after Henry gone to fetch her.

I hears other footsteps rushing to the back and something bumping against the wall. The midwife come in with that bag bouncing on her hip. She ask Mama Shepherd to help get the rags underneath Lilly. Then she ask me if I gots more. I says we gots more in the kitchen so Mama Shepherd go gets what we got and come back. The midwife feeling on Lilly belly and then say she gon check how she coming. She reach down, feeling round, and then she got this funny look cross her face. She ask Lilly how the baby moving inside. Lilly say she ain't know. She think the baby must be tired too. Midwife say it too soon to be tired, specially since he done got himself some turned round.

What you mean tired and turned round? I ask.

He ain't moving round much like before now. Is something wrong? Lilly asks, squeezing the midwife hand.

We need to get the baby out soon. You need to keep breathing through these cramps like you been doing. She take Mama Shepherd out the room and whisper something to her we can't hear. Then they come back and Mama Shepherd tell Lilly she gon need to get up and squat. The midwife say she gotta try to get the baby back in the right place cuz he ain't quite there, off a little. She ask me to get a chair so I gets up from behind Lilly and gets a chair from the kitchen and comes back.

Mama Shepherd and me helps Lilly out the bed and into the chair real slow like. She can barely stand but she ain't gotta go far. She gets in the chair on the edge with me on one side, Mama Shepherd on the other side and the midwife in the middle in front of her. She say to Lilly she gotta be strong cuz the baby need to come out. She feel up in there again and Lilly screaming it hurt and the midwife ain't saying much back so I ask, What's going on?

She say, I trying to see.

I say, What you trying to see?

She say, Your baby stuck. Can't stay in there much longer.

Stuck how, Lilly ask.

Baby got the cord wrapped round em. I trying to tell where it wrapped round.

What that mean? What you mean? I ask. I trying not to get mad but I feels it rising up.

Mean we gotta get this baby out. Now.

Lilly

I feel Ervin's hand squeezing mine and mama on the other side. I look in her eyes cuz I'm scared of what it mean. I was scared for Marcus and me and Ervin. She sayed to keep breathing and the midwife say I need to start pushing but it don't feel right. Baby still feel a little twisted. She say I gots to anyway but then she ain't say nothing after that. She pause and then tell me to push so she can try to loose the baby. I squeeze Ervin hand back. He silent now and I think he holding his breath. I look at him in that light and his eyes is wide like a deer in the woods when you catch it in the lantern light. His jaw set and hard like he clenching his teeth. He trying to be strong for me.

I push down and she say, Good. She count to three and tell me push again. I do. I feels light in the head. She tell me, Good he turned right now. Then she say, Again.

I take a breath and start pushing.

Ervin

Lilly push so hard. That baby come out but it don't come out easy or smooth.

Get the other rags! The midwife yell to Mama Shepherd. She bleeding!

Mama Shepherd grab the rags from the bed. Lilly ain't sitting up on her own. I holds her up. The baby in the Midwife hands but ain't no sound coming out. She get the shears from on top of her bag and cuts the cord that locked up round the neck. I can't tell if it's a boy or a girl. I just see that cord stretching round em and the baby limp. She pull it off and spank the bottom. Nothing. Lilly breathing light.

Lay her down on the bed, Sit her legs up. Gotta try to stop the bleeding. The midwife bout hollering at us.

I picks her up under her arms and Mama Shepherd grab her legs. The morning light shining through the window now. I can see underneath where she was. Blood staining the rags and the chair. The baby still ain't doing nothing. The midwife got her big mouth over his. I can see his parts now from how she holding him. My son ain't breathing but she trying to give him air. My Lilly breathing so light and her eyes ain't opening. I tells her it's a boy. It's Marcus. I hopes that make her wake up. She ain't though.

Lilly! Mama Shepherd say shaking her hand. Lilly! You got a boy. Wake up and see your son, baby.

Mama Shepherd look over at Marcus and the midwife but the midwife ain't saying nothing and looking down.

I hold Lilly hand and rub her forehead whispering she gotta wake up now. Wake up Lilly. Mama shepherd and me both begging her to get up but I sees the blood and it's getting lighter and lighter in the room. I sees all the blood. I puts my face to her face to feel her breath. I can't feels it on my cheek. She warm and soft like I always knowed her to be but I can't feel her breathing. I can't see her chest moving. Then it do. And I feels her breath on my cheek. I waits for the next breath and Mama Shepherd, holding her waiting for it too. We both waiting and trying to get her to breathe again. She don't never do it.

Neither do Marcus. He ain't never breathed air in this life. She ain't never breathed it again. Mama Shepherd holler and cry over Lilly laying up against me and I ain't been able to move.

I ain't wanna believe it. I keep calling her name cuz she has to come back to me. Wake up. Least see her son. Our son one time. But she ain't never lay eyes on him good. When he came out it was dark and she was hardly awake. I shake her arm and hand again. I whisper to her. I tell her I love her and she need to come back cuz God don't need her. Me and Mama Shepherd hold Lilly tween us and the midwife hold Marcus. She finally ask if I wanna hold him fore he cold. I look at him. He ain't had no life in him. She brought him to me and put him in my arm. I keep hold a Lilly with the other hand. I ain't wanna let neither one go.

Mama Shepherd reached over and touch Marcus head. She start crying loud again. I thinks she gon fall out cuz she can't catch her breath. She ain't never lose nobody like this. I already knowed losing your child was a worser thing. But losing Lilly right then was even worser. I ain't never knowed Marcus, not like Lilly knowed him in her belly. But God took him away anyway and Lilly right with him. God keep taking away and ain't giving nothing back.

Empty

I don't hardly remember after that. I think my heart couldn't handle no more hurt so it just put it away somewhere else. Maybe my soul was already too heavy and tired. I made them a casket together and Greenland seemed to feel sorry for me. He sent flowers to her grave and started paying me my full wage again. Even Patrick ain't had much to say. I think they pitied me. All I could do is work. I ain't had nothing else. Mama Shepherd tried to get me to come by for dinner on Sundays but everything there remind me of Lilly.

She remind of Lilly. What Lilly woulda look like when she was older. This whole place remind me of Lilly. I ain't wanna live in that little house no more. I burnt that chair with the blood stains and all them rags. I ain't want none of them memories. I wanted Lilly and I wanted my mama. I wanted God to stop taking away my family.

Greenland told me to keep myself busy so I did. I worked fore day til night when it wasn't no place else to go but that house. I sleeped in the front room by the kitchen. I ain't wanna go in the back no more. It only been them back there. Her hands slide cross my back at night and her laugh come all through the room.

Everyday it crossed my mind bout going back. Cuz ain't nothing there for me cept freedom. And Marcus told me it's worth it to stay and ain't nothing back in South Carolina for me. But he ain't know that the only other person I had was there and I was scared to be alone. I hated it. He had his family. His boys was growing strong. His wife full with another one. He was my friend but even he ain't knowed my heart. He ain't never been nothing but free. He ain't never had somebody he love taken away by man and by God. He had faith in a God that done let everything be taken from me, one after the other. Only thing you got when everything else gone is hurt that I can't even explain.

Most nights I sat behind that house or in the front so I can see the stars. Mama and Lilly up there. Ellie and Marcus. I wondered if Ethan up there cuz he tried to get away one too many times. I knowed he wasn't the staying type. Or did he get free. I wondered if my daddy up there. I looked at the stars and play my fiddle there like they was watching and listening. I might sometimes get a touch of peace then. When it just me, my fiddle and them stars. God ain't gon take the stars. They stay hung high decorating the sky. They ain't going nowhere.

I recalled some nights when I was young and Master John ain't wanna talk too much cuz for some reason things weighed on him and stead we'd play neath the stars. He sayed we can count on them. That they a constant reminder of God. That the big wide creation is. I think he was trying to remind himself but when I needed reminding too, I remember what he sayed.

Moving On

So much changed and so much stayed the same. To look at me and listen you see I changed some since coming here but in my heart everything inside everything was different. Marcus sayed I need to try and find a wife. That it's been more than three years since Lilly passed. Maybe he was right. I got lonely. My body and my mind got to where I need somebody cuz nights was long. There was too much inside and in my mind and I couldn't get it quiet. I'd hear her talking to me like we did when she sleeped side me and walked side me. When we sat in front of the fire and talked bout our baby and how the world was gon be different cuz folks was trying to get rid a slavery.

I don't imagine God made another one like her. Can't nobody replace Lilly. Marcus sayed I'm right. Can't nobody replace her but I can't be by myself the rest of my life. I'm still young. That's what he told me. But every time I tried to love, God show me I can't. I figured I should just listen to God and stop trying to love so I stop getting hurt. Them ladies in town ain't seem to get that I might be cursed. They seed me working as a carpenter and playing the fiddle and that's all they see. They wasn't seeing the stain inside my heart. One what got Lilly face on it and Ellie little feets on it and Marcus baby hands. They wasn't seeing that. They seed I look like a good husband. A widow and seemed like I need a wife.

Marcus done introduce me to Mabel Ann. She a year or so older than me but she ain't act it. She got a real pretty face and a nice shape. She sayed her mama gots some Indian in her on account of her hair not being tight. I sayed that's nice but I don't care bout that. She had a nice backside and front side and come from a decent family. They was in church every week it seem so maybe that was gon be a problem since I only seed the inside when I fancy. And I ain't fancy going more than I need to keep down the talk and stay on top of the important matters. We was in a good place for anti-slavery and I liked that. It keeped me with something to do with my mind and my time. Girl like Mabel Ann might could get me distracted.

We talked bout important things in those meetings. Helping folks through to here and past if need be. We talked bout what it's like down south and how we needed to be together and stick together cuz they ain't gon like us for no more than what we can do for them. They told us bout Nat Turner in Virginia and I wondered if I woulda been that brave if I'd been in a place like him stead a with Master John.

I figured they right for the most part. Seemed like eight a ten white folks feeled that way or least they act it. I ain't know if they had the same pressures as Master John to pretend they so evil. But I also figured they need to be looking to answer to God and stop being evil cuz man ain't gon save them in the end. That fire gon be right hot.

I seed her at them meetings a few times and we talked after for a few minutes. I let myself get some distracted. I admit it was welcome after all this time. She was just as sweet as she look but I think her daddy might not a want her being that sweet. He was wondering bout my intentions. Wondering bout Mabel Ann and what she might be doing too. I wasn't telling him my intentions cuz he might get out that shot gun in his bedroom.

I figured I better tell him what he wanna hear and what she wanna hear. That I intend to marry her. I ain't wanna get married though. I sayed we need to wait and Mabel Ann wanna know why. I ain't got a good reason so I told her I need to get myself together to take care of her. That I had some things I had to do first. Truth was, if I marry her she might die. Like that. I ain't tell her what I think of me being cursed cuz I ain't wanna scare her too.

I spose I had to do something cuz almost a year done past since we been courting and she ain't getting no younger and pretty as she was I ain't the only one with eyes for her. Marcus sayed I need to do something too but to be careful with her cuz she ain't no virgin. I wasn't no virgin either but I was married so ain't no secret bout that. I asked him why she wasn't no virgin and he sayed he ain't know and shrug his shoulder like he ain't wanna tell me. Mabel Ann been there since she was knee high so she growed up there and anybody she been with was likely still there so now he had me wondering who had her and if it been just one.

Marcus got me thinking bout how she wasn't that hard to get and she wasn't hard to convince to be with me. Got me wondering how many others convinced her and if when folks looked at us walking down the street or sitting in church together it wasn't cuz we was a handsome couple but cuz I was a fool in the making.

Another six months passed and Mabel Ann come out straight and ask me herself. She sitting up in my bed with nothing but her undergarments on and asked what my intentions was. I told her they was to love her til I couldn't love her no more and to make her feel that love deep and true. And she ain't think it was funny. She sayed, No. I mean after today, tomorrow and the next day. What is your intentions Ervin? I needs to know.

Any other intentions fell right there. I looked down and nothing. She sayed, Ervin?

What you want from me? A promise? You want me to tell you I love you?

That might be a good start, but that ain't it.

Why you need to hear it when I show you?

It's not the same Ervin.

I don't know what you want from me that I ain't already giving you? I tried to smile and play kiss her neck. Wasn't no need for all that talk.

No Ervin. I'm about to be twenty-seven years old. An old maid. If I don't get married soon I ain't never gon get married.

Marriage ain't everything you think, I sayed to her.

Well it can be.

No. It can't. You don't know about marriage!

Well I should. And it can be good if you give us a chance.

Why can't we just make love and enjoy what we got?

Cuz we sinning. We been sinning and I don't want to live in sin. It ain't right. God don't like it. I don't like it.

I sayed I understand and put my clothes back on. Told Mabel Ann to put hers back on too. Wasn't no reason to stay half dressed. She wanted something and I wanted something but they wasn't the same something.

So Ervin. What we doing? She looked at me all pretty but her eyes had this shadow.

I standed up and put on my suspenders. Told her I walk her home and we can talk on the way back. I ain't wanna talk but she ain't need to be there no more. It ain't feel right talking bout marrying nobody else where my Lilly died. She mighta understand that a man had needs but I ain't knowed if she'd understand me marrying somebody else. I ain't even wanna think of marrying somebody else. Spose that's why more than a year and a half gone since we started courting and I ain't ask Mabel Ann and folks figured asking her was the right thing for me to do.

We walked back to her house taking the secret way so wouldn't nobody see us and she told me how I'm making a mockery of her and embarrassing her and ruining her reputation.

I sayed, I understand. You knowed when we started I ain't plan to make no promises and I can't start making promises I can't keep. If you need to get married I understand and respect it. It just can't be me. Mabel Ann you need to find somebody who don't mind being married.

She hit my face so hard it stung like bees. Why the hell you slap me? I grab her hand.

You have to ask? She turn from me where I been standing back in the shadows of the house and walked away.

I let her go into the house. She ain't sayed nothing else to me. Her folks turned they face from me too. They ain't know the truth. I saved her from me and my curse. They shoulda thank me that they get to keep they daughter.

1834

It was in 1825 I came to Philadelphia trying to become a free man and I think I done it but I still don't have nothing to show for it. I was twenty-seven by 1834. I stopped trying to get closer to folks and the girls leave me alone. Guess Mabel Ann helped with that but I would get lonely and wasn't nobody getting tangled up with me. Sometimes I'd go to church. That's the only way to see black folk on a regular basis. Otherwise it just be me and I got enough a me. We talk more about freedom and what's happening. Things wasn't good round there. Ain't been good in a while. Maybe it just been me think that way since Lilly gone and wasn't nothing much there for me but I ain't think it was only me feeling it.

Days came when I wanted to leave and go back but I knowed there wasn't nothing for me til South Carolina stop loving they ways so much. Stop loving having slaves like they takes pride in it. Nowhere was perfect but least there I been mostly safe cept at night if I was at the edge a town so I stayed where I knowed people and they knowed me.

I stayed cuz I ain't never wanna be no slave again. And Patrick done stop acting like he better than me in the shop cuz I finally done showed him he ain't. He done accepted that he and me gon work side by side cuz I knowed how to do what he can't. All this time and he figure it out but he still make more than I do. I can't say nothing bout it cuz even though he Irish he ain't black. And then Greenland had nerve to say it cuz he gots a family to take care of. I ain't knowed if he knowed his words feel like knives in my heart. Even if some time done pass. He stopped working in the shop cuz he say he need to sell and we do the work. He would take what we do to market and be talking

152

up his shop. He mighta came in and help when we got real busy. Guess he figure if he can underpay a nigger and a Irishman mean he ain't gotta work. Even Patrick ain't got paid right but wasn't much for him to say neither.

Patrick open up and some days I missed when we ain't hardly say nothing. Now he talk all day. It did help the time pass and he could make me laugh talking bout his family and kids and friends. He had a life outside of that workshop. I ain't had nothing but meetings about freedom. Not much social life to speak of. Patrick likely talked more than he should. That's why I knowed things wasn't right round there. He sayed folks upset cuz money ain't right and all sorts of negro folks coming everyday. Sayed folks feeling like the negroes taking jobs they need. I sayed to him we all need jobs and he sayed that might be true but people gon do and say what's best for them. I figured they white too and when it came down to it, that all that matter. Us negro folk ain't have nothing to put up against it. Me and Patrick was both right. Wish we wasn't but we was.

Maybe it was the heat that summer that got mixed with all the pent up rage of whatever was eating them up inside. Maybe it was that new American Anti-Slavery Society they started round Christmas. Maybe cuz Britain done outlawed slavery and Canada is official too for free blacks and those like me who escaped. I went to some meetings cuz I been a slave and can tell all bout my experience first hand. How it was in Virginia when I was a boy and in South Carolina. I told them bout how most slaves ain't had it like I did. They aint got masters who got some light in they heart to do right. That the institution is built on evil and gon curse this land til they does right by us.

Maybe folks ain't like the changes that was happening. But it was like Philadelphia was on fire and I wondered if the whole country was gon be on fire and burn all us up. Its own kind a hell. They sayed it was a mob town like Boston and New York on account of all the fighting against us blacks. Called it a crisis of violence in the papers. That's what William sayed. It been building up years fore that but never like that year. Never the whole city. It started that hot August day and keeped on after. The Flying Horses got turned upside down by that mob.

Black folks and white folks went to that place but that ain't mattered to them mobs. About four or five hundred folks was fighting with all manner of weapons they done picked up from what been laying around, bricks, and stones, and such.

Next thing we knowed, they coming our way to Moyamensing burning and looting and trying to tear down our little piece of town. Two more nights it went on and ain't nobody stopped them from rioting and burning. Nobody came to help us cuz it was us getting our stuff destroyed and beat up in the street. We had to fend for ourselves so we did, best we could. Wasn't no working those days cuz we had to stand guard best we could. Folks got hurt. One got dead by them and nobody ever paid for it. Or the churches they destroyed or nothing. The women ran for help in the city or cross the river while we stood watch. Some folks had they silver and anything else of worth stealed by those plunderers. They ain't liked that we had things. Like we couldn't have nothing nice. They ain't liked we had our own churches neither and could talk about things they ain't want us talking bout.

Most ain't been arrested. They scattered like roaches in the sun. Say just sixty got arrested and I knowed it was several times that many out there destroying and raising unholy hell. I ain't feel like I had nothing to protect. Nothing to save or care if it got stealed. Maybe woulda been best if God had took me one of them nights too, but he ain't. He ain't never took me. He got that house though. And all its memories. He done took it right with so many other houses what belonged to us.

The constables and mayor finally growed tired of the fighting and how they was ransacking the town and tried to stop them but they still manage to destroy one of our churches.

I think that was it. After all the little riots and fights and they cutting our wages trying to wear us down cuz all we wanna do is live in peace with a little human decency. I was tired of this place. It done took more than it give me and I be glad to leave all it behind. Maybe I get a piece of my soul back if I get back to the last place my heart and soul had a bit a peace.

Dear Mister

Dear Mister John James,
I received your letter and have decided to make my
way to South Carolina as soon as possible. The
folks here seem just as opposed to my kind as
anywhere else. I plan to depart in one week's time
from the writing of this letter. I imagine it will take
me several weeks to make my way given the
railways don't stretch far yet. They have some in
Philadelphia but I can't get much out of
Philadelphia, not heading south. It will just be me.
I look forward to seeing you again after all these
years.

Sincerely,
E. James

William always made me sound so smart. I write Master John that letter in early September after I thinked about where I was and where he was and what it mean to be free. After that I had William read me his letters again bout how things could be if I was back there. I ain't had nobody there no way. I wanted to be a man and have some honor in my work. I wanted some respect stead a being hid away like somebody shamed a me like Greenland shamed a me. He show that Patrick round and take him to market and to meet folk like he getting ready to set him up to take over. Patrick ain't bad as Greenland but neither was worth half a Master John when it come to skill.

    I wondered if I can stop calling him Master John. William write Mister in the letter but I ain't never called him

Mister. Always Master and if I was back in South Carolina I knowed I'd have to call him Master, least round other folks. He told me in those letters people miss my playing and ask him why he loan me out so long or did he just sell me. He say it's an arrangement and I may come back if things worked out as such. I wondered if he knowed bout my heart. That it been all broken. Maybe he did cuz I understand how Misses Charlotte heart musta feel. Kinda pain you can't even describe but it eat you up leaving holes can't nothing fill. He sayed she ain't been all better in years. She sick off and on and he took care a her when she like that. Sayed he can't pay nobody worth nothing to help, but that one of the slaves I knowed from church come in and look after her for some extra money. He payed her to look after Charlotte cuz he wouldn't be part of that business of stealing folks labor no more.

I ask William what he thinked cuz he smart and older than me and Marcus. He seed things and understand them better.

He sayed, Ervin, I can't tell a man what to do. I know you never found peace here and it sound like you had peace there, so you have to do what you think is right. That'll be between you and God. But if you go, have a plan for if you need to leave again. You can always come back here. You can go up to Canada too if you don't mind hard land and cold. Lots of folks continuing up that way now.

I know I'd be certain of freedom there but ain't nobody or nothing up there in Canada for me. I shaked my head no, cuz that wasn't the way I intended to go.

I ain't wanna have to come back to Philadelphia. That place done took Ellie and Lilly and Marcus. I sayed to William, I'ma go and hope I don't have to come back but I appreciate you for everything you done for me.

Marcus had me over for dinner on Sunday like he done sometimes so I ain't have to be by myself. He was still telling me I need a wife. But he ain't pressure too hard lately. Guess he knowed I wasn't long for that place. His wife, now she couldn't hardly see me without giving me a word about it and how I needed to make things right or I was never gon find a wife in Philadelphia. I wondered what Mabel Ann sayed bout me. They ain't know I was helping them by not taking on a wife and by leaving.

After we ate Marcus and me took some of his homemade liquor to the back stoop and sat down. I been waiting to tell him bout my plans cuz I knowed what he was gon say. I knowed he be mad at me for turning back. I waited til after I done sent that letter off so I wouldn't change my mind.

He turned to me and looked like I'd done growed a second head. He sayed, You done gone mad Ervin. In that house by yourself too much. You gone mad. You can't go back to South Carolina. Only a crazed fool would go back into the worse place in the states to be a slave.

I know you wasn't gon understand Marcus. It ain't like that where I was.

What if you can't get back to where you was? What if somebody snatch you up on the way? Steal your papers and sell you down the river? To some big ole plantation or some big ole farm where they treat you like chattel? You leave here and you leave your manhood behind, go back to being just a beast to work the land.

That ain't gon happen. I'ma make it back. Same way I came.

What kinda foolish talk is that Ervin? Ain't nobody set nothing up to get people into slavery. It ain't even set up hardly to get people out. They just starting and it ain't ordered. Some folks makes it through. Lots don't and you wanna go back?

This place has been hell on me Marcus. You know it. I buried a wife and two babies. I lost everything here. I ain't got nothing and done ruined my prospects cuz I'm...n evermind. You ain't never been a slave. This all you know. You got that wife and your children.

It ain't been perfect for you but only a fool would go back to South Carolina in 1834. I can't give you my blessings on that brother. You need to stay right here. Need to listen to that young man at the meetings. He say the time is coming. More blacks gon be free and the more that become free, the more can become free. He says we can't give up and can never go back. He talking bout that other William. The young one family name Still. Still knows how to read and write and he can go forward. He has people here, family, friends. He ain't cursed like me. He and folks like him gon be alright when things settle down. But Philadelphia feel like it sitting right on top of a powder keg.

Look around Marcus. They destroyed a church, our homes. Neighborhoods. Killed a man. How this better? And they don't care whether we lose everything we work so hard for. Don't nobody care about us whether we north, south or west.

He just look at me in the dark and sip on that liquor.

You could be happy here if you gave it a chance.

I gave it a chance. I been here nine years Marcus. Nine years and what I gots? I ain't got nothing to show for it. No family. One friend. No kids. And now a broke down house that I don't even own.

You could have more friends if you wanted but you so private. And you coulda had a wife but you ran her off.

You know I ain't getting no wife. And I ain't looking for all kinds of folks in my business. No reason to give them nothing else to talk about. They already talking enough about me and Mabel Ann.

Well that's on you. You drug that woman along for a year and a half and then just cut her loose.

I saved her from me.

For the last time Ervin - you ain't cursed.

Tell that to God.

He stopped again and put down his mug.

So you gon do this then? Go back to South Carolina? You know it don't make no sense. I need to hear you say it's foolish.

I know it's foolish. I know it don't make no sense. I know.

And you still gonna do it anyway?

Yeah. And I need your help.

Marcus shook his head like he was disappointed. I ain't seed that kind of disappointment in a long time. Wasn't nobody to be disappointed in me that I cared about.

You know I hate to see you go and I can't say I understand. But you your own man.

I am.

Reverse

I ain't played so much fiddle since I got there. I played anytime somebody ask. I never sayed no. Any extra money I could make I put away for getting back. Marcus and William got the first leg setup. I was gon catch the new train far south as possible. Wasn't but a few miles but I ain't had to walk it or rely on nobody to get me. I saved every cent I could and put it in that pouch mama gave me.

Patrick sayed I was quiet. I worked just as hard but I ain't had much to say. He asked if I was still upset about a couple months before. It ain't even been a couple months. It only been bout a month. It just now hit autumn and they destroyed my house mid August. He tried to make it seem like it was way in the past but I figure he probably knowed some of them men who was looting and rioting and destroying our stuff.

He ain't bother me too much and neither did Greenland. We got orders in and we did the work. All this time working together we knowed what we doing and it ain't take a whole lot of talking. Glad cuz I ain't wanna talk. Don't nobody need to know my heart.

I had another week or so fore I put on my clothes like I did before and get back on my way. I'm getting ready to go home but it shouldn'ta feel that way. Ain't nobody think it make sense for somebody to go back willing to the bowels of slavery. They figured I just lost some of my senses and I cracked up or something. Maybe they right but it ain't mattered none what they think. Soon I'd be back on my way home.

It was a night not much different than that one in October nine years before I took my leave of South Carolina.

I'd played fiddle longside Master John and still wondered how he musta felt. Now I was going back in the fall. We had to wait to the moon dark cuz we wasn't looking for no extra way to see me.

They coming in the night, crashing in my door. Mama sleep on her bed in the corner and my Lilly sleeping side me. Our babies sleeping side her. They come in loud and angry yelling bout taking things back. That I can't have it cuz if they can't I can't. They saying niggers don't get shit. And they snatching away mama.

She yelling and screaming and they drag her out by her arms. Her feet kicking as she scream. Then they come for my Lilly. I'm froze in the bed. Ain't nobody holding me but I can't move. Like the devil holding me down. And they take my Lilly and drags her from the bed. She hit the floor hard and she's screaming that she's bleeding. I'm bleeding! Stop! And there ain't nothing I can do. Then two more evil men come and snatch up my babies. They snatch up my baby girl Ellie by the foot and laugh and say they like coon baby.

My mouth won't yell, like I got something caught in my throat. My eyes is burning. Cuz only one still there and he already getting took out the box we laid him in to rest. He crying too. It's all I hear. The screams while they take them each away one after the other and ain't nothing I can do. Then they gone. The screaming stops and ain't no weight holding me down. I gets up and runs to the door and open it and there ain't nothing there.

Nothing. Not no street. No dirt. No stars. No trees. No tree frogs. Nothing. Like I'm nowhere. I wonder if I died too and went to hell. I tries to scream but it don't seem to make no sound. I close the door and scream again and it wake me up.

I been having dreams like this since they tore through the city. Hardly could sleep or focus. Was waking sweaty and cold. And it keep happening. I don't wanna close my eyes for too long and it give it time to take hold.

I tried to tell them I ain't worth messing with or worrying about. I told the ones get too close, Keep your women away from me. I know I been cursed.

The devil had some kinda hold. But that devil was bout to get leaved right in Philadelphia. That's what I prayed. Cuz I ain't want it following me back.

Sometimes Marcus come and sit with me at night. He sayed he sad I'm going but he know bout those scares I gets at night. He say, You not cursed Ervin. You just hurting inside your heart and your head.

I told him, It's the same thing.

It's not the same. You a good man Ervin. You ain't got no curse on you.

I guess I gotta wait and see but I hope you right Marcus cuz I don't want this following me round.

Why you think you cursed Ervin? What you think you done that put a curse on you?

I ain't know what I done. Maybe I was born cursed. But God let those Israelites be in bondage for a long time and ain't seem to have no reason either.

He laugh at me but I wasn't being funny. I feel like I'm trying to get out of the promised land so I can make my way back to Egypt. Foolish as it is.

* * *

When it came time to leave my nerves was bad. All this time I been looking to leave but now it come and I wasn't sure no more. Not sure bout nothing. I wasn't sure I can get back safe. If things gon be alright or if Master John gon be alright. I was trusting it cuz he ain't never been much to lie, cept to save me. I figured if he do that he gon be okay. But what about Misses Charlotte? She know they ain't sent me to somebody but I spose she done went along with him all these years. Maybe she wasn't as cold as she seem.

* * *

Night fore I leaved I dreamed of mama again. But this time was different. All them days leading up to leave I been having nightmares. I been getting scared but that night fore I set to leave, mama come to me. She sayed, Not all free men are free

161

and not all slaves are in bondage. Home is where you know you got some love. Love to get and love to give. It ain't always a place much as it is the people. I was home when I was with you. Ain't mattered where that was. Long as you was there. So you carry me with you wherever you go. You carry everybody you love with you and you gon always be home and always have love. Can't nobody stop you from being free in your mind and heart. I'm always with you Ervin. Always have been and that ain't changing. God made me a promise and that mean he made you one too.

She looked like an angel. She was so pretty and I tried to reach out and touch her and hug her but I couldn't feel her the same. I feeled her but not the same. I wanted to feel her like when she was flesh not like an angel. She stepped back and smiled at me fore she took her leave and I waked up. Her pouch was laying under me, close. I ain't prayed really in a long time but I prayed that God see me through. I leaved it at that cuz I figured that covered everything.

Homebound

Nine years done passed since I last seed Reverend Matthew. He had four kids and that baby wasn't no baby. She was helping her mama out with the other ones. I told her last time I was there she was wee size and she said she ain't never met me before. I told her she ain't remember cuz she been a baby. She asked me what Philadelphia was like cuz the newspapers called it dangerous on account of the riots. Misses Clarke got better with her cooking and Matthew got bigger round the waist. It seem them two things goes together .

Girl asked me if I had a wife and kids. I told her I don't and she ask me why. I sayed cuz the Lord ain't see it fit. I ain't tell her no lie. The Lord ain't see me fit for it.

He was raising his kids up to be fair and just. He sayed he don't wanna make no more bad folks. Folks who can't see the love of God in another person or the beauty of God's creation in another person. He say he actually believe what's in that book he read, the Bible. I say some of it don't seem like he say. If it is, how he believe it? I told him how they use that same book to keep us in slavery. He say men will twist even God's words to serve their purpose but that don't mean God's word is changed. Just the men choose to change what it mean. He sayed, You have to see it with your heart Ervin.

Well Reverend Matthew, on account that I can't read, I'ma have to trust you on that.

I took to the floor in the back hall to sleep cuz now wasn't no place else to sleep. There wasn't no nightmares maybe on account of how much praying they do in that house. Fore day Misses Clarke praying and then fore breakfast and fore dinner and fore bed. Most talking I hear from her is talking to

God. Those kids bout the same. That girl even told me she pray that God see fit I have a wife and lots a children. I nodded and sayed, Thank you.

Ain't gon hurt her to do it and maybe it'll least keep off whatever got hold to me. Only Reverend Matthew got some other stuff to say, least round me. He talked about Rebekah and how God made her a promise bout Jacob but sometimes we as people get in the way of our own blessings, trying to force what shouldn't be forced and make things happen like we think they should stead of letting God's plan work.

He sayed I gotta trust the plan and don't be trying to sneak and do other stuff to rush it. I sayed to him I'm coming back this way cuz I snuck and that he sneaking too, right now. He nodded and sayed this was Godly work, correcting sins. That what Rebekah did was working against God, twisting what he sayed for what she wanted. He sayed there wasn't a need to do that.

There was still that promise mama sayed God had for me. About freedom and having something better for me and mine. All I had was me, wasn't nothing mine and I wondered how God's plan was gon work that out. Still it made me feel a little better knowing that even if I didn't understand it, there might be some plan to go with God's promise.

I felt peace there. Like the kind when you ain't fearful something gon happen or somebody gon do something. I sleeped not worrying nobody was gon come in and take nothing of mine. By time we leaved after church on Sunday night I ain't look as bad and my mind could make sense again. He had a set a bibles in the back and some drapes Misses Clarke and the church ladies made for another sister church near the North Carolina border to deliver. She made some boiled chicken and rice and packed it up for that next day and sent apples and meat wrapped in cloth. Rev sayed it would be a few days fore we really stop at someplace along the river and then get on a boat to take us the rest of the way down.

That's how we was gon travel and I remembered walking from Virginia long the river. Marching through to North Carolina. I ain't knowed then I was the only thing keeping mama alive. We riding under those stars and if I ain't survived

I'd be with her and Lilly and Ellie and Marcus. That made me smile cuz either way I'd be okay. Back home or back home. Rev tried to tell me I need to find my peace again. I done told him how God took everything away and he sayed, God restores what he takes.

I ain't say nothing back cuz I ain't wanna be rude but I don't believe that no more. God take and he ain't gotta follow no rules.

Reverend Matthews made a comment bout how Jefferson died more than fifteen years before and said all men were created equal. Then he sat quiet a bit fore adding he had about six hundred of his own slaves on three different plantations. I asked him how he say we equal and hold all those people in bondage. He sayed he wonder how we as a country say those same words and ain't made a move to free every person in bondage. He sayed, I do believe it'll happen. One day. It can't go on like this forever.

Rev, it gon take a whole lot more people like you, white folk, suh, cuz the problem ain't been made by us so it ain't gon get fixed by us either. Still I hope you right.

We was near the ocean. It smelled like too much salt but I knowed North Carolina was close then. We done stop two times. Next time we be close enough to get on that boat and then from there to the last stop with me and Reverend Matthew where we would ride on to the church he was leaving them bibles and drapes at. I be glad to get past Virginia. This whole way had too many ghosts hanging round. They ain't knowed how to get home so they was still doing what they been doing when they was living. We traveled sometimes at night and sometimes in the day. So long to go but I played the part, like him. I played like I'm his and he played like it too. Just what we knowed to do to get through. Specially further we got south. I forgot some bout how it was being down here after all that time up north. They talked different bout us. Like we not there. Invisible. Til they need us to do something then they talk at us like we dogs. Fetch this and that.

Stay low and keep my mouth shut. That's what I tried to do. We was almost to the port and dark was coming on us. Reverend Matthew ask me if I wanted to pull over or keep going. I ain't wanna stop there at night when we could make it the rest of the way. Sides he was a white man and wasn't nobody gon mess with us. We fed the horses and ate leathery meat and some grit patties with bacon juice. It's good when ain't much choice to it. If mama or even Misses Charlotte woulda made it that woulda been better but we ain't have no options.

We ate fast without even saying we needed too and then we set back off. I ain't like these parts. Coming or going. White folks been acting different since the thirties started. Since Britain ended slavery across the ocean and up in Canada. Like they knowed stuff going on and black folks ain't satisfied. They felt threatened cuz maybe we mighta stop doing what they want us to do. We was riding faster. I guess being close to the end of this leg made us feel urgent bout it. I wondered was God talking to Reverend Matthew cuz he was over there praying and looking nervous. His being nervous made me nervous. I ask him why he acting nervous and he sayed, I don't know Ervin. Something's not right. Pray with me.

I ain't tell him God don't hear me but I figured if it help him for me to pray, I'd pray and maybe whatever was bothering him would stop.

Lord grant us safe passage to the end of this journey. Grant Ervin safe passage back to John James in South Carolina. Let no harm come to either of us in the execution of your work. Protect and shield us from evil and cover us with your grace. Amen.

Amen, I sayed and looked ahead and to the side. Trying to believe that God heard us. Heard him. He had a better relationship so I let that be. We keeped going another hour or so by the looks of the moon in the sky when we heard another carriage coming towards us.

Reverend Matthew sayed, Be calm. Just folks making their way home.

I wasn't so sure.

We moved on like we was, til we seed their lanterns in the air. The night was already light but they wanted to see us good.

Who goes there!? A man with a deep voice called out from about thirty feet ahead of us.

Evening. I'm Reverend Matthew Clarke.

Where you headed to this time of night Reverend?

On my way to deliver bibles and drapery to a sister church up the way.

Uh huh. What church is that?

East Hanover Presbytery. Meeting Minister Atkinson.

That's that traveling preacher that pass out bibles?

Yes. That's the one. I've got a fresh stock for him so we can continue spreading the good word of Christ.

Mind if I take a look? We got a lot of traffic coming along the river way. Some folks smuggling property and stolen goods. We just need to be careful.

He held up some kinda badge in the light. Look same as the badge they let men of the law use to catch free black men. I look down to the side of carriage. Let Reverend do the talking.

This your nigra?

Reverend look over at me and nodded. Yes. He's helping me with the cargo and provides extra protection out here. Never know who might be trying to steal your cargo. Can't be too careful.

I see. He walked round back and lifted the dusty tarp. Three boxes was back there. He opened up one and picked through the stacks of bibles fore he opened up another. These feel like some fine drapes, he sayed.

The womens auxiliary group made them. They do fine work.

The man with the deep voice walked back to his horse and the other two men still sat up on their horses shining lights at us.

He fixed himself in the seat then sayed, This road can be a dangerous way to go. You got thieves looking to score, knowing merchants and men such as yourself are heading to the port. You'll want to be careful.

Yes. Thank you. I will.

You want us to ride with you the rest of the way?

My heart was beating fast. I ain't trust them not to take us over, grab me, and do whatever they wanted. Nobody but God and Reverend as a witness to the three of them.

I clenched my hands and it ain't get past Reverend.

That would be mighty kind of you, sir. We'd like to make sure we have safe passage.

I couldn't help but watch as the one with what look like a missing eye rode up to get behind us and the other beside us. Deep voice man rode up front. I prayed Reverend Matthew's prayers was heard and answered.

Charleston

When I was young mama sayed I'd always be home long as I keep love and God in my heart. I looked back at all the time I lived since she sayed that. We was on the way from Virginia to Charleston. She was so alive and even though we ain't have nothing but each other she had some kinda faith.

I thinked bout Marcus and William in Philadelphia. I thinked bout those meetings and what it mean to be free. I wanted freedom more than anything I wanted in my life besides my Lilly and my mama.

On the nights coming down the coast I couldn't hardly sleep. Thinking bout everybody. Mama, Lilly, Ellie, Marcus, even Mabel Ann and how I lead her on wasting her time. I thinked bout me and the daddy I never got to meet but mama sayed I looked like. I thinked bout my brother Ethan and my sister Greta and wondered if they was up in them stars looking down too. I was sad wasn't no way to be sure til I was up there. Then I thinked bout being up there and not studying this life no more and bout mama some more. She told me when I been young and Master John took me to play fiddle with him that I got something to live for and I can be free. She sayed to be smart and save my money and be free. The pouch she gave me was strapped to my waste, patched and stitched up over the years til it hardly look like the one she put on that table for me.

She was watching me.

Some of the way I let myself talk to God. I swore at him for cursing me and taking everybody I ever loved. I told him he's a son of a bitch. That if he loved me, any of us, he wouldn't let this happen. I told him I wasn't doing nothing for him, not so long as he keep it up. I sayed I can't serve a God they give me so I can be in bondage. I heard him though. Speaking back. Telling me that he love all us and keeps his promises. I ain't believe him cuz I ain't seed it yet. He sayed Moses never seen the promised land and I told him just like I feel. I ain't Moses. Let me see it. Let me see the promise you make. I ain't never knowed for sure whether it been a dream or real.

I seed Charleston lights shining on the shore. Only papers I had was fake and they was still in my shoe where I put it after getting on. Matthew made sure I put them right back after showing them and made a show bout somebody being there to get me in Charleston and all. My heart beat like it wanna come out my chest. My head was light and my stomach turn like it wanna let out what I last eat. Charleston by myself. I hoped he was gone be there when I got off that cargo ship. That he might recognize me after all that time. I was bigger and stronger than I was when I leaved at eighteen.

My stomach turn some more in circles, thinking bout what if he ain't there and they take me to market. Strong, healthy with skills like mine I'd never see a day a freedom again. Maybe Marcus and William was right.

The sun was starting to come up behind me and folks was putting out they candles and turning off the lanterns. I stood looking over the edge of that ship. My hands was shaking so I was holding on tight trying to be steady. I ain't knowed if something was gon come up or stay down.

You alright boy? One of the deckhands ask me cuz he thinking I'ma vomit on his ship. Says to keep my head over the edge til time to get off. I can't move. Even when the ship stop my legs and feet can't move.

I ain't talk to nobody I ain't have to on those waters. Like that merchant keep coming round trying to make conversation. Can't trust nobody - even other blacks whether free or slave so I keeped to myself. Now I was wishing I had one friend in case he wasn't at that port or somebody try to steal me right off the boat. Folks was getting off. I stood on that edge looking out. I ain't seed him. Master John wasn't nowhere I can see.

That merchant slow down walking past me to get off. You lost? Need some help? He holding his hat in one hand. Bag in the other like he got things to go bout doing.

No suh.

Well then you may want go head off the ship. Sure can't stay on less you pay passage or work. He laugh like something funny. You got coin for another ride?

I'm getting off suh. Just trying to see the person come to get me.

I waited for him to leave and then followed behind him slow. He looking back at me all the while. He put his hat back on and tip at me. The town done changed since I last seed it. I ain't knowed if the old shops was still there or if the men we did business with still run them. I keeped my head low and walked away heading left from the ship. I looking round the people trying not to look nobody in the eye but trying to recognize Master John. I couldn't see him nowhere and figured he musta change a lot too. That merchant man stop and turn to come toward me. I started walking to the old street I knowed. I ain't had nothing but my pouch and a small bag Reverend give me to hold some food and socks. All I wanted was to get someplace somebody knowed me. Where Master John might come looking for me fore too long pass and folks start asking questions.

That merchant man done start walking slow like he looking for something and gots all day long. He think I ain't seed him following me. Maybe he ain't care figuring wasn't nothing I could do. I can't speed up cuz then folks get scared and my papers ain't true. He started walking up faster behind me like he ain't up to no good. He stopped and talk to this man look like he ain't got steady work then they both started walking to me. I wanna walk faster but white people scared of a negro on the move. So I took longer strides and put my hands in front and open so they see I ain't got nothing to be fraid of. But them two getting closer. I still ain't see nothing I can get to.

I wished Master John had a been there right then and see me. Wish I woulda stayed back where I was longer or that I could stop and wait and be okay. But I done already leave the docks. They looked like they was hunting. Find me by myself and take me off somewhere. Take my money and put me on that block like I was when I was eight. I couldn't do that again. Twenty years and back in this damned city.

I ain't wanna keep walking where less people was. I stopped and turned back round. They was walking on the same side where I was walking and I cross to the other side and tried to get back near the docks. Maybe Master John done got there. I was walking trying to stay outta white folks way, keep my head down, and still see what they doing. I ain't come all this way to be caught by them. They done turn round too and walking toward me at a angle. I can't help but walk faster. I'm looking for Master John. Hoping he don't look so much different I don't know his face. I figured his head be all gray and his face with wrinkles and he likely put on more weight but I'd know his smile if he show it.

I remembered the gap between a couple shops. If I could get in there I'd run through and come back round to the docks. Ain't no way they catch me. I walk faster and turn ahead of them down the tiny alley wide enough for two men shoulder to shoulder. I took off running. I hear the merchant man with the hat call out, Where you running to boy? I just wanna talk.

I ain't stopping. Ain't answering.

I said where you running to? Nobody gonna hurt you.

I ran fast as I can through the other side and catch my breath. Wasn't nobody hardly back on this side of the buildings. Smelled like urine and dead mice. I hurried my way back toward the docks, praying Master John got there. I can't run no more cuz a black man running down the street might cause me never to see Master John. I walked quick like but not too quick cuz it ain't many folk but it's more than none. And I ain't had nobody with me. Lord please let him be there looking for me.

Next thing I knowed that raggedy one in front a me. Then the merchant man come up behind me. They push me to another little alley.

They standing too close.

I asked you a question, the merchant man sayed. Where you running to?

I was looking for somebody.

The merchant man nodded once with his head at the raggedy one and he hit me square in my gut. Got me balled over.

I was trying to catch my breath and he put his knee in my face, holding me by my collar. I feel blood running cross my lips but can't think bout that. I try to grab hold to his waist and push him down but the one with the hat hit me in the back of my head with that case be got and knock me down all the way. Wasn't no use in hollering for help.

Now you gonna stop getting smart. Why are you running nigger? You look like a slave trying to escape. You know what I do to niggers like you?

I ain't trying to escape. My voice was weak like I still ain't catch my air.

I ain't hear ya? Say you trying to escape? the merchant man mocked.

I sayed I ain't escaping. Looking for master.

Your master? In an alley? That's likely. Don't you think that's likely? He asked the raggedy one.

No. I don't think that's too likely. The raggedy one sayed and kick me in the stomach.

The merchant man stepped on my side with his boot. You want me to believe you running to meet your master. Well, where is he then?

He looked around like Master John gon be in that alley they pull me in. I hoped some white woman walk by the alley and maybe make them embarrassed so they let me up. Wasn't nobody coming by.

My mouth like cotton and I had to tense my hands to keep them open cuz I wanted to curl them up.

Yes suh. He's spose to meet me at the dock. He won't be happy to find me in this condition. Likely sue for damage to his property.

Why? We found you like this. We just trying to help you out. The merchant man looked around but ain't take his foot up. Both them blocking the way back to the street. From the ground the stench of urine was even stronger.

I think he lying. He ain't going to meet no master, the raggedy one sayed. His face turned up fore he spat down at me.

So if you looking for your master at the docks what brings you all the way over here? Where was you headed to?

Docks are that way. The merchant man pressed his boot deeper in my side.

Yes suh. I was headed back. I thinked he mighta been in one of the shops. I was just checking.

Uh huh.

You made me nervous following me. So I tried to leave.

You wouldn't get far if you was trying to run, the merchant man sayed.

Then the raggedy one asked, You believe him? I don't believe him. I think he trying to get away from his master and we caught him.

Hmmm could be. You trying to get away from your master?

No suh. I'm trying to get to him. We spose to go home.

Where's that?

Georgetown County.

What's his name? Maybe I know him.

I look up. Wasn't nobody paying no attention to what's happening. I wish somebody might stop and see me lying on the ground. A carriage went by and slowed a little fore it keep going. I was close enough to the end of the alley if anybody cared to find me.

What's his name nigger? Or are you lying like he think you lying? That hat man nod again to the raggedy man and he kick me in the ribs this time. He raggedy and strong. I grunted but they wasn't gon get me to cry out.

No suh. I ain't lying. Name is John James. He's a carpenter.

You know a John James, Robert? He asked the raggedy man.

I understood then. He done this before. Waiting on folks like me to get off by themselves and see who he could catch. I ain't know if he wanted a reward or to sell me. Either way I prayed Master John would show up. Anybody.

I don't know no carpenter by that name, the raggedy man answered. Could be a made up name.

The merchant man leaned over to get closer, looking over me as I tried to sit up.

An old cart bumping down the road pass by close and I looked inside hoping it be Master John. Wipe his face off and get him up, the hat man growled to that raggedy Robert. He talk to him like that I knowed he wasn't no good at all. Robert threw a dingy handkerchief at me then they both drag me to my feet. Wipe your face boy. Get that blood off. I reached up to wash my face and wince cuz it feel like he done crack something in my ribs.

Damnit nigger! I know you done had worse than this. He snatched the handkerchief and dragged it cross my face and neck. Now stand up straight.

I can't. My rib broke.

He said stand up straight less you want both ribs broke, raggedy Robert sayed. He ignorant and a brute.

I forced myself to pull up straight as I could though it felt like somebody was pressing pins in my side and scraping.

Merchant man sayed, Now walk. Ain't nobody coming for you and you know it.

I ain't done nothing wrong but they was gone make sure it look like I did. I ain't had no kinda chance making somebody believe me. Maybe they was right. Maybe he wasn't coming.

We was on the street again. They on each side. Another carriage came down but it keeped going and we was walking back to where folks was thinning out at the docks. Less folks mean I could see Master John better and he could see me. If he was there. Another carriage came down and they shove me further to the side.

The merchant man ask me how old I is and what kind a slave I am. I look him in the eye and sayed, I'm bout to be twenty-eight and I'm a carpenter. He laugh in my face, his spit hitting my lips so I wipe it off. I sayed, I am a carpenter. Trained by Master John James and he'll be here any minute to fetch me.

Well you better hope he come cuz they don't like niggers walking round these streets too long by themselves. You know, you get yourself into trouble that way. But don't worry. You got yourself two escorts now. He laughed like something funny again. Still, wasn't nothing funny.

Get his nose Robert. I could feel a slow drip hitting my top lip and seeping into my mouth. I hate the taste a blood.

The carriage coming down the road started slowing down as it got close so I look up. I wasn't sure but he looked like he was looking at me too. He stop and I falled down to my knees cuz Master John, older and fatter sitting in that carriage.

E? Master John sayed, and it never sound so sweet like that.

What are you doing with these men? What happened to you?

Oh, you know this one? We found him wandering like he was lost and look like somebody worked him over. He said he was looking for you, and we were just trying to help him out, get him back to the docks. The merchant man smiled like he'd done a favor.

I'm sure. Master John got out and helped me in the carriage.

Thank you for your aid. I hope the good Lord delivers swift justice on whoever did this to him.

The raggedy man sucked on his teeth like he was mad I got away. The merchant man sayed to Master John, Keep an eye on that one. I think he might be a little slippery. Not usual for a nigra to be walking by himself just get off a ship.

Why would he be running if he just got off a ship bound for Charleston? That seems mighty backwards, Master John sayed smart.

Could be he ain't the brightest. I'm just glad I found him. In his condition this could've been worse if he'd been left alone. Seem our assistance is worthy of a reward. Wouldn't you say? merchant man asked Robert.

I'm sure the Lord will give you your due. Good day, gentlemen.

Master John ain't wait for them to say nothing else fore he pop the whip and sped up leaving them on the side of the road. I looked back and the merchant man got his hat in his hand and they walking apart from each other.

I was still wincing when Master John finally slowed down. He done went round the block back where I been walking fore I turn around. He stopped in front of the watchmaker shop. I knowed if I had a keeped going I woulda find something familiar and he woulda find me. He stopped the carriage. I

176

wanted to hug Master John but I couldn't. Not then. Not there. Not in my condition. He pat my hand and all I could do was sit there trying not to breathe too deep.

I'm sorry I was late E. These horses are getting old and so am I. Neither of us are fast as we once was. I'm so sorry. Those men back there. I should've left earlier to account for the time. He looked at my face fore he stared off down the street. Won't happen again.

I thinked how easy it woulda been for me to get stolen and be gone.

I know you're in no condition for it but I gotta drop off a couple things here then we'll ride by the doctor and see if he'll fix you up. I wanted to jump out and help like I used to but I couldn't move without it feeling like somebody stabbing me.

I turn my head and see Master John pull back the tarp like we used to do. He tell me how he made watch cases. Lined them with velvet. He came round to show me one like we always showed each other what we done and was proud of. The watchmaker's emblem was engraved on the front and the top and he made it so the top folded with a hinge so he could pull it back without taking up all the top space. I smiled. Greenland ain't had nothing on Master John. I sayed, That's real nice Master John.

Mister Jennings seed Master John outside with me in the carriage and come out acting like he shocked to see me. Ask when I got back and I told him just today. Then he see me good and ask what happen.

Accident on the cargo ship, Master John sayed fore changing the talk to the watch cases. Master John wasn't gon let there be a lot of chit chat bout it. He ask Mister Jennings to help carry the second box. Guess he wasn't up for answering questions bout me being gone and back again. I was alright with that since it wasn't nobody business but ours.

The doctor fix me up and I got to rest the better part of two weeks, mostly doing things I ain't need to stand for and didn't take too much strength. We was in that workshop then, like we used to do and he sayed, If Halley's comet can come back in my lifetime and that's something I didn't think I'd see when I was young, then so could you. I kept that faith. Just like folks ain't got that comet figured out they don't need to have you or us figured out either.

I reckon he was right.

It wasn't long after that when I was moving round right again he and Misses Charlotte start talking bout getting my life back in order and finding a wife and having babies. Lawd.

Georgetown

Like it was yesterday and I ain't been all them years. That's how it was with me and Mister John. He payed me for my work and I saved my money. We faked like we had to for appearances cuz folks round there wouldn't get me being free. Not even allowed hardly. Gotta get the legislature to say a slave can get freed and only if they can prove they can survive without a master. Wasn't nothing me or Mister John could do bout that. I tasted freedom and it forever inside me and Mister John knowed it. He sayed I'm different but it ain't bad. I sayed he different too and not just round the waist and he smile and nod then pat his belly.

Knowing you made me a better man Ervin.

I told him the same was true for me. Then he told me I don't need to worry bout running off trying to be free cuz this world was moving some place dangerous. Sayed folks was getting nervous and he thinked they gon make it even harder. I can't imagine them making it no harder, but seem like white folks come up with all manner a schemes to get what they want and keep what they gots.

Me and Mister John, we maked beautiful music and furniture together. Folks was so happy I was back and we ain't hardly been able to rest for folks wanting us to play. I played happy. I wasn't dead no more inside like I been in Philadelphia. I ain't feel like I ain't got nothing or nobody. I wasn't alone no more. Even Misses Charlotte change. That night we got back it was late but she them biscuits was still warm, made like mama showed her. She made me rice and stewed chicken and even took out the little bones. She asked me if I wanted cornbread

179

too. I told her I did, even though she already filled my plate full. I ain't wanna upset her by not eating what she gave me.

She held that big plate and sit it down at the table and told me to sit. I looked at her and Mister John. I ain't never sat to eat at the table in all the time I was there and so I ain't sit down at first.

Then she said E, please sit. A lot has changed in here. Maybe not out there, but in here it has. You are welcome in this house, our house. You deserve to live like a man and I'm not going to take that right away from you or cause you indignity. God wouldn't like that. I sat down and she sayed I looked taller but I look like I don't eat enough. Truth is I didn't. I couldn't hardly eat these past couple months. Not with everything. Maybe even the year been rough. Food ain't been that important.

That been three months past. I see Misses Shelly when she come to visit with the baby or what was. She the only one at home now. She ain't get no prettier. Still ain't got no lips and her eyes beady. I hoped she get a husband. She done got another woman in to help her how mama did. Miss Annie is what I call her. She like it when I call her Miss, say she like it cuz it make her feel young and special, but she old, like a grandma. She don't move so fast but she ain't got much to do but pick up after three people. One ain't hardly there still. But Misses Shelly don't even seem to miss him none. She and Susanne got they business going good and that girl help her mama with everything my mama used to help with. Misses Shelly act scared to talk to me bout mama. We both miss her. She asked me when I came back how it was being lent out up north. Sayed she'd never heard of nobody doing that for so long but at least the debt was paid. I ain't sayed nothing. Figured Mister John and Misses Charlotte had they stories and those was my stories. No reason to make it nothing but what they sayed. They debts was paid. To me and to God. I can't say the same for Misses Shelly. She ain't seem to see things no different. Stead when she come around we gotta act like we used to.

The one time her husband Daniel come round I like to knock a tooth out if I coulda got away with it. He ain't been there ten minutes and ask me how it was up north. I told him I worked hard as a carpenter. He sayed you mean a carpenter's apprentice or assistant. I sayed yes, apprentice. Damn lie. I wasn't no damned apprentice. I was better than anybody in that town but I couldn't tell him that. He shook his head and pat me on my shoulder then sayed, If you wasn't a negro you'd be a good man. Too bad God cursed your people. But you'll rise in glory like all God's children. You're fortunate to have my brother in law and sister in law to oversee you.

Alls I could think of is he shouldn't be saying nothing bout God or being a good man or that I'll rise up in glory cuz God gon cut him down and likely never see him when he sitting in the pits of hell. A man like him, never home probably got two or three families. I can't say yes suh or nothing else cuz I ain't speaking in agreement to that lie. I'm a good man and ain't nobody telling me no different. Mister John look at me then at him and sayed, you know how you're born has nothing to do with the quality of man you are. Shelly husband sayed, Sure it does. Don't you agree E? I looked at Mister John and Charlotte jumped in and say she made some apple pie just like Ellie used to make and asked me to get it from the kitchen. She sayed to make sure I grab me and Annie some too.

Me and Miss Annie eat and talk together whenever they came over. She help me bring the pie back on the little plates and then we step back to the kitchen and eat our pie in there. Just like mamas. Misses Charlotte learned well. Miss Annie would tell me bout all that's going on since she helped Misses Shelly at the market sometime and served when she did her ladies parties. She hear stuff that should make a woman blush but she ain't seem to care. She say bout anything come to her mind when she ain't round Misses Shelly.

I ain't wanna get too close to her though. Not to nobody else. I figured I'm needed right there cuz Misses Charlotte ain't got no help. Neither do he. Not regular anyway. Sayed he pay for some slaves to come and he pay them and their master cuz that was fair. He sayed he ain't suffering the curse of cheating God by cheating man. I told him it was the right thing to do.

Misses Charlotte still ain't all better but she better than when Mister John told me bout her being sick. She ain't seem to be in too bad a way, not like mama been. Besides the doctor

181

come by every month to see bout her and give her whatever medicine she need. That be why Mister John work so hard. Cuz the doctor costs.

I was glad it was winter and that mean we just gotta do our carpentry and music. Come spring we'd have enough planting to do to keep busy but he done cut back on the farm. I asked him if he growed enough to get through the winter and he sayed with just two of them it been plenty. He wanted to plant more in the spring with me being there. He looked at me and sayed they needed to put some pounds on me.

I told him I ain't trying to get fat where I can't get around. He laughed like it was too late for him. He ain't that fat. Just his belly hanging over his britches some. I told him he need to think bout not having a third helping at dinner every night.

He shrug up his shoulders. Since Charlotte learn to cook some things like your mama, E, I can't stop eating.

I likely woulda been fat too.

Martha

Winter turn to spring and spring to summer and fall and back round again time and time again. Moons and seasons and crops and fiddle and furniture. We got our rhythm and our way and it wasn't the same and was the same all at once. It irked me that I couldn't be open and free. Not here. But that kinda free was what I had. It came with a cost like any kinda free. In my years I learned there ain't nothing free bout freedom. You gon work for it, earn it, fight for it, or die for it one way or the other.

Mister John start pressing me harder bout being a man and not being by myself. Sayed he wanna help me put a little house in the back of the property if I want it. Sayed I could live there with my family. Teach my son to be a carpenter or a farmer or whatever I want. Maybe Misses Charlotte can teach her some of my mama's recipes.

I ain't wanna tell him it wasn't my dream to live back of him. If I was gon have a little house I wanted it on my own piece of land. Ain't had to be much, just mine. Maybe a wife might be alright if she the right one is what I tell him. He laugh every time I sayed it, but I ain't making no fun. Thing is wasn't no right one. Not since Lilly. All these girls looking at me like I got some answer for them. Whispering bout me. I knowed it. Talking bout how Mister John pay me and I was buying my freedom one day. They ain't knowed the truth and it wasn't they business. What we had going was working for me and I ain't need nobody to go messing it up.

Folks already been talking bout why I was still single after all this time. They knowed bout me being widowed but figured it was time I move on. They been saying it since I'd been back a year and ain't stopped and a few years had done passed. Some of them wondered if I like men, some wonder if I got injured up north. If they did something to me. But I just ain't wanna be bothered with getting involved in that way. The one girl I did see regular was a secret and really for only one reason. She was pretty too. Not like Lilly but in her way. I figured she ain't want nothing more then what she had and so I settled for getting what she could give. We was both satisfied with the arrangement, least that's what I thinked til Mister John ask me my intentions. I realize then she been talking cuz her master come asking Mister John bout me. She done messed up a good thing.

She wasn't a girl I planned to marry and I wasn't gon use up no more of her time. I told Mister John we wasn't talking no more on account of differences of opinion about some core beliefs about life. He look at me strange and then nodded cuz he remembered how his brother-in-law sayed that a couple weeks ago about some business he had over near the southern edge of South Carolina. Then he been at home a little more for the next week or so fore disappearing again.

That week we had service for all the black folks outside cuz the weather was getting nice. The girl I been seeing ain't come. Probably on account of me. Her sister was there giving me an evil eye when I come up and sit down.

I ain't knowed it was gon stop that day. The whole world. It just did. I wasn't ready for it. Mister John laugh at me for two full weeks afterwards cuz of how I acted.

That day in church the traveling minister came over from north part of Marion and his daughter came long with him.

Martha

My daddy knew the good book better than most folks who could read. At least the parts that was important for black folks to learn. He preached what our master let him preach to help our people to have faith and to be obedient. Our rewards

184

was waiting in heaven for a life lived well and in service here. I believed what he said. Every word. He preached it at home and in other people's churches.

Mama didn't get to come with us but I went with him to aid our mistress. When daddy wasn't preaching he was helping the master out with whatever business he had in whatever town we went through. I got to meet all manner of people, white folk and black folk. All wanting to get a little closer to heaven. It was warm when we showed up in Georgetown. Warm for mid March, but it's like that in South Carolina. Hot as fish fried in a barrel. Traveling to these places like this I get to see us in our Sunday best, clean and with the feeling of almost freedom for just one day. I traveled with daddy to farm towns and big plantations. Some weeks he speak to rooms of ten and other weeks to rooms of two hundred. Folks in the back can't hear but they gotta be there or in their quarters since somebody gotta account for them during church time.

When I came that day with daddy to Georgetown, he was there. Sitting in the back row. High cheekbones and full lips. Kind eyes. Smart eyes. He seen me looking at him and I sat down in the front row quick before somebody else noticed. Four white men leaned up against the church, their arms folded looking round at us. They was studying the women like we wasn't there for God. Unholy eyes like they wasn't leaned up against God's house. I didn't want them studying me. All through church I wanted to look back. I could feel him looking at the back of my head. I wondered how my hair looked up under my bonnet.

Daddy called me up to sing the song I always sang before he finished up the service. Something to remind our people to keep hoping and looking forward to freedom that don't end, everlasting freedom with God. Least that's all it meant to daddy. It meant more to me. Freedom shouldn't have to wait til I was dead. Til any of us was dead.

I sang I can't stay behind! Then the church sang
I can't stay behind, my Lord
Dere's room enough, Room enough,
Room enough in de heaven, for you
Room enough, Room enough,

We sang together I can't stay behind.

I been all around, I been all around,
Been all around de Heaven, my Lord.
I've searched every room--and Heaven all around
De angels singin'--all around de trone.
My Fader call--and I must go.

Shout back, member
I can't stay away!
Shout back member
I can't stay away!

O, my mudder is gone! My mudder is gone!
My mudder is gone into heaven, my Lord!
I can't stay behind!
Dere's room in dar, room in dar.
Room in dar, in de heaven, my Lord!
I can't stay behind.
Can't stay behind, my dear,
I can't stay behind!

O, my fader is gone!
O, de angels are gone!

O, I'se been on de road! I'se been on de road!
I'se been on de road into heaven, my Lord!
I can't stay behind!
O, room in dar, room in dar,
Room in dar, in de heaven, my Lord!
I can't stay behind![11]

The church sang with me and outside we keep our own time, clapping and tapping. I seen him back there with tears in his eyes as I got to the end and he didn't want nobody to see. In that back row couldn't nobody see him. Nobody paying him no mind. But I see him. I see him crying, even if just a little.

I wonder how much he wanna be free too. How much he wanna be home.

Ervin

She done come here. Tall and strong with a big wide smile. When she opened those round lips to sing she turned into a pretty songbird. Singing about going to heaven. Way she was looking and singing wasn't like no peaceful songbird. She was strong in her voice. It was full and rich and throaty. Made me wanna shout back when she sayed to. Made me wanna sing when everybody else did. Made me wanna clap even if that song pain me. I ain't feel like that in a long time.

The spring breeze kick up dust and made it get all in our eyes and mouth. She probably thought I was crying but I ain't had time for tears. They don't do no good it seem. Nobody care none if I cry or stay dried up from the inside. It ain't matter if none of us cry. But I could listen to her sing and my heart feel a bit a something.

Church end and everybody went to talk to her and her daddy. They was surrounded for least twenty minutes hugging and greeting and talking. I could see her lips saying thank you over and over. I wanted to talk to her too but so many folks been up there and I ain't want them talking bout who I was talking to. I let folks wander back to they little gossip circles and I waited by the back row of seats even though the men done start picking up the chairs. I know they thinked me strange. But they so content and the ones who ain't, ain't talking neither. I can't tell them bout my years of freedom or coming back to be a slave under a master who treat me like a man. They ain't gon understand that song mean something different to somebody like me. Too many I love in heaven.

And what's your name?

I look up from the stick I done start whittling and that peachy color dress standing there in front of me. I been scared to look in her face cuz she might see too close in my eyes. How she get there without me knowing? I look at the bow on her shoulder, white with blue in it. I figured it been a dress her mistress passed to her. Too nice for a slave otherwise.

Ervin.

I'm Martha, Ervin. I looked around. She talking to me without her daddy around. I still ain't look straight at her. She come up to me and striking up a conversation without no shame. And at the church.

I said I'm Martha.

Nice to meet you ma'am. I sayed and bob my head a little.

I noticed you seemed moved by the song I sang today.

It was uh...it was nice. You got a real nice voice, I sayed.

Thank you. Were you back here singing?

I ain't really know the song, but I sang a little with everybody else. Easy enough to catch on.

She smiled then. That smile. She had them pretty teeth slavemasters try to steal when they teeth go bad. I was surprised they let her be out here instead of back home making babies. That was worth more than seeing after a mistress. Any old slave woman could do that.

How old you is? I asked her.

Twenty-three.

And you ain't got no husband or no children yet?

I almost did but he – she stopped and look around at the two men still standing against the church looking at us. Should we talk out of the way?

It wasn't even a question. She start walking off soon as it came from her lips. Then she look behind her to see if I was coming too.

I looked at the folks looking at us. Mister John was talking to some other men by the carriage. He done notice me too. He likely seen the sweat forming cuz of my nerves. They sayed I ain't cursed but wasn't nothing to prove otherwise yet.

How bout under that tree? She started walking to the weeping willow on the other side of the church and I walk slow behind her, keeping a couple steps back. I ain't want nobody talking bout nothing.

Why you so nervous Ervin?

I ain't nervous. Just don't want your daddy or nobody thinking I'm doing nothing untowards.

As I was saying I was about to get married but he got sent away. Not just another nearby plantation. All the way to Tennessee. Given as a gift to my mistresses sister. Wedding gift.

There was pain in her eyes too.

How old are you? Martha asked me.

Thirty two.

And you ain't got no wife or kids? She asked like she really wanted to know, not just cuz she looking for a husband.

No. I ain't got neither. You find out soon enough I'm widowed. Lost my wife and children.

Oh. I'm sorry. I didn't mean to pry.

Ain't nothing for you to be sorry for. You ain't do nothing.

My master and mistress coming here to look at buying some land. We come through here regular but this the first time daddy got to preach when you was here.

I looked away cuz I ain't usually come to church when we had the traveling minister. Everybody was always in your business. If I could stay away and work in the shop I'd do that but Misses Charlotte insisted I go to church with them and she sayed I should go to the negro service today. She insisted.

I looked over and she with Mister John and they was both looking at me. They done set me up.

Martha

He don't act like he want nothing. Not from me. Not from anybody. He seem content by himself but I don't believe it. God didn't make us to suffer this life alone. No partner. No help. Misses Charlotte must not of told him about me like I was told about him but it was okay. We both had things we needed to do. Things we wanted.

I need a husband proper whether I'm free or not and whether he is. Don't neither of us need to be alone and we'd be good together even if he don't know it yet.

Misses Charlotte made a fuss to my mistress about having dinner at their place, like it ain't already been planned. They was doing it on Ervin's account.

Looks like we'll get to know each other some better after all, I said to him before walking over to my daddy. He looked a little curious but still didn't say much.

Ervin

Now I understood about that other girl. They was just trying to see if it was serious fore they brought this songbird in. She like them sirens John told me about. Gon distract me.

I got in the cart and Misses Charlotte tell me I can ride with Martha if I want to but I don't wanna sit tween her and her preacher daddy so I tell her I'ma ride back with them.

Martha look disappointed. She probably ain't expect me to say no but that was the best thing. She ain't really knowed bout me and the curse I likely still got.

The evening seem long and short at once. I sat eating with Martha and her daddy. He wanting to talk about God and I ain't wanna talk about that and what I wanna talk bout, I can't with him here. I was curious about her too. She'd done come all that way and went through all that trouble to meet me and her daddy thinked it was okay too. Mister John and Misses Charlotte too. Ain't nobody asked me nothing. I ain't surprised. They knowed I ain't been serious bout nobody since I got back and Mister John been trying to see who I might take a liking to but it ain't been nobody yet. He figured he and Charlotte could make a match with this songbird. Lawd know she been prettier than a flower in April but I ain't understand why she had to come all that way and I wanted to know if her master really buying land here or just looking. If she wasn't really coming wasn't no need to bother. But if she really was gon be there, maybe. Maybe.

Her daddy seemed content just like he is. I sayed to them I spent time in Philadelphia and he ask why anybody wanna be in that dirty and dangerous place. He heard about the riots and sayed we all need to settle down and respect our places. I looked at Martha and knowed she ain't think the same but I couldn't get to where she was or where she might be trying to go with him keeping such a trained eye on her.

Sir, would it be alright if me and Martha walk round the farm? I can show her what we're putting in this year.

I'd like to see what you're planting too.

Daddy, perhaps you can walk behind us so Ervin and I can talk. He frowned up his face and ain't try to hide it at all.

Whatever either of you got to say you can say in front of me. You can show both me and her the farm. I push back my seat and then pull hers back too so she can stand before we start walking ahead of her daddy. At first we ain't say much, but then she ask me bout Philadelphia and being free and the light that catch in her eye made my whole world stop.

Me and Martha

I done talked to Mister John and Misses Charlotte and they both knowed how scared I was. Misses Charlotte told me she a good woman and it's time. Mister John told me I'm a good man and I'll do right by her. I hoped they was both right. She turn my world round and everything I ain't never knowed I wanted, I wanted. Six months of her coming there with her daddy but it wasn't til the third time her daddy finally let me walk her round the property without him trailing us by a man's length. I sneaked a kiss that day and it was like fresh butter on warm bread. I never wanted it to stop and she told me I got nice lips. Soft. If I was pale I mighta blushed. I held her hand and we walked and talked til her master sayed it was time to go cuz dusk would be there soon and he ain't wanna be riding at night. Those Sundays went too fast and a month between was too long.

Last time they come Mister John and her master sat in the living room talking quiet and they was whispering. I sat with Martha in the nook I used to eat in as a kid. Bigger table in there with a seat for two. Martha sat where mama used to sit and where Miss Annie sit when she come. I know Miss Annie think I done forgot about her on Sundays when Martha here, but I can't please all the ladies and like she sayed before, I ain't getting no younger. She ain't had no reason to worry. She knowed I always come by after they gone. She get lonely over there in that house with just the youngest girl and Misses Shelly.

But Martha done changed things.

Ervin, she sayed, you like to keep it all to yourself. Ain't no need to hold it all yourself anymore. That's why you got me. That's why we got each other. Ain't no more loneliness you gotta feel.

That was what Martha told me the month before I ask her if she be my wife. Last time before that we was walking and I wanted to tell her I was nervous, that maybe I was cursed, and she might wanna think bout finding another man to marry. Stead I ain't say nothing cuz I ain't wanna scare her off. I wanted to keep her and I knowed it was selfish to not tell her the truth about me being cursed but maybe for once God was gonna give me something good. If I ain't say nothing bout being cursed maybe the curse could just stay away and we both be okay. Maybe even Marcus had been right and I wasn't cursed and this could prove it.

Martha could tell I was hiding something and that's when she sayed it. I told her she the best thing that happened to me that whole decade and the decade was bout to end. I ain't wanna start the new one without her. When she leaved I told Master John I wanna go with her to north Georgetown county where she live. He ask me how I'm a work and I told him I can split my time. Be with him in the week and with her on the weekends. Have to live in two places but it be worth it to see her more than once a week and to keep making money like we make. I ain't gon get that kinda coin myself near Peedee river and Yahany. All they doing is planting rice and I swore I wasn't planting no rice if I can help it. Bout anybody who a slave round here working rice patties if they on a real plantation. Godawful break ya down work. I told Mister John he just hold my workbench and table and I be there and when planting time come I'll be there. I earn my way working long side him.

He ask me if I was sure I ain't wanna build a house right there. I could be safe with my children and family and buy Martha's freedom more easy. But Martha had family where she been. Lots a family and friends and her mama and daddy specially. She sayed she be heart broken if she had to leave and I understand being heartbroken. Mister John understand too so we make a plan for me to take ole Yancey back and forth. He been the oldest gelding but he was steady, even if he was slow.

It be worth it though to ride on up to my Martha on a Saturday morning or Friday afternoon and see that smile and those bright eyes looking at me. It be worth it to hear her humming and singing like she do and seem like ain't no cause.

She just catch a tune and it come out. And she can cook. Ain't nothing like a woman can cook. And she ain't been stuck with none of them regular rations of cornmeal and greasy pork fat. She been the mistress favorite so she get stuff from the main house and sleep up in that house too, for now. Getting some favor in this life was all some of us could ask for.

She ain't sayed it but I think she might be a little like my sister Greta. Not directly but something like it. Don't matter to me - she ain't free. Her master sayed we can build a little house on the land to live in cuz he can't have slaves off property out there. He knowed I belong to Mister John so he ain't spose to ask me to work at his house too less he paying cuz I had to pay rent to him. Mister John done ask about buying Martha freedom and he sayed maybe, it be up to the misses. I figured them misses don't be giving up nothing less they want it gone or they heart change for some reason don't nobody understand but them. I never did get it but I likely wasn't spose to get it. Get them. None of them. Not even Martha.

Since that wasn't gon happen no time soon I had to make it official so we could see each other regular and right. Her daddy ask me if I was ready.

When I was with Martha I feeled like a man all the way again like I had some peace in my soul. I ain't thinked I'd ever wanna get married again and give my heart to somebody and take the chance of God hurting it again. But she made me wanna try.

So we did. Mister John and Misses Charlotte and me rode up to where they farm was. We got married in the little chapel her master got on the plantation. It was right around the harvest moon in September. Fall just come in and the sky was clear and some of the heat done broke. That plantation remind me of the one where I was born. Big with overseers and lots more slaves. Wasn't hardly no joy there. But that day we celebrated with her mama and daddy and her brothers and sister and cousins. I wondered how long they family been there for her to have so much.

She sayed, This ain't all my family. This just what's left and some of them here ain't family by blood, just by luck.

Her master gave me one rule bout living there. I was told I couldn't talk about going to Philadelphia or being hired out all those years and I need to stay away from the other men. I'd say yes to anything he ask if it meant Martha and me could be together. I sayed yes to him and yes to her daddy bout taking her for my wife and I planned to keep her til death made us part.

I kissed her like I ain't want her to get no other breath cept from me. And she laugh after, embarrassed before we jumped over that broom Mister John carved out of a light chestnut and put our initials in. I guess Mister John just wanna give me something he made with his own hands and Misses Charlotte tied dried birch twigs to the handle. I told him it was too fancy to be sweeping up the floor with and he sayed we can put it up on the wall after we married and when the house get built. Wasn't a big rush since we was staying with Martha mama and daddy and her younger brother in they little house. We still jumped it after her mama waved it over our heads to keep away anything bad and give us good luck and a good marriage. Martha later told me the same thing I told Mister John. It been too nice to sweep the floors with so we planned to do what Mister John sayed and put it on the wall. I'd fix her up another broom for everyday.

We danced to Mister John's fiddle under that big moon and that night the world been alright.

Family

Her mama and daddy and her brother stayed at her aunt's cabin that night. Sayed we needed the place to ourselves and some privacy. I ain't argue a second cuz it been time. I ain't want it to but Lilly cross my mind like she did when I wasn't even looking for her to. I remembered our wedding night all those years ago and how long it been to finally make my way back round again. But I was happy. Finally. And Martha and me was gon do things we ain't told nobody else bout. Our secret dreams and talks bout what we was gon do with our family and for our family when we bought our freedom. Where'd we live since we couldn't stay in South Carolina if we got free.

I told her we should go way north and she think we should go west. I sayed, Ain't nothing out there but them Indians Jackson marching cross the land. She sayed, We can make something out there. A place for us and our family Ervin.

I hated leaving her come the start of the week. Sundays was hard cuz it mean I had to get back on that horse and head south for the week. But if we was gon buy her freedom, I had to work. It wasn't bout buying my freedom cuz I ain't had to pay for mine but her master wasn't like Mister John. They think it alright to keep all them people as property. Chattel.

I knowed folks was struggling more with money cuz they was stretching out accounts and orders was less than before. So they seed us slaves like we was notes in the bank, holding us like we gon pay off one day. They sayed it was bad on account of that President they call Martin Van Ruin. Why they mess with that man name like that? But couldn't nobody tell what they stand for on stuff important to me, like slavery. They was scared to take a stand, I figured. More worried bout power than what's right. Mister John put it that way too. He sayed he was gon vote for sure now that bout every white man coulda vote. Sayed he was gon vote like he been voting for me and Misses Charlotte too. We just had to wait and see what happen the next year.

Mister John was getting old and Misses Charlotte still suffered from whatever took her down when I been up in Philadelphia. But she teached piano still and by then she been teaching the kids of those kids who she teach when I was young. She tried to teach me when I come back and I told her I ain't had time or give her other reasons. Finally she asked me why I really ain't never wanna learn piano and I told her cuz you gotta be stuck inside playing and I ain't like being stuck inside. You take a fiddle anywhere. I told her how my fiddle seen its way to Philadelphia and back. I couldn't do that with no piano. She couldn't argue with that and stop asking.

It was near Christmas and for some reason I start thinking bout mama. The sweet potato pies she'd make and sell for holiday parties and when they'd go do they shows. I swore I smelled them. Sometimes ladies show up for them parties cuz they knowed her pies was gon be there. I wanted some of that sweet potato pie. The cinnamon and nutmeg smell up the house cuz she'd be baking all day and night long when I come to visit. Didn't feel like Christmas without them pies.

Mama still rested back in them woods and I visited her to talk. I ask her how she like Martha and if Lilly and Ellie and Marcus was doing alright. I ask her if she still feel good and if anybody else we knowed done come to join her. I told her bout Miss Annie cuz she getting old and ain't doing so good. Told her to look out for her in case she came up there. I talked bout how Misses Shelly don't ask her to do nothing she ain't decide to do herself and even then Misses Shelly tell her to sit down. I think she been scared Miss Annie gon die right there in the middle of sweeping the floor or washing clothes. It ain't help that Miss Annie done went blind in one eye so she was always missing something and bumping into things.

I told mama Misses Shelly try to tell Miss Annie to rest cuz wasn't nothing they need so bad but Miss Annie ain't hardly know what to do with herself but work like she been working all her life. She ain't had no family and only time she see friends was Sunday or if Misses Shelly come this way with her. That been the only time I got to see her but Misses Shelly told Mister John cuz she ain't know what to do with her. That Miss Annie was a stubborn old girl who wouldn't sit down even when she got the chance.

I told mama this cuz I knowed it woulda make her laugh thinking bout Misses Shelly trying to get somebody to do less work, rather than more. I told mama about me and Martha plans and what we gon do with our freedom. I wondered who she think was right - me or Martha, north or west. She wouldn't care either way if it mean me being happy.

I let her know one more thing I ain't whisper to nobody cuz even though it been almost three months I was scared. Scared to speak it and curse it. I told her bout Martha being with child and I prayed she help Martha and my baby. Only ones who knowed sides me and Martha was Martha mama and likely her daddy. I sat there on that ground a while waiting for her. Waiting to feel her hand on mine, hear her muffled laugh, or for her let me know she heard me. I bow my head down missing her and the gentlest breeze come through them trees, like to kiss my cheek. I looked up cuz I feeled her but wasn't nobody there.

Then I told her I still waiting on the promise cuz I hated our baby was gon be a slave cuz Martha a slave. Even if Mister John handed me my papers that same day it wouldn't change nothing for them. But I was gon have another chance at a family even scared as I been.

Mister John had three grandbabies, all girls. He reckoned it was gon be that way cuz if Priscilla had more she likely wouldn't make it. I told him she best not have no more then cuz those three she got need they mama. She done turned out nice, like her mama and daddy. She got a lady to help her in the house with them children but they payed her too. Mister John sayed he had a good long talk with Priscilla and her husband bout it and they see his way on the matter. Thing is here ain't no black folk free hardly so they gotta hire out somebody else slave. I told him like I seed it. It better than the other way and that slave get some money and might can buy they freedom one day.

Then I started thinking bout Lilly again and Philadelphia and being free. How I ran up there when I been eighteen only to be back in the same place I been. Fourteen years done passed since. I was gon be a daddy but this time I wasn't gon be alone. I had her family and Misses Charlotte and Mister John and Miss Annie. I hoped Miss Annie stay long enough to see this baby come to the world. But I wasn't telling none of them til that baby take a breath, cry, and decide to stay. I done made up my mind that my babies decided they ain't wanna stay before.

They got they first whiff of this world and changed they mind. They souls turned round. I couldn't make sense of it no other way. This one though was gon stay. They was gon get to see they mama and daddy and grandmama and grandpappy and all that family. They wasn't gon be coming into the craziness that was Philadelphia. Wasn't no wars going on. They couldn't trade slaves from Africa no more. Over in Britain they made it against the law and last year they got rid a some of them apprentices they was holding. That mean tides was changing. My baby was gon wanna see that new world. I wanted to see it too. Maybe in my baby lifetime it be over, this peculiar institution, as Mister John called it.

Like I sayed it been round Christmas so Mister John and me got a turkey at the market. That's what we joke about when Misses Charlotte asked us how we got one. We wasn't hunting men, so that's how we did it. The house was full so it mean me and Misses Annie was at our little table in the back. Even if she tried to be ahead of her time, Misses Shelly still wasn't gon outright break the rules and definitely not her husband. I ain't been sure bout Priscilla's husband. Maybe if it just been them over.

We ate just as good though. Same food as they had, just to ourselves. Sweet potatoes Misses Shelly made long with green beans with bacon juice. We had white rice and the turkey and cranberries and cooked apples with cinnamon. That musta been what I smelled making me think of the sweet potato pie. I stayed with Misses Charlotte and Mister John Christmas Eve here and soon as the sun start to light up the sky I got on the horse to get back for Christmas with Martha. Night before I gave Miss Annie a spool of yarn so she could sit down and have something to do. I figured that why she ain't hardly sit. And she couldn't help Misses Shelly with the cutting and sewing on account a being halfway blind and her hands wasn't still.

Miss Annie been so stubborn. Everybody sayed she need to rest some cuz she ain't gotta do nothing no more. Ain't nobody asking her to do nothing but sit down and rest. Only thing she might gotta do is make food and even that she ain't have to do all the way by herself cuz they ain't want her with no knife in the kitchen. I sayed if she wanna make some pretty things with that yarn she can do that. That'd be enough. She grab my hand, sayed, I love you Ervin. I wish I'da had a son or grandson like you.

I love you too. If you want I be your grandson.

She sayed, I like that very much E. Call me grandma Annie stead a Miss Annie. I like that a lot.

Yes, ma'am, grandma Annie, I told her. I wish we ain't wait so long for that. I coulda done with a grandma long ago.

God, Please

Martha was big and round. Some sayed she been carrying like it's a boy but I think it's a girl. Can't say why. Just do. I done load up the horse with a little cart behind it to carry wood and tools and had it at our place so I could work and be close to Martha case the baby come. I told Mister John I ain't wanna be far cuz if something happen I need to be right there. It was a week fore the fourth of July when Martha start cramping again. Just a few days before the midwife on the plantation sayed she think it been too early but Martha told her she knowed she was with child when it happened. So when she start cramping again Martha ain't think it was just them preparation cramps. She sayed it was real. Sophronia, her mama, got water on by the fire and I run to get the midwife.

My songbird was gon give birth and I was running cross the family farm part of the plantation to Narcine cabin. Levi, Martha daddy, gone to tell the mistress the baby was coming. Case they had any problems they could get the doctor. He sayed we need to do that so the doctor could make his way to the plantation. Only some doctors treated black folk on account they thinked our bodies was different. So if that doctor been tied up elsewhere wasn't nobody else could help.

I waited on Narcine to grab all her stuff together and then I picked up the bag with one hand and bout dragged her with the other hand back cross the farm to our cabin. It wasn't even done yet. Windows was cut in but I ain't made no shutters yet cuz I wanted to make sure I put floors down first. My wife and baby wasn't gon be on no dirt floor if I could help it. Mister John help me on a few weekends to bring down wood and put that floor in and now the other slaves jealous cuz I had floors but I told them if they can get the wood I help them put some in. The master of that plantation was looking like he couldn't figure out who working for who. Mister John just told him that stead a paying me for some extra work I was doing he was helping me with that so we equal. Whatever made him happy. It ain't matter. We got a floor and I made two beds push together and a bassinet. Martha laid up in our bed with layers of rags covering it and rolled up blankets behind her head.

Narcine came in beside me and grabbed the bag from my hand before going to Martha. You think it's coming today? She ask her like she been trying to catch her breath.

Martha looked at her breathing out her mouth short and loud. Then she sayed, This baby coming today.

Narcine check her belly on the outside and then told me I might wanna step outside with Martha daddy. Levi was pacing outside our cabin when I step out. He sayed, This be my fifth grandchild Ervin. Fifth one. It still get me. I smile nervous like back at him cuz I can hear Martha groaning through the windows wide open. Something I planned to fix for the cool come in.

Yeah, it's today, Narcine sayed loud enough for us to hear outside too. Then she told Sophronia to check the water to make sure it's warm and she sayed it could take a while.

The sun went from high in the sky to where the tree tops block it from view fore it sets. We was still waiting. Levi and me was both getting hungry. Sophronia came out and went to they cabin and brought back some biscuits for us fore she went back to see bout Martha and our baby. I got up and peek in the window but wasn't nothing to see sides Martha sweating in that late June heat and breathing hard while she sit up in that bed. Least she sitting up now. Mean she might be getting close.

My own clothes was drench with sweat from heat and worry and Levi sitting there rocking and drinking water. I ask him if the other ones was like this and he sayed, They all different at the start but it all turn out the same. I ain't sayed nothing cuz fore then, mine both turned out a way I ain't want to happen again. He look at me then sayed, Ain't nothing we can do to control this part. All we can do is stay out the way.

Martha scream out and we both bout jump out our chairs startled. I run to the window to look in and Sophronia looked back at me. Wait, she sayed.

I keeped looking in through the window. She was still screaming and Narcine sayed, Keep breathing Martha. This baby coming soon and you gonna need all your energy to push it outta ya.

I couldn't sit still. The piece of wood I was whittling ain't look like nothing after I keep whittling at it cuz a my nerves.

You wanna pray? Levi asked me.

I looked at him. You sayed wasn't nothing we can do.

He shrug and sayed, But might be something God can do.

I told him, If you want to you can pray for us. God likely hear you if you ask. I put my head down with him studying my fingers and all they callouses. I can't tell ya what he mighta sayed but I heard him whisper Amen, same time I heard Narcine tell Martha to push. I ain't wanna look in that window so I stood side it and sayed a prayer too, to myself and God. Just let me keep them, God.

I was gon say more but a whaling cry cut me off. I look in and Sophronia holding the baby while Narcine cutting the cord. I looked at Martha and she was awake looking at them. She was awake and our baby was awake. I ran back inside to see them. See both of them. I took Martha hand, scared to say anything that might mess something up.

Narcine looked at me. It's okay. You got a girl. She turned back to tend to the rest of what need to happen with Martha.

You did good, I whispered to Martha. I looked up at Sophronia holding my baby and ask, Is she alright? Can I hold her?

Let me get her cleaned up some first then she need to get to her mama to eat. She hungry, been fighting to get out for hours.

I wanted to hold her but I touched her head with my hand and my hand look so big on her. She was so tiny. Smaller than my other babies. But her lungs was strong cuz she hollered the whole time. Sophronia wiped her down fore giving her to Martha to eat. They sayed I could wait outside but I sayed I was gon sit with them, my wife and my child.

Narcine tried to argue that she wasn't done and other stuff was gon happen but I ain't care bout none of that. I cared bout them two. That's all. Martha and Victoria but we call her Vicie. That what she gon go by.

* * *

It been almost three months and Vicie and Martha was inseparable. Vicie attached either at the hip or teet. But least she growing good. She come out so tiny I was worried but ain't speak it out loud. I wanted to take Vicie and Martha back to see grandma Annie since she couldn't travel like she was. We was all gon go next time Levi do church. I couldn't wait to show everybody my baby. She was pretty like her mama and had them big bright eyes babies got. I think she smiled at me sometimes but it been hard to tell if it been a smile or gas cuz she smile then she burp. I ain't wanna stop looking at her cuz I mighta miss something or something mighta happen. I thanked God for letting me keep them.

* * *

If we ain't go in October we'd have to wait til spring cuz we wasn't taking the baby out after it got too cool. Levi, Martha, me and Vicie got in the carriage with they master to go back south for Sunday. Martha ain't sang in church since Vicie came but she was gon sing that day. I ask her, What you gon do with the baby when you up there singing?

Martha sayed, I ain't gon do nothing with the baby. You gon do something with the baby.

So I asked her, What I'm gon do with the baby?

She sayed, You gone hold her til I'm done.

What if Vicie get hungry and need her mama?

A song ain't but a few minutes and much as she eat, Vicie ain't gon starve in less than five minutes.

For a young woman she got a lot a sass. I just sayed, Alright, cuz wasn't nothing else to say. She a songbird, that's what she do.

She got up when it been time to sing and look at me but she ain't smile too much. I knowed she been thinking bout that song and it been a while. I done heard her practicing that song for the past couple times we been together. I ask why she wanna sing a sad song like that and she say it ain't sad. Going home ain't sad especially when you ain't got nowhere else you belong.

Poor Rosy, poor gal
Poor Rosy, poor gal
Rosy break my poor heart
Heav'n shall-a be my home.
I cannot stay in hell one day
Heav'n shall-a be my home
I'll sing and pray my soul away
Heav'n shall-a be my home.

Got hard trial in my way
Heav'n shall-a be my home.
O when I talk, I talk wid God
Heav'n shall-a be my home.

I dunno what de people want of me
Heav'n shall-a be my home.

Martha sang it through again and the church come in when it been time and sing long with her. Made a beautiful sound but even with me holding my new baby and looking at my pretty wife I thinked about what heaven was holding already and how mama had always feel like home. Right now I ain't wanna go there with them, not yet. I was feeling like home was standing in front of me and falling sleep in my arms.

Church let out and folks start coming up to me and Martha quick. They sayed how they like the song but went right to the baby. She wasn't sleeping no more with all them eyes looking and hands touching her fingers. They was coming from every side trying to see my Vicie. Our baby girl. I ain't feel that proud since I been in Philadelphia.

I seed grandma Annie sitting out the way. She ain't try to press through all them people to see Vicie cuz she was gon see her later anyway. When we got back to Mister John and Misses Charlotte she give us a blanket for our Vicie she make from that yarn I give her.

Time

Time ticked by like it want. Fast sometimes, slow sometimes. Christmas rolled round again and that Harrison won out for President. They sayed he the oldest president round. Mister John sayed they close to the same age and he can't imagine having actually got out and campaigned. Sayed Harrison went all the way to Charleston to get votes at his age. Mister John don't hardly like going to Charleston no more even to sell furniture. He done start to slow down some. Misses Charlotte too. They still younger than grandma Annie by at least ten years but they all got silver heads and lines scratched cross they face.

I worried he was gon leave here too. What happen if I ain't had my freedom or something gone wrong and I wind up in a situation that wasn't no good? He tell me don't worry cuz slavery ain't gon last forever and he done made arrangements. I ain't knowed what them arrangements been. Could be good, could be not. I ain't met no other folks down in them parts like these James. Some talked about slavery being uncomfortable but wasn't many willing to treat us right, pay us, give us a chance. Not like Mister John and Misses Charlotte. If they went on to heaven what was gon happen to me and Martha and Vicie?

More months went pass all through the winter. We thinked that maybe the break in cold might break that flu been pestering everybody. Newspapers sayed Harrison done took office official and one month later to the day, right fore Easter Sunday he done succumbed to pneumonia. It wasn't that I cared so much bout that. Folks dying all the time and them affairs of white men ain't count much for me. But it scared me cuz like Mister John sayed, they was close in age and the flu been taking folks out like it ain't done in almost ten years. It took a president out, what it gon do to Mister John or Misses Charlotte or grandma Annie? She couldn't take a common cold.

Misses Charlotte sayed, You can't worry about what come natural, aging.

I told her, I ain't worried about aging. I worried about age making you and Mister John like to get sick.

She sayed, It's not about age, Harrison just happened to be elderly.

That ain't make me feel no better. Mean it could come for anybody even my Martha and Vicie. That spring and summer I keeped them close, much as I could. I keeped Vicie in my arm when we was back near Peedee and Martha on my other hand. When she was done helping the mistress each day we sat there in front of our cabin and talk, Vicie between us at our knees. She needed a brother or a sister and we been working on it. She was still a tiny little thing but her legs was strong and she been trying to pull up. I figured she be walking in a month if not sooner.

Martha say don't rush it cuz then we just be chasing her round and having to keep her outta stuff. But I wanted to see her walk and I wanted to chase her round and watch her run and tell her to get outta stuff. Martha told me that cuz I only home on the weekend and she the one gon have her hands full all week.

I told Martha I wanna big family so we need get going. She teased asking if I'm a be able to buy freedom for all them children. She say maybe we need to go head and get free then have them children. But I ain't been able to save as much as I want. Getting back south, building us a home, then the depression we just getting outta mean they ain't been as much to save. Not to buy freedom for two females and Levi and Sophronia, if they was even willing to sell them.

If I coulda take her away from there I woulda but that wouldn'ta make her happy less her mama and daddy go too. That cost enough then add on children and I gotta make a lot more caskets. Least this flu so bad this year we getting more business for it. It ain't good but at the same time it helping me put money away for us. Martha couldn't hardly make no extra money since she waiting on her mistress all day. Sophronia watch the baby cept when time to feed and she take Vicie up to the big house so Martha can feed her and then get back to work. I tried to stay out the way of that house and the master. Mind my own business and take care of my family. That's all I could do.

Since we got married he sent off Malachi who might be some relation to Martha but don't nobody know how. Malachi got mad at the overseer and grabbed the whip when he was bout to lash one of the younger men on the field. Grabbed it and yanked so hard that man fell right off his horse to the ground, broke his arm. Had it coming for sure. The master ain't knowed how bad he was, power hungry and evil. Whip a man for walking too slow, or too fast, wiping his brow, or needing to take a piss. A broke arm wasn't hardly enough if you ask me. Master couldn't let that be an example though so he sent Malachi to some plantation just on the Georgetown side of the line outside Charleston.

Me and Martha tried to tell her brothers don't be no trouble. Don't give them no reasons, like mama use to tell me. She sayed she ain't use to understand it til she was older and we had Vicie. Sayed she ain't been exposed to everything some other slaves got exposed to cuz she work with the mistress. But they so many slaves here they all got different stories.

When the heat a summer finally broke we celebrated. We waited til the harvest moon and I played the fiddle in the evening on Friday cuz the moon was still full in the sky. October done come round again. I was getting old. Most men on the plantation fell ill and started dying from the hard life when they reach my age. The women ain't had it much better, maybe they get to forty. I ain't want my last days to be watching men my age dying. I wanted to live long like Mister John or Levi. He was near fifty but he ain't been in the field since they plucked him out as a teenager. Same with Sophronia. I wished I coulda told them in the field it wasn't like this everywhere. I wish I coulda told them bout Philadelphia.

I whisper it to Martha brothers who whispered it in the fields. Not so they would go but that they have hope cuz they was free folks out there. If they wanted to try they could. I did, but wasn't nothing there for me. Others made it okay. In other places they had black folks who mighta been slaves but they could get they freedom. They was folks of all colors working to get us free, not just buying freedom, but being free. I wanted that kinda freedom for me and Martha and Vicie.

We danced like tomorrow wasn't never coming cuz we wasn't never guaranteed nothing. We had right then. That moment. I knowed I could make good music, laughter, fun that last for an evening and if tomorrow come, it be a good memory for somebody to carry them through some other sorrows. Maybe when they working hard and they bodies tired they might hum them tunes and it give some more strength.

That's what I did. I played the fiddle and Levi banged on some drums his master got him for a Christmas gift fore I met them. And my Martha sang. And we made merry til the mistress come out and told us it was time to go in for the night. By then we was all bout tired anyway but the merry was set in our soul.

Martha sayed she was exhausted from dancing and I wondered if that was all she was tired from cuz she ain't dance that much. Not like other times. I ask if she think it might be another reason and stead of answering she sayed good night.

Fall

Martha already been tending to that woman all the time and when Vicie got past a year back in June she spect Martha to pick up her duties like before, accompanying her on engagements that take her from the plantation. She sayed it ain't as much as before and we lucky winter coming. The mistress prefer not to travel long ways with the short days and cold weather. That don't stop her from going now and keeping her social diary. After one of them trips at the start of November, Martha come back home with a cold. The mistress too. Then them sniffles turn to the flu. We knowed cuz the doctor come to see the mistress and sayed it been that influenza.

Everybody getting it this year cuz it's an epidemic, that what her doctor sayed. He told the mistress she need to rest cuz she up in age. That mean she want Martha waiting on her hand and foot but Martha sick too. So she call up another slave woman Nora to help us with Vicie since she want Sophronia back in the house cooking and she figure it best to have Martha help since Martha already sick too. It ain't make no sense. She want it all back to normal for her comfort but don't nobody else matter. And she ain't trust nobody but Martha, so Martha up there taking care of that woman while trying to take care of herself too. And I couldn't take care a my wife cuz I had to work. All I could do was to tell her to rest much as she can. Take every chance she get.

When I got back end of that week they sicker then before and Vicie done got sick too. Doctor sayed the mistress got pneumonia. Whatever she got, Martha got and seeing how Vicie sound she got it too. They calling in the doctor for them but we gotta wait cuz he in high demand right now. Folks falling ill like

211

the plague. Ain't nothing I can do but sit up beside them and watch them like I used to do Ellie. And pray. Pray God keep them and he don't let me fall ill too. I do what Levi do. I pray. He work for the master and when he ain't tending to his needs he somewhere talking to God or trying to make Martha more comfortable when she working in the house too. He say he do some of her work so she can rest but it ain't enough. She need time to recuperate and take care of herself. Levi say that what the doctor say the misses need to do so he figured it been the same thing Martha need to do.

The master scared bout his wife, but me and Levi and Sophronia scared bout Martha and Vicie. Wasn't nothing for this thing to take out somebody. I knowed cuz of the caskets we been making on prospect. Mister John sayed we ain't got orders for all them yet, but we will. He been right so far even if I wish he wasn't.

It was hard to get through then and it ain't much easier to think about. We did all we knowed to do. We tried the concoctions the healers on the plantation cook up and the medicine the doctor give and Vicie start getting better. Her little body would shake so bad with that cough in her chest and I'd hold her body to mine when I was there. Nora would sleep on the floor mat with our little girl bundled up against her. She wasn't scared a getting sick. She sayed that little girl wasn't going nowhere. Not on her watch. She wasn't but eighteen but she got that strong spirit and she fierce on her belief she ain't gon lose Vicie to this sickness.

Martha tried to keep doing her work but when she been carrying a fresh towel and water to the misses to clean her up she catch a coughing spell and fell in the hall, water everywhere on the floor. She couldn't even call out or nothing cuz she can't speak over trying to get her breath. Levi done find her after hearing the water bowl fall and looking for the sound. He helped her up and back to our cabin and that's where she stayed.

Doctor finally come and give us the news she got it bad. She took penicillin and he open the shutters and sayed keep them open so she can get fresh air. I sayed it's cold out and he sayed that's part of the point. Somebody in Europe done some studies about cold air and stuff like what been going on. So we keep them shutters open and got wrap up in blankets. When I wasn't there Nora keeped them open while she looking after my baby and my wife. She done what nobody else could. Sophronia and Levi had wanna be there to help but they couldn't on account they had to keep working in that house with the master and misses.

When I been at Mister John house I wasn't all the way there. He knowed it too. I was slow in the workshop and not just cuz of the cold. Wasn't no happy songs coming from my fiddle and I had to let Mister John know I couldn't play no engagements but he sayed I needed to if I wanna do what I say I wanna do. Even if my heart wasn't in it my head need to be. So I tried and put myself in a happy place. I thinked bout before Martha and Vicie fell sick and how we danced and played the night away and I use that to be happy for a while. Til the quiet come and I find myself with just me in that room I been sleeping in since I was eight. We put a window in when I was fourteen and Mister John helped me make shutters. At night I push them open to see the stars. I loved looking at the stars. I figured if Martha awake she was looking up at the north star too. That's what we sayes we'd do.

I looked and find our star and feel the cool air on my face. The air was still and quiet like it be in December. Christmas round the corner and January was gon come soon. Grandma Annie done fall sick with flu too but she ain't had to do nothing but rest and things turned round that Misses Shelly was taking care of her. When I got round to see her she whisper she might stay sick a bit longer and keep this up as payback. I told her no, she need to get well. Don't nobody else need burying in 1841.

She laugh and ask if that mean she can get buried in 1842 but that wasn't at all funny.

December twenty come and so did Richard, Martha younger brother. He come bumping in a cart with some white man side him. They was rushing up to the house and then Richard jump out and tell me I gots to get back quick. Doctor done told them she ain't got long. Mister John tell me to go and I ain't take nothing with me side my coat. We ride back quick to the Peedee area and the plantation. Richard and me run to the cabin and everybody inside sitting and standing round the bed.

What's going on? I asked and ain't nobody sayed nothing.

Somewhere in the middle of all them people I heard her say, Ervin? That you?

I push through them all and told her, I'm here so you ain't gotta worry.

Sophronia put her hand on my shoulder and Nora sayed she sorry. Nora was holding Vicie but Vicie ain't understand that her mama was laying there getting closer to my mama.

I put my fingers round Martha's and told her, You is a good woman and a good wife and a good mama and a good daughter. You is good in every way. You need to choose to stay here so we can do what we sayed we gon do.

She smiled at me but it look like it took all her strength. She tried to squeeze my hand but it feel like Vicie. She tried to say something and cough instead.

You just stay Martha. You stay. You don't go nowhere cuz we gots things to do. Remember? We gots plans. For me. For you. For Vicie. For your mama and daddy and Richard here. We gots plans for all us. Remember? We made them together Martha. We made a promise to each other. We promised that the north star was ours and we was gon see the promise of it together. Martha? I squeeze her hand and she squeeze back a little. Remember Martha? I leaned to whisper in her ear. We sayed we was gonna have a farm and our family was gonna be there. Safe and free. Remember? We gon raise some chickens and pigs and plant fruit trees and grow our own food and build our own homes and our children gon live free on our own land. Martha? Remember Martha? You gotta stay. Remember what we sayed we was gon do together?

I squeeze her hand but she ain't squeeze back. Martha? We gon do all this together for us, for Vicie, for our family. We gon do this Martha. You just gotta stay. Stay with me. Stay here with me. With us. Just give me a little bit more time. I promise we gon do it.

Ervin? Ervin? I pushed Sophronia hand off my back and stayed where I was. My lips pressed to her ear. These was our plans. Our plans. We been making them since we started walking round the house where I live with Mister John and Misses Charlotte. These was ours. They was meant to be keeped like we promised we would.

Our Father

There ain't no way to get used to losing folks you love. A piece of you get lost with them and can't ever be found or put back. Almost make you wanna put a box round your heart so it don't love then you ain't gotta worry bout the hurt that follow. But this time I ain't by myself. I ain't feel alone in all my pain of losing her, Martha. They carried the hurt with me. And through it all there was Nora. She cared for Martha when she was sick and I believe she the reason Vicie got better. Vicie ain't never been the same but God let me keep her. She sickly now but she here with me. God took Martha but he ain't curse me to be by myself this time. Stead he give me somebody who understand something about love and pain. And she want a family big as I want.

Some time pass and me and Nora got married in the same place me and Martha got married. She younger by a lot a years but that mean she got lots a time for making our family. She survived that flu without more than a sniffle even with all the sickness everywhere around her.

I admit my heart been a little heavy. Hard to lift it up to where it once used to sit. Hard to open it full again like I did with Martha. Hard to trust it won't be done like it been done before. But Nora was an angel. That's the easiest way to describe her. Like God done plucked her and put her there. Not no sweet angel, but like one of them angels you know watching and protecting. She fierce and feisty and she ain't gon let me let up. Mister John sayed I needed that in my life. He was telling me lots of things. I spose since he turn seventy he start counting his days too.

He told me I need to make the most of what I got. He made sure he introduced me to everybody we done business with, specially Mister McKissick. He don't just have me in the back. He would tell everyone of them if he can do it I can do it too. Sometimes they seem confused. Sometimes they let it be with a nod cuz they been knowing us working together so long. I wasn't gon be able to do what he been doing for us after he gon. It's South Carolina. Nothing much else to reason bout it. But I could still do some and some of them folks would keep giving me business private, even if it was a secret.

Now the fiddle, they ain't seem to care who I work with for me to play my fiddle. I got my own business with that most of the time. One party lead to the other and when I told them what I charge sometimes they try to negotiate but I'd say, Well that's my fee for playing like this for an evening. I understands if that's not something you're comfortable with, suh.

Then I start getting my stuff together cuz three folks in one night was gon ask me and I only need one or two to come through. And since ain't nobody else play like me round them parts and I had the reputation, they was gon wind up paying for it, eventually.

That's how it went. Nora by my side and playing the fiddle on the side while I figured out that being a carpenter wasn't gon be forever like it was. Misses Charlotte and Mister John was too old to do what they been doing. I worked them fields and hired help in the spring and at harvest time to make sure we had enough food to eat with some to sell or trade. I took the goods up to the market to sell. Sometimes with him, usually not. They knowed me and when they seed me set up they'd ask bout how Mister James doing. Most times I sayed, He doing alright, just ain't up for being out and about.

Most Sundays I'd see Grandma Annie but I figured that was gon be the last year for her. I wanted her to see my baby with Nora and she was trying to hold on to see that baby too. She sayed she already started on a blanket for her grand. Vicie loved seeing her cuz she sneak her sweet stuff she done bake. Only thing she do round that house is make them fat with baking pies and cakes. But don't nobody complain cuz that's all she need to do.

Nora was gon have that baby in late March or early April most likely. I done build Vicie a regular bed and that bassinet was for the next baby and lots more.

Wright come along in 1846 like we expected and he and Nora was both fine. All the way. God let me keep both of them. Finally. Nora told me we was in for better days and she wasn't going nowhere. Now I had a boy and a girl and for all my wishing for a big family I told God I'd be satisfied if he just let me keep them. Nora sayed, We gon do like we sayed and that's it Ervin. We sayed we gon have a big family and ain't no reason to stop now. Them wasn't no easy times by no count, but we worked hard, both us. God seen fit to give me her and Vicie and Wright so I figured my curse or my debt musta come to some kinda end. Nora say it been foolish for me to talk bout being cursed all them years. Maybe it was but that's how it feeled in the time, even if it ain't been true. I can't know for sure one way or the other. I just knowed how I feeled and what I seen.

Me and Nora had Robert in '48 and Sidney in '50. Ellison come in '51, giving us four boys and Vicie. Nora hardly had time to catch her breath with all them boys or on account of me and her making them.

I showed off all my babies to Mister John and Misses Charlotte and Grandma Annie when they come along cuz they was getting so up in age. When I was there working during the week me and Mister John and Misses Charlotte sit around inside talking bout what was happening in the states, like the compromise and what it mean for freedom.

Mister John sayed, E, maybe you can get to California.

I sayed, All the way from South Carolina with five children and a wife? If they catch us on the way they'd sell us off separate maybe and it ain't worth losing my family to follow the same way they march those Indians to they death.

He paused a long time fore saying, You're right, Ervin. Now they have those laws requiring you be returned but there's no guarantee you get returned here. Could wind up anywhere. He put his wrinkled hands to his forehead like he did when he ain't got no answers and trying to figure something out.

Ain't nothing to figure out here, Mister John. We gon ride out our course. Ain't nowhere safe to go for me and my family. We gon stay here and make the best we can outta the situation.

Mister John curse like I ain't never heard him curse before. He sayed Britain ain't need all this to do what's right. Now folks of every ilk was gonna die cuz some men didn't believe all men should be free. He sayed, Ervin listen it makes no sense what we've come to. We don't see it yet but the writing's on the wall. That Uncle Tom's Cabin book stirred up something in folks. You watch Ervin, we're gonna have brother against brother and families torn apart. Our land torn apart because of this. And this damned state'll be the start of it. What kind of place tells a freed slave they have to leave the state? Even if they don't choose to enforce it all the time, they can at anytime. It'll be the death of whatever good might be in the South.

He rambled on for a long while and I watched him close cuz he done got so worked up he might fall over. Finally he sayed to stay out of this mess cuz I need to stay alive and keep my family alive. If I didn't everything me and Nora was working towards would be in vain.

I told him even though the business be in Priscilla name I'd do alright building boxes for those boys wanna keep my people as slaves. They can pay me and that be how I get some get back.

He laughed and pat my hand. He sayed, You do that. Get your whole family free. He told me to work with Mister McKissick who in the business of reselling and got some kinda deal with the church.

Wasn't but a couple months after that he ask me again whether I was gon leave South Carolina. He done told me if I did try and I made it I'd be free - forever cuz a that Lincoln's proclamation. I just had to get north and then I wouldn't need no papers to be free. I told him I can't go now. I gots four boys, a girl, and a wife. I can't go nowhere. Sides, this home. As much as what was wrong with it, it was home cuz the people I loved was there and wasn't leaving or couldn't leave.

His eyes went down, like this time he wanted for me to go fore all this come back on us in a bad way. Rather than argue he sayed, I understand, Ervin. You are a good man. I only wish for you to feel freedom.

I sayed, I do feel freedom Mister John. Maybe not like you, but I do. I want my children and Nora to feel real freedom. That's what I wants for them. I don't care if we gotta work the land and farm. Long as we on our land. We'll do what we need and my family gon get through.

He ain't look so sure. I believe it been round that time Mister John decide he ain't wanna be here no more. I couldn't blame him. He was old. Misses Charlotte was old. They been good people and they got a good long life. Priscilla say she don't expect them to be here much longer either. I don't imagine I know what it feel like to be her, bout to lose your parents after they done live a long good life. I imagine it still ain't easy. Losing folks you love ain't easy no matter when or how. She got lots of years with them. Lots of time together, specially after they got older and even more the past few years.

We knowed it was coming but like I sayed, when death come for folks you love, don't nothing make it easier. My second girl Sallie been born that year, 1855, and we still wasn't free. Mister John been bout eighty years old and by then he was always tired and achy. His body making noises every which way. He ain't get up so early no more cuz I did most of the work in the shop. He handled the business end when needed but his hands couldn't do what they used to. They was stiff and hurt all the time. Tween all that working with them, we wasn't surprised. Mine likely seize up one day too after doing what he been doing all these years. I was sitting at the table eating breakfast and looking out the window while the sun start to give the sky some rose color when Misses Charlotte come out crying. She sayed, He's not waking up Ervin. I do believe John's gone. Can you check? She wiped her eyes. All the years I done knowed her and I ain't never seed no tear fall from her eyes.

Yes ma'am, I sayed and she walk with me back to they room. I seed enough death to be sure. He was there looking like he was sleeping. He ain't look dead, just sleep. I touch his hand and his face and then pick up Misses Charlotte looking glass and put it to his nose. Nothing. I sit it back down and look at Misses Charlotte who already look frail.

Misses Charlotte, you right. Mister John is gone.

I looked at him again. He look peaceful like he ain't had no worries. I wondered if he seed mama. Then I ask Misses Charlotte if she want me to send word to Priscilla. She nodded and I help her sit down in the chair by the bed. She ask me to roll over her writing tray and she start writing a note for me to take long with me, case I get stop. Being my age they ain't stop me so much no more as when I been young and going back and forth to Martha. Had my note from Mister John and her master so I been covered both ways til they start knowing me. Got some business for Mister John that way too, after while. But this was gon be different. Wasn't no more Mister John.

She writing with her hands with big knots now from all them years on the piano. I told her, Don't worry. He with God. And I actually believed it. He ain't had to worry cuz if he ain't made it, wasn't much hope for the rest of us and it be pretty lonely, quiet, and boring up there in heaven.

I had to get outta there. I couldn't stand to see her sad but I ain't wanna leave her alone neither. I couldn't be there with him lying on that bed and no life in him. I think bout all the people I ever knowed and loved who was up there in heaven. Mister John being the newest. I grabbed the biscuit on the plate and got the rest of the way dressed fore heading to Priscilla. It take a good two hours there and two hours back. Plenty a time to be by myself.

He was gone. The only man like him I ever knowed. Levi step in best he could but he ain't raise me up like Mister John. He ain't teach me about being a man. Teach me how to make money and earn a living. I ain't had no father but God seed fit to give me two in that place. They both teach me about taking care of my family. Thy teached me bout forgiveness and kindness and decency. Now one was gone. God had both mama and Mister John, long with Lilly, Ellie, Marcus, and Martha. I ain't cried though. He lived bout eighty years. He lived good and long and right. Ain't nothing for him to be worried for. Me neither, but he was gone. I'd never play fiddle with him again or sit in that workshop and make pretty furniture with him again. Never laugh with him or listen to his jokes. He was gone. Misses Charlotte old and alone and my best friend done leave.

I know I was gon be alright but riding to Priscilla I couldn't hardly breathe. I been hers on paper. I prayed the Lord's prayer for peace riding to her. It was hard getting past Our Father. My throat like to swell up and wouldn't nothing come out. I never knew my father. He ain't never been more than an idea, like a ghost you can't never really glimpse. I thinked of what a father spose to be to his children. About how he sposed to take care of them and provide and protect them. About how the men I knowed who was slaves wasn't never given the chance to do that. They was punished for protecting, not allowed to provide. Mister John told me bout being a man, taking care of a family. He gave me a chance most ain't never got. To earn money and feel that kinda pride. To be respected by somebody I work with not just for. I wish I had known what it was like to be a daddy more though cuz I ain't perfect. Sometimes I ain't got patience and I can't be there but a couple days a week. It ain't seem hardly enough. I was scared my boys wasn't gon be ready. Scared they might get taken. Scared my Nora might not survive the next baby coming. Scared my Vicie wasn't gon live long cuz she ain't never been all well and still little.

I was scared for all the things I ain't got no control over cuz I ain't got no control over nothing cept how I wake up each day, God willing, and do what I been given to do. The rest outta my hands. So I pray trying to get to that part where God kingdom come, and wanting it right now like they must have it in heaven. I want it now down here. It ain't get here. We was still trying to get bread, get the basics of life. I tried to forgive everybody who done took our life away either all the way or cuz we ain't got no free will. Nora and my children's master who ain't never gon let me buy they freedom. He done sayed as much, that they too valuable and he trust my family too much. That they can't live without them.

I ain't met no other man like Mister John. The two reverends I knowed, McKissick and Matthew, come close but round here, not so much. It took me bout the whole ride to get through that single prayer one time. I asked God to take care of Mister John and help Misses Charlotte get some peace. I asked mama to welcome him and make sure he meet Lilly and my babies up there. I asked God not to take nobody else no time soon.

They buried Mister John in the cemetery by the church. His casket was beautiful. I spent almost as much time with it as I did on mama's but I never could get it right for him. I wanted it to be as good as he woulda done. Misses Charlotte told me it was better than any she'd seen. My Nora held my hand on the side of the funeral where they lay him in the ground. The kids gathered round behind us. Misses Shelly sat in the front with Priscilla and her family. We was all getting old. And behind me and my family was Grandma Annie in a chair, half sleeping but for the cold air that wouldn't let her get comfortable. She seem she might just outlive us all.

Uncivil

Priscilla bringed the news. It was a couple weeks past the new year when she come with that paper to her Daddy house. Misses Charlotte done got a lady to keep house and watch her who live there. She on paper as a slave like me but she get paid like me.

Misses Priscilla come in waving the paper and calling for me to come inside. I follow her in the house and she already sitting next to Misses Charlotte and Tabita in the living room.

You are not going to believe this, she started.

Misses Charlotte sayed, Come on, now Priscilla. Don't tease. What's it say? The important stuff. Me and Tabita done heard rumors we wasn't part of the United States no more and folks was trying to start a new one on account a slavery.

Listen good. I'm going to read it just as it's written.

These ends it endeavored to accomplish by a Federal Government, in which each State was recognized as an equal, and had separate control over its own institutions. The right of property in slaves was recognized by giving to free persons distinct political rights, by giving them the right to represent, and burthening them with direct taxes for three-fifths of their slaves; by authorizing the importation of slaves for twenty years; and by stipulating for the rendition of fugitives from labor.

We affirm that these ends for which this Government was instituted have been defeated, and the Government itself has been made destructive of them by the action of the non-

slaveholding States. Those States have assume the right of deciding upon the propriety of our domestic institutions; and have denied the right of property established in fifteen of the States and recognized by the Constitution; they have denounced as sinful the institution of slavery; they have permitted open establishment among them of societies, whose avowed object is to disturb the peace and to eloign the property of the citizens of other States. They have encouraged and assisted thousands of our slaves to leave their homes; and those who remain, have been incited by emissaries, books and pictures to servile insurrection.

For twenty-five years this agitation has been steadily increasing, until it has now secured to its aid the power of the common Government. Observing the forms of the Constitution, a sectional party has found within that Article establishing the Executive Department, the means of subverting the Constitution itself. A geographical line has been drawn across the Union, and all the States north of that line have united in the election of a man to the high office of President of the United States, whose opinions and purposes are hostile to slavery. He is to be entrusted with the administration of the common Government, because he has declared that that "Government cannot endure permanently half slave, half free," and that the public mind must rest in the belief that slavery is in the course of ultimate extinction.

This sectional combination for the submersion of the Constitution, has been aided in some of the States by elevating to citizenship, persons who, by the supreme law of the land, are incapable of becoming citizens; and their

225

votes have been used to inaugurate a new policy, hostile to the South, and destructive of its beliefs and safety.

On the 4th day of March next, this party will take possession of the Government. It has announced that the South shall be excluded from the common territory, that the judicial tribunals shall be made sectional, and that a war must be waged against slavery until it shall cease throughout the United States.[2]

Priscilla paused then and look at me, Tabita, and Misses Charlotte.

What that mean, Misses Priscilla? I asked her.

She already had tears in her eyes. It means South Carolina is leaving the United States of America to form its own nation.

Misses Charlotte sayed, They can't do that. Can they? Just decide to not be a part of the country my daddy and your granddaddy fought to create?

Priscilla shook her head confused. I don't know. This is what it says. I can't see how they would do this without a fight. I fear this means there's gonna be a war, mama.

I had six boys and two girls. Charles and Eli wasn't but two and one and we was gon be in war come spring, likely, if South Carolina had they way and could get other states to follow.

You think it gon happen, Misses Priscilla? War? I was too old to fight and my boys too young. Only thing I had was my kids and Nora and I ain't wanna lose them to nobody war.

I don't know. We'll have to see, she sayed.

Tabita scared just like me bout if that war get lost then what happen if something go wrong with Misses Charlotte and Misses Priscilla and we wind up in the wrong hands. I told her that's when it time to run. She young enough.

Mister John been right like usual. They wasn't gon let us be free. A year and a moon after they officially leaved the country that war started. It ain't come much our way. Charleston was mainly where it was but those Union boys had a hard time with Charleston. I figured if they ever took it this war be over. It ain't make no sense. Men who ain't hardly have nothing willing to die so other men could keep something they shouldn'ta never had. Least them young men who ran off to fight when Lincoln put it out they could be free if they made it to the Union line was fighting for something worth it. Took him long enough to do it though. With all them young men gone they ain't had enough help. Got slaves doing twice the work and starting them younger.

My girl Sophronia come along more than a year after he made that proclamation and little Ervin still been on Nora. Nora asked, What if we leave Ervin? Get away and our kids be free.

I sayed, We can't with all these youngens. Vicie was grown and married and Wright was grown but the rest wasn't quite there. One still on the teet and two on the hips and then the bigger boys who wasn't quite big enough.

If it been a few years later and I been a few years younger, I mighta took the chance. What if that war went on forever or the Confederate States of America won? And then we ain't got no protections from being part of the United States.

It been more than two years since them Confederates fired on Fort Sumter. Things changed since the war started, specially being near the coast and less than a day's trip to Charleston. They was still planting rice but now they needed men to help where so many of them able body white men went to fighting that war. My older boys was rented to other plantations in the area. Sometimes for a day at a time and sometimes for a week. It depended on what was needed. The girls not so much. Vicie worked with Nora and Grandma Sophronia in the house for the family but she lived in her own cabin with her husband Thomas. They does everything from cooking and cleaning to taking care of the grandchildren since they seem to be there all the time now. They daddy done gone off to fight for the land his wife family own and she bringed all six of them kids and spect other folks to take care of them, least the hard parts.

Since they was waist high my four boys been learning to farm with me. I been doing this going back and forth so long I ain't been able to teach my boys much cuz they belong to somebody else. My boys Ervin and James too young and they with Grandma Sophronia, Grandpa Levi and Nora back on the plantation. We worked the James farm since they was young when I could get them away from the rice patties. But they pay for themselves with what Misses Priscilla pay for they day labor. The master get most and they gets some too.

I teached them what Mister John teached me. I did for them what Levi tried to do for his family in his own way. Work hard and take care of your family. We knowed how to grow real food and not just rice. I run that farm and we got enough to sell to the soldiers and regular folks at market. Don't matter who buying but we ain't negotiating with them men trying to keep us slaves. Different markets in different places. We can't charge nobody higher than the price we set but we can negotiate lower and so that's how we does for the ones fighting so we can't be free.

Life keep going on with that war. Bunch of the men from round there took off headed north. If they could get out of Confederate land they was free. Hardly nobody my age run cuz it was a hard trip if I be honest. Priscilla keeped me apprised so I can keep the other slaves on the plantation and at church apprised too. I told them to keep it to themselves til it was time. We in South Carolina and Priscilla know all the news. She sayed Lincoln done signed something else making us all free whether we was in Union territory or not. I sayed, We gotta win the war first for it to matter.

She told me Sherman was making his way through Atlanta and Georgia and heading this way. It might only be a matter of time before it was over. When '65 come in I prayed the end come with it. I wanted my babies to know freedom. All of them. From Vicie to my new baby James. They all should know freedom and if Priscilla was right, they might see it. I might see it for I leave.

A few weeks later she come back in her carriage and it barely stop fore she was dragging herself out. Jonathan, her son-in-law calling after her to slow down fore she hurt herself again. She move with a limp like she fell or something but it ain't hardly slow her down.

228

She call out to me while I been in the workshop. She sayed, Ervin. Ervin. You'll never believe it, Ervin. A bunch of negro soldiers came right into Charleston. They they Ervin..

Catch your breath Misses Priscilla and slow down. Sit down now.

She sat in the chair and grabbed my arm fore starting up again. Ervin, It was a group of negro soldiers that came to Charleston. Can you believe it? And the mayor surrendered.

Charleston? Negro soldiers? And the mayor of Charleston surrendered? You not playing with me today Misses Priscilla now are you?

No Ervin. And those soldiers came from right here in South Carolina and, let's see, Massachusetts. Together they were the first to enter Charleston.

I sat down in the other chair in the workshop. We was sitting just like I used to sit with Mister John, talking and playing. But it was different. This might be the end.

Less than two months later and that war finally ended. Misses Priscilla sayed that mean the Union won and we was in Union territory. I ask her if that mean what I thinked it mean. I was scared to utter them words like I might curse it.

She sayed, Ervin. It means that you are free because you are in Union territory now.

Say it one more time Misses Priscilla. I need to hear it again.

You're free Ervin. All of you are free!

I stared at her with my heart beating fast in my chest. Then I jumped up. I gotta go Misses Priscilla. I gotta tell the others. I won't be back tomorrow cuz tonight we gotta celebrate. I can't believe it. I'm free Misses Priscilla. We all free!

She laugh long with me and the lines cross her face too. Her hair was old yellow now. We was all getting old but least we got to see the day. I hug her and ran in the house to tell Tabita and Misses Charlotte. Tabita screamed like she done seed a ghost and Misses Charlotte ask if I was sure before she let herself get too happy. Priscilla give me a pie she sayed she been working on the recipe for since she met my mama. She claim she still ain't had it right but that it was still a good sweet potato pie. She sayed to take it to celebrate.

I ride so fast to Nora. The war was over and we was free. That night of December we carried on til the sun come up cuz it been the first time most of us ever been free. We danced and singed and it ain't matter that the night was a little cool cuz we was free. Every last one of us. Free to leave or stay. If we stay we get paid now to do work we done free. My people.

Bout midday the next morning when wasn't nobody out there doing nothing in the field and ain't nobody showed up in the house the master of the plantation call a meeting.

He sayed, You all are free. It's true. I can't keep you here against your will so you are free to leave. Half the men and bout three of the young women start walking away. He look at them then start up again loud enough for them to hear. Before you go consider your prospects. How will you earn your keep? What will you do for money? How will you feed yourself? Your family? Where will you live and sleep? Where would you even go? Each question he ask and I see the light go outta one more set of eyes.

Thing is, he was right. Ain't nothing change cept couldn't nobody steal us. But most ain't had nowhere else to go. They families been on that plantation for generations, passed down from one owner to the next. They was all free but wasn't hardly none of them free. They was free to stay here and work like they been doing for a few cents a week or take they chances but wasn't no place to live. No land, no property. Ain't nobody had much a nothing, cept the mulattos who got willed something from they daddy's. I ain't knowed nobody like that up here by PeeDee - either Marion or Georgetown. Not personally.

We was free on paper, but I knowed already you gotta be free in your mind first or nothing else was gon matter.

Forward

Nora asked me that night while I lay side her, What's next? We gon do what we talked about? Our kids need a place to call home and not under a master by another name.

Fisher come and we ain't got off that land yet. Ain't had nowhere to go. Nobody to get land from. The contract with the owner of that plantation be up at the end of the year. She tell me we needs to do something cuz she ain't see much sense being free and still doing the same as before. Working for that family who don't treat her or Vicie no different.

Ervin, she sayed, if we don't do this now we gon miss our chance.

She ask me bout Mister Eli McKissick and his family and that land he got. She knowed Mister McKissick like me and respect me. He been settling his accounts through me since '61.

Misses Priscilla daughter and son-in-law Jonathan ride with me to see Mister McKissick and his son in Marion some weeks later to bring a new set a caskets to his farm. They ain't want nobody to bother me with the wounds of the war being so fresh and all. I asked Mister McKissick how he doing with that land he got for farming. Over 300 acres he ain't even using. He sayed he doing good with it and he already willed some to his son now that he grown and done got his education at Mars Bluff Academy. The older Mister McKissicks sayed things changing but he hope not too much.

His son look at me out the side. I know he ain't think like his daddy. He engaged to get married and planning to go to the ministry. I knowed by now they was some who followed the love of God and some who claimed to but ain't never lived it. Some was like Matthew who believed it and some was like the preacher at the plantation we still lived on who ain't seem to live it a day of his life. Mister McKissick hoped to will it to his kids one day.

I sayed, Yeah that be nice. Have land to will to your children.

He sayed, Yes indeed. Sure is.

Jonathan look at me and cock his head to the side fore saying, We better get these inside.

Mister McKissick son, Eli, me and Jonathan carry those three caskets to the back area he use for storage. I could feel the weight like I ain't used to. Jonathan bear the load mostly and they wasn't heavy as some since they was made from thinner pine. We was walking back and Jonathan whisper I better be careful asking about that land. I asked him why and he tell me cuz white folks ain't selling or giving land to negroes. Sayed it cause troubled.

I told him, Well it's new to be able to. We ain't been free but five years after a couple hundred years as slaves. Everybody gotta get used to it.

He look at me with that look mama give me all them years ago. Pity. Like I ain't know no better.

Just be careful Ervin. Folks around here won't take well to anybody involved in it. At the cart Eli looked back at his daddy sitting up in that chair then back at me. He smiled a little and sayed, I plan on going to the ministry, you know?

Oh yeah? Ain't you young to be getting all tied down like that?

It's never too early to serve the Lord.

Your daddy getting up there. Ain't he gon need you to care for the farm?

Like he said. Things are changing. Nothing wrong with that. Hopefully by this time next year I'll be married too.

You really don't plan to waste no time, I told him.

No I don't. Jonathan can you help him with that end? No disrespect but you don't need to be trying to get that down by yourself.

After the third one was in the storage I turn and ask that Eli a question. How much land you got Mister McKissick?

He laugh and sayed, Why? You want some? Just kidding.

Maybe.

You know we in South Carolina don't you?

I told you, Jonathan sayed. We ain't up north or out west. They don't take well to that business for your people or ours. I'm telling you it's best to leave it alone.

Mama promise from all them years ago echo in my ears like the dreams me and Martha made that I carried on and put into Nora's heart. Now she the one keep me going with that dream. She reminded me of what we sayed years ago and why it mattered. Wasn't nothing taken well when it come to living better so this wasn't gon be no different. At the same time, we was free. When I started them dreams even freedom wasn't more than a dream itself. But it happened. Like God got them Israelites out but then theyw as wandering aimless. I ain't want that. I wanted the promise. I wanted the promised land.

Sometimes you gotta do something that don't sit well to make things right.

Ervin, we don't need anything happening to you, your family, or our family or Eli here. Tell him Eli. He needs to stop this foolishness and don't let anyone else hear of this.

Them two was both young enough to be my sons. Old enough to be men. Jonathan done took a wife and Eli was fixing to. I was near his age when I find myself falling in love with Lilly and full of dreams about living free in Philadelphia. I ain't had nothing. I come with nothing and leaved with nothing but the change I made. Change I'd been saving since I could save.

That young Eli McKissick looked at me and ask me what I know about farming since I been a carpenter.

I know how to grow just about everything you need and can raise hogs and chickens. I helped Mister James on that little farm about all my life and I teached my boys too. They work that land we live on now. We know how to farm and make things grow.

We need to be getting back Ervin, Jonathan cut in like he was getting nervous. He was right bout how things was but I still wanted to know.

You ain't sayed how much land you got Mister McKissick.

He laugh again and sayed he got a good amount but he wasn't thinking about selling nothing right then.

Come on Ervin. Let's go before we both find ourselves in trouble, Jonathan sayed with his voice deeper and start walking.

Eli

Nora wrap her fingers round mine after dinner and look me straight in the eye. She told me, We deserve this and we done worked hard for it all our lives.

Well we ain't getting no younger. Our time done passed, I sighed heavy like cuz seem like wasn't nobody thinking bout letting no negro buy land in them parts.

No, Ervin. Our sons and daughters deserve it and they sons and daughters. It ain't about us no more Ervin. You right. We getting old. We gotta do this for them. If we don't do it who else gonna do it? Who else can do it? You got folks who like you and you been saving up since you was that Eli McKissick age, younger even. If it ain't now, when's it gonna be?

Stop woman! They just as soon kill me as let me have some land. They might come kill you too. God knows what they might do to them kids.

I stormed out. She ain't understand. I promised to provide and protect but it wasn't fair to have to choose. I looked in the window and she was sitting at the little table quiet. I ain't mean to yell but I did. I looked up at them stars from the front of our little house and wonder if maybe mama made a mistake or if God whispered in the wrong ear. I wondered if I might not see it after all and all that I been working for was in vain. The door open and Nora come out. She done grab a bowl with pecans and start shelling them. She sat in the other chair out there and look where I been looking.

You know not every north star sposed to lead you to Canada or further north. It just lead you where you sposed to go and can't nobody else say where that is. Ervin you got favor. I know it may not seem like it with all you been through and what you done lost, but sometimes God don't do for you he do through you. Don't close up God's path to bless our children. Our people. He used everybody in your life so you could do this.

I sit there for a while longer looking off. My hands aching a bit after all day and looking more and more like Mister John's used to. I turned my head up to them stars. I sayed, I've been cursed and broken. I thought for a while I was going the right way. That God ain't curse me afterall. Won't let me have the one thing I been dreaming of since I could dream. He took my dream Nora. He took everything.

Yeah? Here I am. You got two handfuls of children and you got money saved up. Not everything is gone. When you ever heard a God just handing it to you? There's seed. It don't grow less it get put in the ground and get sun and rain. You got the seed but you gotta work it if it's gon grow. That Eli might not a tell you yes, but from what I can tell he ain't tell you no neither.

He didn't say no. Jonathan done most of the talking.

So you don't know what that Eli think, really. Ervin you got the means to do this and I know you got favor, or else we wouldn't be sitting here right now. Question is, what you gonna do with what you still got?

I could hear my songbird Martha in my ear singing that sad song she try to say wasn't sad.

Got hard trial in my way,
Heav'n shall-a be my home.
O when I talk, I talk wid God,
Heav'n shall-a be my home.
I dunno what de people want of me,
Heav'n shall-a be my home.

I'm a go tomorrow and talk to him again, I told Nora fore we went to sleep that night. I figure it be Saturday and I'd find him easy enough. I ain't tell nobody else bout it. They might a tried to stop me and talk some sense into me. I ain't been up there since he sayed he was engaged to be married to Miss Ellen Fountain. They set it for the Saturday after

Thanksgiving so everybody could make it from out of town. He still had some months fore then so I hoped I could get his ear.

My nerves turn my stomach the whole way. My mind was racing with all manner of questions. What if he say no? What if he say never? What if he say he can't and won't nobody else? What if somebody else hear about what I'm trying to do? What if they come after us? What if he want more than I got to pay? What if I can't never get land or a place of my own or for my family to be safe and call home?

I got closer and I could hear mama voice, Ervin, now stop all that talk. What's for you is for you. You have just as you believe you'll have. If you believe you gonna get some land from that man, a way will be made. Just like a way was made for you to be free.

I sayed back it was a war that was made so we could be free.

So all them men died so our people can be free, and all you wanna do is have your children working up under somebody, tied to somebody else land with nothing to ever call they own? That's what you want for my grandchildren? What about your grandchildren?

These women. All up in my head. Trying to tell me what they thinked I should think. Wasn't none of them with me going out here to that farm, praying a white man might listen and be more of the good in God than of man or the other god some men serve that ain't good. I prayed I'd make it there and back and when I come back to Nora it be with a plan.

I ain't never asked God for much. A little happiness, a little peace, somebody to love, and someplace to call mine. That's all. It done took all this time but I had three of them. If I get to four…

That song play in my head the rest of the way to see that Eli McKissick.

Got hard trial in my way,
Heav'n shall-a be my home.
O when I talk, I talk wid God,
Heav'n shall-a be my home.
I dunno what de people want of me,

Heav'n shall-a be my home.

On the porch sitting with his betrothed been that younger Eli. He ain't no kinda farmer, sitting out on a Saturday late morning stead a tending to them fields clearly that clearly needed tending. I wonder where his help been. I knowed he had an old man still living there and a couple others but if he wanted to get that done he need to get working, all them. Farming wasn't nowhere on his mind. They sitting there reading the bible.

Good day Mister McKissick. Miss Fountain. I took my time getting off that horse after I lowered the bag I carried with me to the ground gentle like. I always made sure I had some business I was tending to even on social trips or the ones that wasn't about official business. They ain't like to see no black man riding round by himself without no business.

I can put together these picture frames for you while I'm here. I likely won't get back around for the wedding and this is my gift to you.

You didn't have to do that Ervin. Come all the way out here.

It's my pleasure. Where can I work?

You can use the storage area back there if you want, Eli sayed. He ain't look like he wanna get up from that young girl company. I seed the door open and somebody poke they head out. Musta been Miss Fountain chaperone.

You mind showing me a good place to set up?

He jump down from the steps and come to me. You been here enough Ervin, you know where to go. I've got company.

I know, suh. I wanted to talk to you if you just have a few minutes. I'll put these together and then be outta your way. Promise.

What is it? He asked me and look back at Miss Fountain sitting up on the porch and she looking back smiling.

Mister McKissick, it probably don't come as no surprise that it's hard for folks like me to get land here in the low country. Won't hardly nobody sell what they got to us freedmen.

Well, that's not a surprise. What's the point though?

I know you got a lot of land and it don't seem that's your passion, Mister McKissick. Seem the good book and God is the path you following. What you gon do with all that land while you serving God?

It's to be farmed. I'm sure at some point it'll be at least.

I think it should. I think you right. You got over a hundred acres ain't being farmed though. Tween you and Misses Poston.

He looked at me and fold his arms across his chest.

What are you asking Ervin? Come out straight.

My mouth feel like the cotton out in the field my boys been picking all summer. I tried to find something wet to swallow so I can speak. Sir. Mister McKissick I wanna buy some of your land.

He laugh and sayed, Ervin me and that lovely lady over there plan on having lots of babies and we are going to need this land. And like my daddy hand it down to me, I plan to hand it down to my children.

I nodded. I know that's how it goes.

Yes. That's how it goes.

I learned how to build furniture, and caskets and all manner of woodwork from Mister John James. I work with him bout forty years til he passed. You know that?

That's a long time.

Yessuh it is. I was eight years old when a slave trader come and bought me and my mama from a plantation in Virginia. My daddy was sold before I ever seed the light of life and my brother and sister got sold before we come here to South Carolina. I understand a parent wanting to give they children something. Leave something with them for them to carry on.

I took a small nail and hammered it into the corner of the frame where they was lined up. Your daddy had some slaves didn't he?

Mister McKissick push his shoulders back. That was him. Not me. I never agreed.

I'm sure you don't Mister McKissick. I known your daddy and been doing business with him going on, well long as you been alive. Liked his name and even though he had slaves your daddy was a decent man. Not everybody was like him. I know. He made sure that family stay together and I know he let you kids teach them kids to read.

Eli start to argue but I stopped him.

I ain't gon tell nobody. See I learn long ago ain't nobody perfect. Ain't nobody all good or all bad. Some lean a little more one way or the other. Some a lot. I also learn can't none of us escape answering for what we do with this life so I ain't got to judge, God take care of that as you know.

His mouth part to say something but I wasn't gon stop talking.

I found out your daddy name mean God is my Oath. I named the first child I had born free Eli cuz of the promise and faith me and his mama had that one day we was gon be free. That God wouldn't keep any of his children in bondange. Eli. That's your name too. The land you got is made possible from people like me. You gets to enjoy it, pass it down cuz people like me wasn't allowed to have any or own nothing. Not your fault Mister McKissick but sometimes things can be made right by one right action.

Do you know what your saying? First it sounds like your blaming my daddy for your predicament. Second it sounds like you think I should give up what's rightfully mine because of what someone else did.

I'm not asking you to give up nothing. I'm willing to pay for whatever I get, fair, just like anybody else. I'm just in need of a chance.

And you think you can pay for land?

Depending on how much land and what it cost? Yessuh.

I'm sorry you came all this way Ervin. I appreciate the wedding gift. It's good work as always and it'll be perfect for our portrait. I'm sure my fiancé will like it too. Now, far as selling land. You know that's impossible to do around here. Don't you?

Well I believe if we believe something's the right thing to do and decide we gon do it, God will make a way. I spose for me, each day I gotta walk with some measure of faith that God ain't completely fail me after everything I been through to be standing in front of you today suh.

I drove the last nail into the picture frame and stand it up for him to see. Congratulations on your upcoming marriage. I pray you be happy and have all them babies you want.

Mister McKissick nod his head. Thank you.

I'll see my way out.

My heart sat heavy in my chest riding back to the plantation. Wasn't nothing I could say to Nora that was gon make it better. I ask God to help me believe what I just told that Eli. If he ain't plan to fail me I pray he make a way.

Nora been waiting in the door when I come back. One hand sitting on her hip and she leaned up against the side. I got off the horse and start making my way towards her. My hat in one hand and the empty sack I carried that wedding gift over my shoulder. She studying my face but wasn't nothing I could do to hide it.

He ain't gon sell. I walked past her and sat in the chair. Nora took a pot off the fire and then filled a bowl with soup and set a piece of cornbread on top.

Maybe he'll come round. Give it til after he married and then take something over to him. Folks like gifts. Soften them up. And from what you say he might like food too. I'll make him a pecan pie. What you think his fiancé like?

I don't know. They was studying the bible when I got there.

Let me think on that one. And what about-

I had to cut her off. Let me eat this fore it get cold woman. I took it and set outside on the chair. I wish Levi was there. He always made sense outta no sense. He somehow found a way to be at peace in a storm but even he wanted to be free. He would talk about that great city. He talk about the birds flying north and laugh that they ain't know enough not to come back, then look at me. He take what he learned from the bible and make it fit whatever he was talking bout and make you laugh at the same time. I look at the other seat out there where he used to sit fore he passed on. He missed seeing himself and his family free by a few months. We was fighting that war and he'd rock and talk about if he was twenty years younger he woulda run off to Union lines.

241

He give me his story bout how he'd run off when he was about to turn twenty cuz his master sayed he was selling him to somebody else, and everybody knowed slaves died on that plantation and wasn't nothing done bout it.

I asked him what happen and he lift up his shirt to show the stripes cross his back.

They sayed if I tried again they'd send my mama, brother, sister and Martha mama away. Sayed some might go to that same evil plantation and some might go further, so far I'd never see them again. Oh but if we coulda gone together. They knew I couldn't. Mama was full with child and my sister and brother wasn't but yea high. He put his hand to his knee and keep rocking. Got that far off look in his eye.

I rocked in that chair imagining Levi beside me telling me something smart about how to handle this or be at peace with it. Either one. I ain't get much from him bout this though. He ain't had no life experience like it. Wasn't even something he coulda thinked about.

The sun started fading and the kids running in and out that little house. They been working all day. I hear mama say, They don't mind working hard, Ervin. Like me. Like you. But what they gon have to show for it? Making that man rich and he ain't giving them nothing to get ahead. Just enough to survive. Don't you want more?

I'm going for a walk, I yelled inside.

Can I go with you? My Eli asked me. He looking up excited with his eyes big. He wasn't in the fields with his big brothers. Least not yet. He stayed with Nora, inside the house and in that kitchen.

Sure. We can take a quiet walk. Daddy need to think.

Bout what?

I look down at him. His whole life ahead of him and he ain't never knowed nothing bout being a slave. Life ain't look much different but it was a big difference between being owned by somebody else and owning yourself.

I gots a lot on my mind Eli.

Me too. I gots a lot on my mind, Daddy.

We walked along the other cabins and toward the end of the long path headed to the turnoff and the road. Folks was on the stoops and kids running outside. I lost Eli to some other kids playing. He sayed he was done with what was on his mind.

I'd get him on the way back. My mind wasn't done yet.

Pie

Nora baked three pecan pies for me and I made matching serving trays. I carry them pies in the trays like Nora stack them up so they wouldn't get messed up. She made sure to tell me they gotta stay pretty. I looked at the stack and that horse. Wasn't no way to keep them pies pretty going on a horse alone. I told her I'm gon take the wagon and Eli so he can help hold them pies steady. Eli so happy cuz he don't hardly get to go no place but church.

He looked all around but ain't say much. Me neither. I ain't wanna talk about where we was going or what for. I ain't wanna tell him about the dreams me and his mama got cuz they might get jinxed up. Naw. It been better to hold my tongue along with my mind and think on something else like Vicie being married and me being a granddad. I ain't never think I'd be an old man but there I was with a five and three year old all the way to grown children. I ain't have much to show for it. Least not nothing that lasts. I had my reputation and respect and I had to believe that was gon be enough.

We pulled up to that long dirt path leading to the McKissick farm and I taked a real deep breath. You alright daddy? Eli look at me with them big eyes.

I'm alright son. Sometimes I just gotta catch my breath.

Why? Where it run to?

I laughed and sayed, It just get away from me sometime and I gotta snatch it back. It been what Levi sayed when my oldest boy Wright was about Eli's age. Now half my kids was grown.

Let's go see the man got the same name as you.

Why he got my name?

Well cuz it means something. That's the reason you got your name.

What it mean daddy?

It mean God is my oath.

Why you name me that?

Cuz, Eli. You are God's promise. You was my first child born free. After my whole life trying to feel free you was born free.

I like that.

Ervin! You're back. Wasn't expecting you.

Good afternoon Mister McKissick. I hope you and the Misses is doing good on this fine day.

Fine as can be expected for all this heat.

I wanted to bring you something now that you married and all.

Another gift? Mister McKissick fold his arms like he was scared to take it. We love the frame you gave us during our engagement. We don't really need anything else right now.

You ain't even seed what I bring you.

Is that your grandson?

I smile a little and sayed, You know folks think Eli my grandson all the time but he my second to youngest. Believe I mention him last year.

That's right. You look like a strong boy.

Mama made you pies. Sayed I couldn't have none cuz they was for you. Eli frown up his face.

Hush up now, Eli. Ain't no place for that. Sorry Mister McKissick.

I do like pies. What kind are they?

Pecan, I telled him.

My favorite.

I made you serving trays too. Right now they holding the pies.

You still doing much wood work?

These hands can't do all that detail no more. And I can't stand not to do good work so I had to stop selling and making stuff.

What about your boys? You passed it onto the older ones I'm sure.

Maybe they can whittle and make something simple but I couldn't really teach them right. Wasn't enough time with them in the fields all day and me working at Mister James all week. They can farm though. They learned that on the plantation and I teach them the rest.

I see, he sayed fore he step back again. I open up the bag and pecan pie caught up in his nose. You trying to bribe me to sell some land with some pie Ervin? You gotta be kidding me.

Good food sometime make for good conversation. That's all I want is some of your time to talk. Eli go head and see if you can find one of them four-leaf clovers.

But they hard to find, he complained.

That's what make them special. Now go head.

Eli hunched over where grass and weeds was growing all together and I stood looking around.

You surveying my land? Eli McKissick asked.

I'm just looking, if that's what you mean.

Why do you keep asking about it?

Cuz that little boy deserve to have something that lasts cuz I work hard my whole life trying to give him something that ain't gon by next week or he lose once I'm dead.

Eli McKissick look back at the house and start chewing on his lip. Let's walk Ervin.

I look over at my Eli still hunting and Mister McKissick start telling me how he and his wife trying to have a child. It ain't easy as it seem. They only been married a few months but he hopeful still.

We plant the seeds but we can't make it grow, I told him.

Mister McKissick nodded his head slow and sayed, But we plant them anyway and what grows will grow in it's season and time.

We walked a little more and he say he been thinking about me wanting to buy some land. Sayed folks wouldn't like it but that wasn't no surprise.

How much would you be willing to sell?

Right now? I'm not. I thought about it and it's too risky. For me. You. The family I'm trying to make. It would be hard on all of us. Ervin they'd run us right out of town.

Well I think it might not be so hard as you think and for my family, it likely be better than what we got now.

I know you want my help Ervin. I wish there was a way to help but we are in two different worlds and in one of them...

In one of them what Mister McKissick?

Ervin, don't misunderstand me.

In one of them a man can be free and own land and leave something for his family. In the other a man can work someone else land so he leave something for that man family.

That's not it. You're not understanding.

I think I understand just fine Mister McKissick. I hope you enjoy the trays. We'll be taking these pies. My boy and me are hungry and we ain't get none.

All three? You don't need three pies for you and a little boy. Come on now.

It's all I have and all I got to give him. But you right. It's more than we need. You probably take one and we wouldn't hurt none. You'd enjoy some sweet pie and we'd enjoy some sweet pie too. But I gotta take back all three.

Because I won't sell my land to you?

Cause if I don't make a deal and I ain't got these pies I might not have a wife come morning.

That's ridiculous.

Well you ain't been married long yet. Y'all still in your sweet time. But it might be ridiculous. Might not be. It just ain't a price I wanna pay. For you it's your reputation in the community. How people might treat you. More than how God gon see you and how he gon judge the seeds you plant. But I ain't gon judge. My price for not coming to terms with you might end with an angry wife. You got your own thing and I can't judge what that price is to you.

You can't come to my home trying to make me feel guilty.

No disrespect suh. I can't make nobody feel guilty. I ain't got no such power to put on any man some feeling that ain't already somewhere there.

Why God? He asked turning himself away.

Then he say he gotta pray on it. This wasn't no light decision and he need to talk to his wife.

I understand. Those two important things to do. What you want me to wait or come back?

Come back next month. Not before four weeks. Give me time. I don't wanna rush anything.

I understand Mister McKissick.

I took two pies out and put them in the wagon and then hand him the two trays with one pie.

Thank you for considering this. I be back in a month. I just ask if your answer be yes you tell me then how much land you willing to sell and what I need to pay for it.

Fair enough. And thanks for leaving a pie.

Have a good day Mister McKissick. I nodded to him and then call to Eli. You find a four-leaf one yet?

No suh. Ain't none nowhere.

Let's go then. Maybe you find it next time.

More Pie

The heat of August hanged on us like that Spanish moss on old oaks. Oaks that been here longer than me and Nora together. She wrapped up two pies and told me don't come home with none this time. Eli held them pies in his lap and we set off up the road to the McKissick farm again. Me and Nora been praying too and we keep saving what we could save. I had a good feeling bout going back to see him this time and bout them pies not coming back, even if me and Eli had to eat them both fore we got home.

I pulled up and stop the cart a good ways from the house. I had my promise with me holding two pies, in my heart, and up in heaven. I took a deep breath and let it out slow.

You catching your breath again Daddy? Eli asked me.

Yeah. I ain't planning on going home with no pies this time and this an important talk I gotta have. You know how I tell you a man spose to protect and provide for his family? This here trip is so I can provide.

You providing pies to Mister McKissick? He ask me all confused.

I'm trying to provide for yall and I'm hoping these pies help.

Wasn't nobody around. Not in the field but in the heat of the day in August, I wouldn't a been out neither. Better to get up fore the sun and get done early.

Wait here and don't let nothing happen to them pies, understand me? I sayed for I got out and walk up to the side door. I knocked before stepping back and clasping my hands to keep them from shaking. I already knowed what I plan to say. Done practiced it a hundred times in my head.

I knocked again cuz ain't nobody answer. That wasn't no way to be. They ain't had no children yet so that misses can come see bout the door. I wait some more and they still ain't answer. I finally hit the cowbell hanging on top, hating to make a ruckus but I ain't come all that way just to turn around for no good reason. After some time I heard slow footsteps coming to the door. So I stand straight and fix my shirt and collar.

That young Mister McKissick opened the door and look at me. He ain't say nothing and just walk away with the door open.

Hi ya doing suh? I brought you two fresh pies, for you and the misses, I sayed.

I looked round and from the sight and the smell it ain't seem like no misses been there. After some time with this strange silence I sayed, I just set them here on the table. Uh, everything alright Mister McKissick? You look a bit outta sorts.

No Ervin. Everything isn't alright. You wouldn't understand though. Thank you for the pies.

Mister McKissick you might be surprised about what I understand. And you told me to come back in a month so I did.

A month ago things were different. A month ago I had something to look forward to. I had dreams of a big family with my wife. Everything is different.

I know what that feel like.

How? You got ten or eleven kids and you got grandkids and you still have your wife.

I do. But I ain't always think it was gon be that way. Not with my first wife, nor my second.

Eli McKissick lift his head just enough to glance in my face. Then he looked at the pies.

He ain't stop me so I went on. I sayed, I was about your age Mister McKissick when my Lilly died. Ain't make no sense and I was angry for a long time. Angry at God, at people, at myself cuz wasn't nothing I could do about it. I ain't had no power over nothing in life or death.

How'd you - what'd you - he stop and collapse in that hard wood chair.

Mind if I sit down too?

Doesn't matter. Nothing does.

Don't say that Mister McKissick. I know it don't feel like it do right now. Like God done abandon you and leave you empty. I know. Most folks ain't gon understand but you sitting up in this house by yourself with nothing but all that talk in your head. It'll make you crazy. You need to get a woman in here, maybe one of your sisters to help you out. And you a man of faith so you might wanna call on that too right about now. You still gon have hurt and pain and anger but maybe it'll soften it some so you don't stay broken so long.

My sister is coming this week. Ervin, I thought I found the love of my life. The woman I would grow old with, and we'd have lots of children and I'd share what I have with them. Instead she's gone and those dreams with it.

I got eleven kids living now Mister McKissick. My boy Eli out there now digging in your yard. You still young. Nothing I say gon make it better but maybe it'll plant a seed a hope.

I plan to study the bible Ervin. Learn God's word and preach it. That's been my plan for a while. How do I do that when right now I think God forgot me.

Forgot you? If I can sit up in your house after being a slave most all my life and losing wives and babies along the way and still think some part of me ain't been forgot, then you can too cuz I know you ain't been forgot.

Mister McKissick sat in that stiff chair quiet turning a pie round with his hand. He stare into that pie like it got some secrets. Finally he open his mouth, still studying that pie. I know why you're here Ervin. I haven't had much time to think on it over the past few weeks but I already been leaning towards selling you some land. With Ellen gone well I don't much wanna hang around here. I know for me I can always buy more land. I also know for you that ain't the case. I prayed on it like I said I would and come to peace with it. I just don't know why Ellen's gone now. I was doing right in all areas of my life. Trying to at least. Why do you think Ervin?

His eyes was bloodshot red and he look like he done lost ten pounds.

I can't answer that. Lots I can't answer. I just know that we ain't got no control over it, specially when ain't nothing we can do to stop it. I done lost lots of people I love but I keep

251

getting more folks to love come in my life. You a good man Mister McKissick. God see that.

Are you leaving the pies this time?

Well the misses done tell me I can't come home with them cuz I gotta make a deal. Either way they getting eat up.

Ervin. I've never really fit in around here. I mean I want to be a minister after all. But it's because I do believe in the promises of God even if right now I have some doubt. But I don't feel guilty about having doubt. Just means I have to seek more. I don't want to be on the wrong side of right when this life is over or be asked what I did for the least of those and I can't give a good answer. I believe you when you say what you want for your children and grandchildren. Same thing we all want. Difference is I can easily have them. I work, I make money, and I buy what I want. It's not that easy for you Ervin. You'll be hard pressed to buy land around here from someone else.

I know this suh. That's why I'm here with you.

I've got close to a hundred acres Ervin. A fair price for that is between $650 or $700 dollars. I know it sounds like a lot but you asked for fair and that's fair. Same thing I'd tell anyone else.

I accept fair Mister McKissick and if that's the fair price then we can make a deal. I need a little time to gather up the rest. Just a little.

I need time too to get myself together and get this house in order. Plus, I'm going to spend some time deciding where I'll go next, and getting my affairs set up for that.

I ain't never done nothing like this before Mister McKissick. What I need to do? How we do this?

I'll get it surveyed to see exactly the boundaries and then we make a sale and record the deed. You just make sure you can settle the account, Eli sighed.

Damn. Pardon my language. Thank you. Least I ain't going home with pies.

Ain't the worse said in this house of late, and while I could eat two pies, I shouldn't. You and your boy want some fore you head back?

That'd be nice Mister McKissick. She do make the best pecan pies.

Home

Thanksgiving come round again. We ain't buy nothing special cuz we saving every cent. We made do with what we had cuz what we getting worth more than a turkey or some cornbread and rice and gravy. Young Mister McKissick sayed the surveyor was coming out right after Thanksgiving to say how much land and where exactly. All that we been praying for and hoping for was happening. He done made plans to go to Cains, far and close enough at the same time.

We counting down days cuz Nora and the boys contract end December 31 and I wants this done fore then. He sayed the Monday after the land get surveyed he should have the answer for me then we could make the sale that next week or so. We had enough long as the price ain't change. Nora made pies for everybody she could for Thanksgiving and we was saving every nickel and dime making little things easy enough for me to do with my hands like they is. It pain me to do it now but once this was done I wouldn't have to do it no more. Just gotta get settled up and get that first crop in for spring. Like I been saying, we had to plant seeds, otherwise wasn't nothing gon grow.

The plantation owner surprise us day after Thanksgiving with some leftover turkey and Nora made soup with that and some sweet potato and pole beans we growed in our garden. She looked at me with them kids sitting round eating soup all messy. She sayed, This the last Thanksgiving here Ervin. Look at us. We been here a long time in this place you built with your hands but still ain't yours. Next place built is ours. For keeps. We been saying it and it's happening. Don't wait for Mister McKissick to send word it's done. He got enough on his hands trying to keep them wolves at bay while he do what don't nobody think he should do. You ride out there next week and find out so we know.

She got so much energy and life. All them kids and how she work day and night and still got time to think about things like this. I was tired. Trying to be there and find ways to earn extra money and do what a man do. We got along good. Always did. I did what I did and she did what she did and one ain't work without the other. That cabin we had was made by my hands and them kids was good. The land I was gon buy was possible cuz I had been working fifty years trying to save up what I could. Cuz Nora come and won't let us quit on these dreams and right now right by my side doing all she can for us. It been so many lows mixed with the highs but wouldn't no high be like this.

I wish you could come with me Nora, I sayed coming up behind her and wrapping my arms round her waist.

And leave the boys watching the boys? I don't think so. You handle the business and I'll take care of right here so there's a right here to come back to.

I started humming. I been talking to them big boys about buying and farming our own land since they worked with me at Mister John's.

What you humming? Song Ellison sang a few Sunday's pass at church?

Yeah, I sayed and started singing it out loud and my Nora join in. Then Sophie and the boys was singing too.

Dere's no rain to wet you
O, yes I want to go home
Dere's no sun to burn you
O, yes I want to go home
O, push along, believers
O, yes
Dere's no hard trials
O, yes
Dere's no whips a-crackin'
O, yes
My brudder on de wayside
O, yes

O, push along, my brudder
O, yes
Where dere's no stormy weather
O, yes
Dere's no tribulation
O, yes[3]

Nora already done sayed I can't wait too long from when he get that information back from the surveyor cuz we ain't need him second guessing and changing his mind.

She been right about that. Right about most things so far.

This time when I went up I took my three youngest boys James, Ervin, and Eli. I had to know how much land and how much it was gon cost. Lastly when we was gon make it final. If I coulda buy it that same day I woulda so wouldn't nobody change they mind. Ain't nobody hardly believe it was gon happen. They keeped telling me that white man ain't gon sell one a us none of his land. They don't do that round here less you the child a one of them. We wasn't that, but I sayed he gon do it.

Like he been expecting me, he open his door and come out when we riding up in that cart. James holding the pie this time. Was only one cuz we ain't had much to spare. Sold all the rest.

Ervin James. Can't say I'm surprised to see you here. I suppose you came to find out the details.

I smiled and slowly got out the cart and walk over to him. My knees and back was stiff from the ride but I stood straight as I could.

Yessuh. Come to find out how much you got to sell me and how much it's gon cost me and when we can make it official.

He rubbed his chin and then look around like he trying to see somebody. I looked too just in case.

You worried? I asked him.

I shouldn't be. But I am. Come in. Your boys gon be okay out here?

Ain't nothin for them to get into. I already holding the pie. Don't yall do nothing that gon make me come after ya.

256

Ervin and James drop the sticks they was holding. Eli asked for them to help him find a four-leaf clover.

Mister McKissick pick up a paper and hand it to me. This is the report. Shows the property border and how much land it is, approximately.

What's it mean? I see 109. What that mean?

There are 109 acres to sell you. On three sides it borders other people and on one side it borders my land. It's a good size of land Ervin. Enough to farm and have space for your family.

Yessuh it is. My heart beating out my chest. There it was on paper. Is it still the same amount?

I can sell it for $700 no less. That's as fair a price as I can give.

That's fair and I accept. When can I buy it off you? My family contract end on December 31 this year and we need our place fore then. Even if we gotta set up a tent, it be ours.

He laughed and sayed I ain't gotta do that. I can use one of the old cabins til we build. He sayed one occupied but not the other.

What about you? What you gon do Mister McKissick?

Well, you probably gather already it's not the best for me to stay around here. I visited Georgia and eventually I'm a make my way there to study. For now, it's still up to Cains. Maybe it'll give folks to cool off a bit bout this whole thing. This last week has been especially hard. We were supposed to have made a year on the 27th. Reminds me that staying here ain't for me.

You doing what's right Mister McKissick and that ain't gon go without its rewards.

I pray you're right Ervin. Come here noon on Tuesday and we'll take care of the business. I'll be off the property by end of the year but hopefully by the holidays. I'm heading to my sister's so we can spend it together. I think being alone for Christmas this year would be too much.

It be good for you to be with family Mister McKissick. I'll be here noon on Tuesday.

Oh and it'll be me and Mary Poston. I was able to get her to add some land on account it helps her out to sell some. That's how we got to 109.

I smiled cuz he smiled. Maybe doing right by us might help him fix his heart.

* * *

We was standing outside waiting for Wright wife to come so she can watch the young ones. Nora was coming with me to see us get the land we been dreaming of together for twenty-five years. We had seven hundred dollars including the three or four or five dollars my sons each chip in. We had enough and could get a home for all us.

Nora wrapped her hair up nice and put on a dress she was always saying she was waiting on a special occasion for. I told her wasn't no more special occasion then today. We got bundled in our coats for the ride over and was feeling warm inside. We talked bout how we gon farm and grow our own stuff and sell it and make it so our children and grandchildren could feel free and work they own piece a land if that be what they wanna do. They could feel proud cuz they gots something to call they own.

What you think gon come of it Ervin? When we buy this land and we start planting in the spring.

I can't rightly say Nora. I'm just glad to do it. I just wanna see it.

We'll have to wait and find out then, she smiled but looked all nervous like I feeled.

* * *

Two other carriages was already pulled up to the house when we got there and Nora took a deep breath and start fiddling with that dress.

Come on now. You look fine and it look like it high noon so we better get inside.

Oh Ervin. I'm so excited I think I might be sick.

Don't mess up that dress Nora. I'm feeling my nerves too but it been too long to get here and we gots one chance. This it.

We walked up to the side door and it was wide open. They all at the table waiting.

I see you brought your wife Ervin. Seems a worthy occasion. Mister McKissick looked at both us and smiled. He look brighter even since the weekend.

Yessuh. She need to be a part of this. Something we dreamed of since we was much younger.

Another man been sitting in the corner and Mister McKissick sayed he there to be a witness.

Mister McKissick shrugged, Well then let's get on with the business at hand. Oh and this is Misses Mary Poston. I mentioned her last we spoke.

Yessuh. Nice to meet you ma'am and thank you for being willing to sell us some of your land too.

Eli here told me about you and what you're trying to do and I figured it helps us all out a bit. She ain't hardly speak loud enough to hear but I get the gist. She stayed in that seat looking at the paper filled with words me and Nora can't read.

Can you read it for us Mister McKissick?

He picked up the paper and start reading to the end then he ask if it all sound alright. Me and Nora looked at each other and then start nodding at the same time.

Yessuh, I sayed. And we gots the money in this here purse.

You should go into town and visit the leather shop. They have some fine bags there. I think you've patched that one anew, Eli sayed studying it while it rest in my hands.

I held the bag up some and look at it too. Wasn't much of the original leather. Pieces of fabric I done got across the years both leather and cotton was holding it together. Nora had put a new tie on it right before our little Eli come along.

It's been through a lot but it's a good bag. I pull out the dollars first and start counting them and then Nora count the coins. Mary and Eli looked on. Six hundred sixty eight bills sit on the table with thirty two dollars in coins. Coins I'd refused to spend that mama made selling clothes almost fifty years before and coins I made playing the fiddle. Dollars from working under Mister John all them years and then some from my boys and from Nora and them pies and washing other folks clothes. It all sitting on that table, our whole life counted out.

Mary recounted the cents and Eli recounted the dollars. Mary stopped and looked at Nora. Seems you made an error in your counting. Nora got all tight lip like she did when she nervous.

I counted it. We ain't cheating you. I mighta count it wrong but we ain't trying to do no wrong Misses Poston.

She hold up four coins and slide them back to Nora. You gave us too much.

I see Nora shoulders drop and a little smile cross her face. That mean we settled? Nora asked them.

We just need to sign these papers, Eli sayed.

Nora watch me holding the pen in my hand. They had three sets of the same papers to sign. One for Eli, one for Mary and one for me. I put an X on the line they say had my name. Then Eli and Mary sign and then that witness come and put his name down and initial by my X.

After he finish all three I step back. That mean we settled now? I ask and pray wasn't nothing gon happen to change it.

The witness sayed, It'll soon be recorded in the county records for the deed. Til then hold to your copy of the agreement.

Ervin James you are the owner of 109 acres of land in Marion County, soon to be Florence if they have their way.

I can't say I care much where it is, long as it's mine. Long as we can live free and in peace on it. Thank you Mister McKissick. Thank you Misses Poston. You both done a great thing today. God gon bless you both.

I shook his hand and thank Misses Poston again. She nodded her head at me and Nora. We took the copy I sign for us and we bout run out the door fore they can change they mind or get scared about what they done.

* * *

Me and Nora pack up the things that belong to us, clothes, furniture and what we bought with our own money and we load up the wagon. Everybody who could, come out to see us off. We hugged and kissed and cried. We took the children who all still live with us and went to that cabin. We told the others to come too even if just for a night to feel what it like to sleep on your own land. They'd be coming to live soon.

I had all my family that was living. My children and my grandchildren and it ain't matter that it been cold and the cabin need cleaning and been too small. It ain't matter the floor was hard. We piled into that little cabin and eat Christmas dinner. We ain't had no other gifts to tie up or give but that ain't matter neither. On the floor sleeping side by side was my younger boys James, Ervin and Eli with Sophie. Heads on feet and poking each other in the back and ribs. Ain't none of that matter. They was all there. Vicie and Wright and Robert with they families and Sidney with his wife Annie full with they first child. Ellison and John sitting on one side of the fire talking half to us and half to themselves. All eleven of them with me and Nora on our land. Finally.

The sky was clear and it look like we just pass a new moon letting the stars shine like a rich woman jewels. I hear mama say, You did it Ervin. You got the promise.

I smiled and thinked to myself, Yeah Mama I did.

Vicie asked, You alright Daddy? You finally did it, what you been talking about my whole life.

That been near thirty years for her, but it been since I sat across that wooden table from Mama and she sayed God had a promise for me and I ain't been but sixteen. They put me down as being just fifty-five but I knowed I been closer to sixty-three and them stars been looking at me all them years and me right back at them.

Been that long, huh? I'm alright Vicie. Everything's all right.

Nora grab my hand fore she start knitting. She couldn't stop smiling and me neither. We was like a king and queen in our own little kingdom. Sitting up with the princesses and princes, talking and eating and making a new set a dreams til the stars fade and the sun find its way back to the sky.

The End...

261

And the Beginning of a Story for Generations

Your review of this book is greatly appreciated.

Epilogue

About Jamestown

The following section includes information about Jamestown and the purchase of the land, Eli McKissick, and photos from the property today. I utilized Ancestry.com primarily for my genealogical searches and for documents, such as the land deed.

In addition, members of the James Family Heritage Reunion were of assistance in providing background information on Jamestown such as the application for the site to be listed on the national historic registry as the Jamestown Historic District.

Ervin James had eleven surviving children. The James line began with his eleven living children of which two were daughters and the rest sons. These included Vicie (daughter), Wright, Robert, Sidney, Ellison, John, James, Ervin, Eli, Sophronia (daughter), and Fisher.

Ervin James founded Jamestown with the 1870 purchase of 109 acres of land which was divided into lots. The land was farmed and hunted for food, and most men worked offsite in agriculture, or even out of the area, returning wages home. The community felt it better to have the choice of where to work for wages over the sharecropping system which tied laborers to unfair contracts with landowners, often former slaveholders. These contracts made it difficult for freed blacks to leave, seek better opportunities, or create ownership.

The first few images are the deed for the purchase of the land and part of the submission for Jamestown to be listed in the historic registry.

The Deed for 109 Acres of Land

Jamestown Historic District

  Ervin James, the founder of Jamestown, was one of the fortunate African Americans in South Carolina who was able to purchase land. He bought a sizable tract of land on his own from Eli McKissick and Mary Poston near Florence, South Carolina, in 1870. A deed recorded on January 23, 1871, documents the transaction.[19] Both McKissick and Poston owned land adjacent to the tract of land that James acquired from them. Like James, African Americans in South Carolina at the time hoped to obtain their own land in order to escape forced labor contracts. Sharecropping was not an attractive alternative to working for wages because it still bound African Americans to white land owners. Above all else, freedmen desired their own land and the ability to establish their own communities free from white control after the war. Perhaps unbeknownst to him at the time, Ervin James' purchase would develop into more than just a family farm. During the last two decades of the nineteenth century, James' tract of land would evolve into such a rural African American community.

  For freed blacks who did not have enough money to purchase their own land as James Ervin did, another option existed. Cooperative purchase allowed individuals, typically family members, to buy land collectively and then divide up the purchase amongst themselves into smaller portions of land that each individual farmed as his own. Cooperative purchase often led to the establishment of small rural black farming communities that operated outside the direct authority of white southerners.[20] The original tract of land purchased by Ervin James was eventually augmented by his sons through cooperative purchase. Ervin James' five sons, Sidney, Ellison, Eli, Fisher, and James James as well as Ervin James' son-in-law, Alonza Wright, divided up the original tract of land that their father had purchased into six twelve-acre plots for each of them to farm individually[21]. Throughout the last decade of the nineteenth century and the first decade of the twentieth, these six men made several cooperative purchases to increase the collective land holdings of Jamestown. All six names appear on a deed recorded on March 26, 1891.[22] In that year, the men bought several tracts of land from J.A. Grice and his wife Sarah E. Grice, the daughter of Eli McKissick. A subsequent deed recorded on May 29, 1891, documents the purchase of more land from Rebecca A. Gibson acting as trustee for the will of Nathan S. Gibson.[23] Gibson owned land that bordered the James family holdings.

  The practice of cooperative purchase continued into the next generation of the James family. On June 29, 1915, Ephraim Ford, Eli James, James James, Robert James, Pat James, Elliott James, Mitchell James, James Wright and Betsy Williams collectively purchased land from J.R. Moody.[24] The presence of several surnames other than James on the deed suggest that several other African American families had established themselves in the community by that time or had married into the James family. Jamestown had become a community. Land divisions were made during the earlier years of the community to establish individual homes and tracts of land for separate families to work. However, over the years property was passed down to the family heirs in each generation who, for the most part, collectively owned the land of their ancestors.

---

[19] Deed Book DD, p. 494, Florence County Courthouse.
[20] Magdol, Right to the Land, pp.174-5.
[21] Oliver James, telephone interview with Tom Brush, 23 March 2000.
[22] Deed Book E, p. 413, Florence County Court House.
[23] Deed Book 4, p. 362, Florence County Court House.
[24] Deed Book 21, p. 231, Florence County Court House.

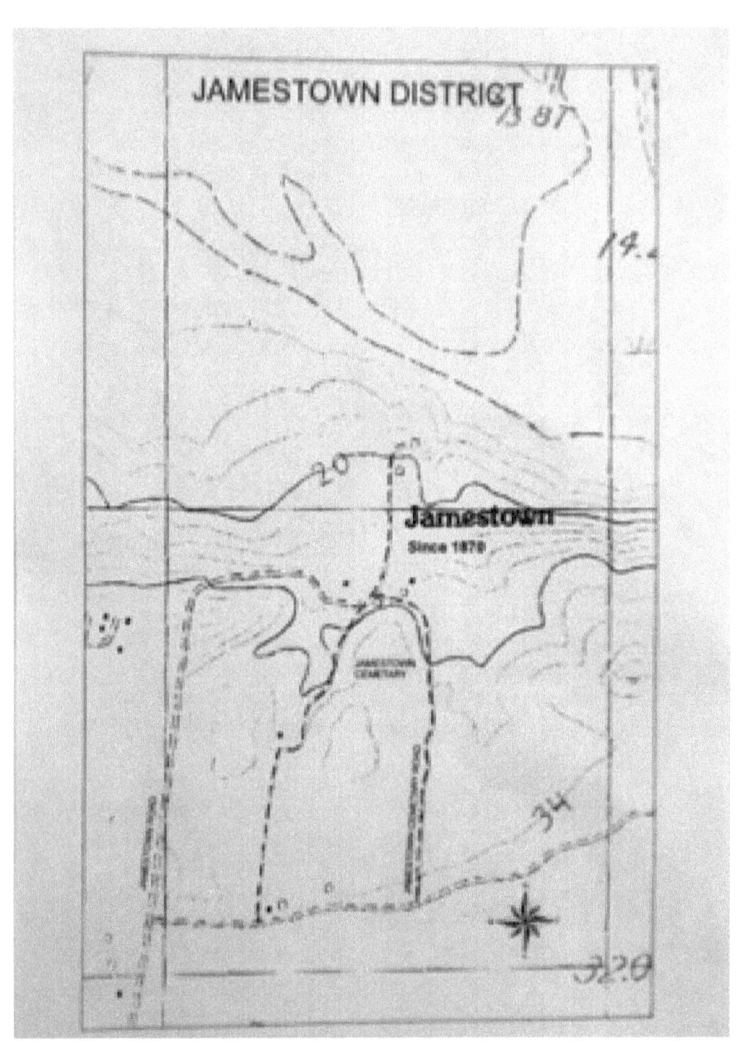

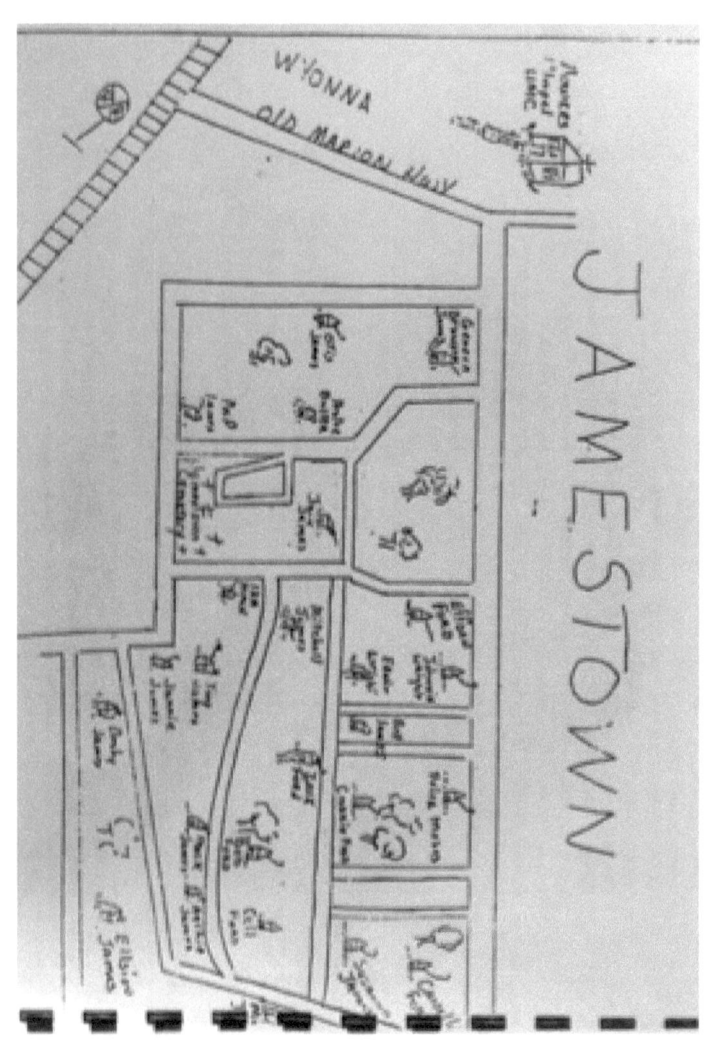

Photos from Jamestown

(Jamestown Historic District marker. Photo credit: Rebecca Washington)

(Home on Jamestown property. Photo credit: Rebecca Washington)

(Circa 1930. Eliza Ford James and Archie James who was the son of Robert James and grandson of Ervin James. Photo courtesy of Dorothy Elo.)

(Dorchester Williams, born and raised in Jamestown and the last to live there. Photo courtesy of Dorothy Elo)

(Jamestown Cemetary marker. Photo credit: Rebecca Washington)

About Rev. Eli Murchison McKissick

Provided from "Twentieth Century Sketches, page 217 (edited), on Ancestry.com

Rev. Eli Murkerson McKissick was born June 20, 1852. He is the son of Mister Eli McKissick and Misses Clarsey McKissick, originally of Marion County, S.C., but now of Florence.

He was educated at Mars Bluff Academy, Mars Bluff, S. C. under such teachers as Professors Scott and Clayton. He resided with his father while attending school and also afterwards until 1872, when he went to Georgia. Some of the time while with his father he was engaged in farming. He was converted at the age of thirteen years, under Christian parents, Rev. J. B. Campbell being the pastor at the time. When fourteen years old he felt called of God to the work of the ministry. As stated above, he moved to Georgia in 1872. In July of that year he was licensed to exhort. In June 1874, he was licensed to preach, Rev. George Yarborough, of the North Georgia Conference, being the Presiding Elder. He served as a supply on the Ocmulgee Circuit, in Georgia, for the years 1875-8. He moved back to South Carolina in 1879."

He was married on November 27, 1869, to Miss Ellen Fountain. His second marriage was to Miss Hester Palston, on August 12, 1872. The following are the names of their children: John Mack, James Thomas, Eli Matthew, Mattie Belle (7/4/1876-5/17/1952), Ellen, Lula, William Oscar, James Harmon, Willie, Corinne, Irene, and Harry."

Reverend Eli McKissick and Hester went on to have thirteen children after their marriage.

A Brief History of United States Slavery

The first African slaves were brought to the colonies by the English in August 1619, before the Mayflower. These enslaved Angolan Africans were stolen twice. They are thought to be prisoners of war taken from Africa by Portuguese. Privateers stole twenty or so of the lot of Angolan Africans from the Portuguese and loaded them onto their ships - The White Lion and the Treasurer, both owned by wealthy and powerful Robert Rich. He was the Earl of Warwick, an English nobleman. The ships arrived in Jamestown, Virginia four days apart and traded slaves for food.

However, slavery and the presence of Blacks in the present-day United States stretches back even further than 1619. The Spanish brought slaves during their early conquests in the 1500s. For example, African slaves were brought by the Spanish to Saint Augustine, Florida in 1565, and in 1526 the Spanish attempts at an expedition was ruined by the slaves rebelling. Both Africans and Native Americans were enslaved in what is now the United States of America, sometimes side by side.

Where the enslavement of Native Americans ended, traded for the removal of them by force and war, the enslavement of Africans continued. It became a part of the American culture and systems, impacting the country today. The impact of the Native American experience has also left its mark in a country that wishes to erase the connection between the native lands and the people it seeks to ostracize and keep out. Slavery and the relegation of Blacks as less than people and less than equal was codified in the Unites States Constitution, where Blacks were counted as three-fifths of a person for the purposes of census counting so that Blacks didn't provide an unfair advantage in representation.

There is some argument about whether Fort Hood, Virginia or Jamestown, Virginia should be the place noted. And, given that race-based slavery which made descendants of slaves automatically slaves, was not put into legal code until the 1700s, the forced exploitation of slave labor was not technically slavery, however, in all its ways, it was enslavement.

The slave trade became big business in America. It is estimated that between six and seven million slaves were brought to the Americas. In 1807, pending the January 1 enforcement of the Act Prohibiting Importation of Slaves of 1807, a record number 23,864 slaves were brought into the United states. And even once the trans-Atlantic slave trade was made illegal, the buying and selling of slaves was common. There were some who continued trading from places such as West Africa and Cuba, at risk of being caught. With these restrictions on trade, intercontinental trade was now how traders made their money. It is interesting to note that the United States slave population is the only one to increase through these natural means during the period of slavery.

With the end of legal trans-Atlantic slave trade in 1808 shortly after Ervin was born, the availability of slaves was reliant on trade and natural growth through reproduction. According to National Geographic, the enslaved population was 16 and one-half percent of the whole population, numbering 1,191,364 in 1810. This is an increase from about 700,000 in 1790. Growth after 1810 can be attributed primarily to reproduction within the existing slave population. By the 1860 census there were almost four million slaves in the United States. This same census showed there were 400,000 free blacks, meaning there was about a 90 percent chance a black person was a slave.

The men and women who landed on these American shores came before this country was even a country, before it sought freedom from Britain and some even fought for America's independence.

Slaves, however, did not benefit from this freedom. Slave codes dictated much of slave life. The only rights slaves had were to life and a minimum standard of basic necessities such as food, clothing, and shelter. It was not considered murder if a master killed a slave when punishing them, even with 50 lashes, which wasn't an unusual punishment, but was enough to kill a man.[4]

But when Ervin and Ellie left Virginia in 1815, slavery was not just alive, but was thriving anew after Eli Whitney's cotton gin invention which transformed cotton in the south and increased the demand for slave labor to meet the growing demand for cotton. By the time the last census before slavery ended was taken (1860), only one in four white families was estimated to own slaves. It is peculiar in that people spoke negatively about the slave traders in retrospect; however still engaged in the purchase and selling of slaves. It wasn't simply when they were short on money, but also for self-interest and as a way to make money. Wealthy and powerful men in politics were often involved in the selling and brokering of slaves.

The 1820s brought about renewed interest in abolition with the Missouri Compromise. Missouri became a slave state and stoked anti-slavery sentiments in the north. This continued until the abolitionist movement officially emerged in 1830. This official movement and the energy around it may have coincided with greater sentiments around the role and place of Blacks in society, including in the areas where protests erupted in the late 1820s and early 1830s. There are historians who believe that the religious movement called the Second Great Awakening also played a part in the increase of those supporting the abolition of slavery. With this Protestant revival came the idea that all men are created equal in God's eyes.[5]

During this institution that lasted some 246 years, slavery took on many forms. There were the larger plantations like the Virginia one that sold Ellie and Ervin. There were the smaller slave owners that only had one or two slaves, like Ellie and Ervin were sold to. They had different experiences generally. Neither were free, but the relationship between master and slave was different. There were masters such as John James and Shelly Bowers who formed partnerships, making the institution that can never be justified, more bearable due to more humane treatment. It is my belief that smaller slave owners such as these allowed for a view of the humanity of the slaves, which ultimately helped end the institution for those individuals or their children.

This wasn't the lifestyle or experience of the average slave. By 1860, the last census, it was more common that slaves were on a plantation than a farm. The population of those on these plantations are estimated at approximately a half million.

In addition to white slaveowners, there were some black slaveowners as well. The 1830 census showed that over 12,000 slaves were held by 3,775 free blacks. One slave owner in New Orleans named Andrew Durnford was an opportunist who owned 77 slaves. Unlike others who bought slaves as a way of 'freeing' them and keeping them out of slavery by whites, Andrew owned slaves for the same reason whites did. He only freed a total of five slaves.

The Emancipation Proclamation was issued in 1863 during the midst of the Civil War, but was not enforced in many places until after the Civil war. It was June 19, 1865, more than two months after the Civil War ended that the last slaves were freed in Galveston, Texas. The thirteenth amendment wasn't ratified until December of that year, which made general slavery illegal while legalizing slavery of incarcerated individuals. Legal slavery of incarcerated individuals remains until today.

Slave codes turned into Black codes, meaning that those who'd already been free now suffered setbacks that they hadn't before. These were extreme restrictions on the ability of freed to earn a living or even live. Some codes prevented them from selling goods such as in South Carolina. Codes prevented blacks from living in towns or cities, voting, working in fields other than agriculture or as domestic servants. These codes systemically relegated all blacks to second-class citizenship and black codes weren't reserved to only former slave-owning states. Northern states had their own black codes, though not as extreme as the ones instituted in former slave states.

Southern states who'd left the union to continue their right to own slaves were admitted back over the next few years following the end of the Civil War. Tennessee immediately agreed to the terms set for the Union, however other southern states resisted and were subject to oversight by the military. In

1868, South Carolina, the first state to secede, along with Alabama, Arkansas, Florida, Louisiana and North Carolina were readmitted to the Union. The window of reconstruction of the south was difficult for many whites but gave opportunity for blacks that hadn't been available before then, and soon after would be gone again.

Slavery is a stain on our country, one that we cannot seem to get out. It has caused suffering that extends through generations to this day, supported by outright systemic codes to biases born from centuries of the promotion of an ideology that blacks are and should be considered second-class citizens.

To break free from the chains that slavery hold on us as a nation will require a reckoning by those who have always held the power and an acknowledgement that it was a wrong and inexcusable institution. The effects lingered long past the last freeing of slaves on June 19, 1865, bled into ideals that allowed it to take root in the first place, and then continued through black codes, Jim Crow, red-lining and other policies that reduced the rights and freedoms of former slaves and the descendants of slaves. It is these maligned ideals that must be rooted out so that healing of our nation and our Black citizens may begin.

Sources for *A Brief History of American Slavery*

The First Africans in Virginia Landed in 1619. It Was a Turning Point for Slavery in American History—But Not the Beginning

Slavery in America

How slavery flourished in the United States

Black and slave population of the United States from 1790 to 1880

The American Past, A Survey of American History, Fifth Edition by Joseph R. Conlin.

Abolitionist Movement

About the Author

Bernette Sherman is a multi-genre writer and creative with a passion for creating and inspiring others to do what inspires them. She resides in the metro Atlanta area with her family.

Connect:
Website: BernetteSherman.com
Instagram: www.Instagram.com/IAmBernette
Facebook: www.Facebook.com/IAmBernetteSherman

[1] Allen, WF, Ware, CP, Garrison, LM. Slave Songs of the United States. Original edition, 1867. Electronic edition, 2000. Accessed September 24, 2020. https://docsouth.unc.edu/church/allen/allen.html

[2] Confederate States of America - Declaration of the Immediate Causes Which Induce and Justify the Secession of South Carolina from the Federal Union. The Avalon Project. Yale Law School. Webpage accessed 10/05/2020. https://avalon.law.yale.edu/19th_century/csa_scarsec.asp

[3] Negro Spirituals. by Thomas Wentworth Higginson. Accessed October 10, 2020. https://www.theatlantic.com/past/docs/issues/1867jun/spirit.htm

[4]Conlin, Joseph R. 1997. *The American Past. A Survey of American History*, 5th ed. Chapter 19.

[5] History Editors. (2019, November 29). *Abolitionist Movement.* Retrieved from https://www.history.com/topics/black-history/abolitionist-movement

www.ingramcontent.com/pod-product-compliance
Lightning Source LLC
Chambersburg PA
CBHW030957260626
47169CB00002B/579